LOCHLEVEN

Janet Walkinshaw

By the same author

Long Road to Iona & Other Stories
Knox's Wife
The Five Year Queen

LOCHLEVEN

A land torn apart by religious strife

To Lauren
with thanks for
a splendid tour
Janet

iii

Published in 2018 by FeedARead.com Publishing
Copyright © Janet Walkinshaw.

A CIP catalogue record for this title is available from the British Library.

Cover design: Hoggettcreative.co.uk

Cover photo: Tony Brotherton

Contents

John, 5th Lord Erskine = Margaret Campbell

Alexander Erskine

John, 6th Lord Erskine,
Earl of Mar
= Annabella Murray

others

James V King of Scots - *liaison* - Margaret Erskine = Sir Robert Douglas of Lochleven

Lord James Stewart,
Earl of Moray
= Anyas Keith

Euphemia Douglas
= Lord Patrick Lindsay

William Douglas,
later Laird of Lochleven
= Agnes Leslie

others

vi

Prologue
1568

Margaret Erskine gave orders that an extra allowance of ale was to be sent to the guards' quarters. They were already not entirely sober. The May Day festivities had been wild and intense, spilling over into a second day as if to make up for the physical restrictions and isolation of living on the island.

'There will be no danger tonight,' she said.

'The Queen?' asked Captain Drysdale.

'She has gone to her oratory in the tower. She must be left in peace.' Margaret had her back to him but sensed his puzzlement. Perhaps she had put too much sympathy into her voice.

'Some nonsense saint's day,' she added.

Captain Drysdale obeyed her orders, as he was bound to do. Soon afterwards, she saw him playing handball with some of his soldiers.

Now, she waited in the gathering darkness, standing motionless on the wall walk of the keep. It was a balmy night, one of those mild May evenings when the spring which had begun to stir some weeks earlier settled into early summer and the days were already long. These were the days when the occupants of the small island in the middle of the loch were at their most restless.

A few servants were still moving about the courtyard but Lochleven Castle and all its parts, the kitchen, the brewery, the bakehouse, all were beginning to shut down for the night. The men playing handball had gone inside. From the guardhouse there came a roar of laughter. A man went from sconce to sconce lighting the torches. Above her head there was a sudden rush of wings and loud cries: a skein of geese, flying in low, skimming over the water to land somewhere out of sight on the marshes of the mainland.

She saw a flash of movement at one of the lower windows of the Glassin Tower. A few minutes went by and then a woman emerged from the doorway. She crossed the courtyard, heading for the postern in the wall that led to the jetty. An ordinary countrywoman, judging by the clothes. Except it wasn't. The Queen's height distinguished her from the lave of women, even though now she was hunched over in an attempt to look older, or smaller, or both.

The Queen passed through the doorway. A hand reached over from outside and pulled it shut behind her. Soon she reappeared in Margaret's vision standing beside the boats which were here pulled up on the beach. Not the jetty then. No, that would be too obvious. Better one of the spare boats which no one would immediately notice was gone.

As Margaret watched, the disguised Queen was helped into a boat by a man similarly drab in workman's clothing.

'Willie,' she thought. 'Good lad.'

Willie Douglas pushed the boat out onto the water, released the painter and leapt aboard. He fitted the oars into the muffled rowlocks and began to row, swiftly and silently. Within seconds the boat had gone from sight as darkness spread over the water.

Chapter One
1534

Word came that King James had been sighted and would reach Stirling Castle within the hour. It was a small private party which was expected, James and his closest friends. He had already stood down all the fighting men who had been with him in the north. The main part of the court would bypass Stirling and go on to Edinburgh.

The Great Hall was warm, for the fires had been lit in the early morning. Margaret Erskine, checking that all was prepared, straightened the heraldic canopy hanging over the King's Chair of Estate on the dais. She smiled. Soon her own arms would be amalgamated with the royal arms of Scotland: the lion of the Stewarts side by side with the strong hand and dagger of the Erskines.

'What will you play tonight?' she called over to her father's musicians lounging by one of the fireplaces. They had been there for hours, claiming that instruments needed to be kept warm as an excuse to stay there all day. Her father indulged them.

'*Une gay Bergier,*' the viol player replied. 'And *Adieu mes amours.*'

She nodded approval. Appropriate, she thought. The King had left all his old loves behind.

'We've written a new tune celebrating the King's successes in the north. A pavane.'

Soon they would be writing songs for a different celebration, in praise of her wedding to the King.

As she left the Great Hall she saw her mother entering the Chapel Royal. Lady Erskine beckoned. The chapel was empty save for one of the priest's helpers

3

pouring water into the piscina. As soon as King James arrived there would be a mass said in thanksgiving for his safe return.

All was clean and in readiness. They watched as the man made his obeisance to the altar and left by the side door. Without looking at her daughter Lady Erskine said, 'Margaret, you should know that your husband is coming with the King.'

'What is that to me?'

'He wants to talk to you.'

'I will not see him.'

'He is your husband.'

'Not for long.'

'Are marriages to be so easily broken, on the whim of a king?'

'It is not a whim. He has always wanted to marry me. We expect word any day that the Pope has granted my annulment.'

Margaret turned to go but Lady Erskine clutched at her arm and glared into her face.

'Don't delude yourself. Do you think you are the only one of the King's women? He will whore with any backstairs skivvy. Do you think you are different?'

'The King will marry me.'

'Robert Douglas is a good man. You should count yourself fortunate to have such a husband. Not many men would have waited so patiently for you to recover from this insanity.'

Margaret shook herself free. 'If I am mad then so is James.'

There was a sound from the retrochoir and the priest appeared. He paid no attention to the two women but knelt before the altar to pray.

Outside in the courtyard people were milling about, intent on their duties while from above their head came a shout of warning. The King was nearing the town. Margaret ran up to the wall walk to watch her lover's arrival. There they were, riding hard, King James's standard out in front, fluttering in the sun. Behind it the King himself, with his squires in red and yellow. Around them an escort in Erskine livery, for her father had sent men to meet him. There was the Huntly standard and those of the Setons, the Maxwells, the Hamiltons, the Lindsays, men the King had grown up with, men who were his friends. Near the rear, she could just make out the Douglas banner.

That night the music was livelier, the dancing more vigorous, the lovemaking of the couples who slipped out of the overheated room into the surrounding darkness was sweeter, all the more so for the easing of tension almost palpable in the men who had been riding with the King for the last three weeks. King James had subdued the north, demonstrating that he was the King for all Scotland, that no part of it was beyond the rule of law, his law.

The court revelled.

Then a word to the herald who called for silence, and the King was on his feet, beckoning to his host.

'My Lord Erskine, my dear and loyal cousin.'

Now. Margaret felt her cheeks grow hot and her heart beat faster. Now James was going to announce their betrothal.

But no. It was not that. Not yet. He was talking about King Henry of England.

'His Majesty has been pleased to offer me the Order of the Garter.'

'Doubtless Old Harry thinks to bribe our King into marrying his daughter.' Margaret turned her head too late to see who had spoken such foolishness, but the crowd had shifted and all were now waiting for the King's next words.

'Since I obviously cannot leave Scotland I will send my Lord Erskine as my proxy to do duty at the ceremony.'

There was a murmur of approval. It was indeed a great honour, both for the King and for her father, a preliminary no doubt to the more important announcement. She shifted impatiently and made to step nearer the King, but he was now signalling to the musicians to start up the dancing again.

'A pavane, my friends. Written by our host's musicians in honour of our successful progress to the north.' He stepped down from the dais and took the hand of Lady Erskine.

Margaret found Lord Seton by her side. He drew her into the dance. She had always liked George Seton. A companion to James from an early age, they had all grown up together. Now he was mourning the death of his young wife.

'Margaret, I wish...' he began and then stopped.

'Wish what?'

Seton shook his head, whatever he wanted to say he could not say. He seemed unwilling to meet her eye. Was he yearning for her? She felt a spark of amusement but kept her face grave. They danced on in silence.

When the King had signalled the end of the evening and walked out of the Hall, he said quietly as he passed Margaret, 'Come to me tonight.'

In the King's chamber the fire had been banked up for the night. On the table there was a jug of wine and a plate of tiny marzipan and lavender pastries.

Margaret poured herself a glass of wine. She had drunk little at the banquet, feeling herself already intoxicated with the atmosphere and the anticipation.

She idly turned the pages of the book lying open on James's table. He was an avid reader. As the helpless pawn in his childhood of one faction of nobles after another, he was deprived of a disciplined education. Now he was proud

6

of the extensive collection of books which he was building up.

This was one of his favourites, a book published in the time of his father. James had used to read her lines from it when they lay together. She remembered them and now she could pick them out in the heavy black print. *Up rose the lark the heaven's minstrel fine, In May to a morrow mirthful.* All our Mays will be mirthful, he promised, and all the birds of the air will rejoice with us. She closed the book reverently and ran her hand over the leather cover. Perhaps he would read to her tonight.

Now the warm glow of desire was overlaid with slight irritation. What was keeping him?

There he was at last. She had not expected her father to be with him. Lord Erskine ignored her.

'Well, John,' James said. 'When can you travel south?'

'Not immediately. Perhaps it would not do to appear too eager.'

'True. I would not want my Uncle Harry to think I dance to his bidding.' They fell to discussing the details. As Keeper of Stirling Castle, Lord Erskine had to ensure its security whenever he left, and then there were his duties in Edinburgh in the council and the Chancery Court.

'Have your people check the vaults at Edinburgh and pick out some suitable gold to take as a gift. Let me have a list. We can have it cleaned up and, if necessary, engraved. When you get there don't stand for any nonsense about precedence. If they try to place others ahead of you, do not stay, just take the documents of the Order and come home.'

Why were they talking business that could wait till the morning? At last her father rose and without looking at her left the room. Margaret slid into the King's arms and he kissed her, hard and passionately. His longing was as strong as hers.

7

'My Meg,' he murmured.

'James, are you going to make the announcement tomorrow?'

'Later,' he said, nuzzling her neck. 'We'll talk later.'

'I thought you were going to tell everyone tonight.'

He pulled down her bodice and kissed her breasts. 'Later,' he repeated, pushing her down onto the cushions piled in front of the fire.

'No, now.'

He kissed her again. 'Ssh.' But she pushed him off and he sighed and let her go.

'There have been developments.'

'My annulment?' She felt joy flooding through her. 'My annulment has come through? The Pope has agreed?'

'No, not yet. I mean, not that.'

'Is there to be more delay? But James, why can we not announce our plans now? I can see we cannot be married till the annulment comes through but that surely is only a matter of time.'

'Meg, I love you, you know that.'

'I love you, too.'

'But a king is not his own man. He must always think of the kingdom in everything he does.'

'Of course. And I will be by your side helping you. You always said so. How much longer, James?'

He stood up and began to pace the room. He tried to speak but the words wouldn't come. He looked down at her with a sombre expression. Then she understood.

'James,' she said, keeping her voice level and quiet. Screeching at this time would not help. 'What are you talking about?'

'My marriage.'

She reached up to the table and lifted her wine glass and took a sip. My marriage, he said. *My* marriage. The wine was a sweet Madeira, the wrong wine for a throat gone suddenly dry.

'Yes, James, go on.'

'There are many who would be unhappy were I to marry a Scotswoman.'

'There would certainly be some sorry to see you marry me.'

'Not just you. Any Scotswoman. Do you not see, Meg, if I was to marry *any* Scotswoman, her family would become too powerful and the other lords would not like that.'

'My family are already among the most important. Nothing would change that.'

Her voice was trembling but if he mistook it for anguish he was wrong. She was angry. She knew what was happening. She may have been a girl in love but Margaret Erskine was nobody's fool. He was telling her he was not going to marry her.

He dropped back down onto his knees beside her. 'I do want to marry you. Nothing would make me happier, but I cannot. I cannot.'

'You are the King. You can do what you want.' But she knew the game was lost. She should have known it was lost months ago, when he had put off and put off making the public announcement, when he had been slow in agreeing the wording of the letters dispatched to the Pope applying for the annulment of her existing marriage. Had he perhaps been hoping all this time that she would decide *she* did not want to marry *him*?

'The council are pressing me to consider a French marriage.'

'And are you?'

'I hardly think of it. It matters little to me.'

'And when is this to happen?'

He shrugged. 'Some time. There is no urgency. Let's not worry about it.' He raised her hand to his lips and kissed the palm of it.

She shook him off. 'When?'

'I believe David Beaton has already started making enquiries.'

Ah. David Beaton.

David Beaton, who it was said forgot he was the Scots King's ambassador in France and thought he was the French King's ambassador to Scotland. Of course David Beaton would want the King to marry a Frenchwoman. Beaton loved all things French.

'I see. You've already begun planning. Before you said anything to me. Does everybody know? My father?'

'I wanted to tell you myself.'

'Now you have told me. You will not marry me.'

'There is the old treaty. The treaty requires that I marry a Frenchwoman.'

'The treaty was there when you lay with me the first time. And the next. And the next. And it was not mentioned when our son was born. It was not mentioned any of the times we talked of marriage.'

'Margaret, it has to be. It is best for Scotland. We need the alliance with France. David Beaton has the right of it.'

'Has he been telling the Pope to refuse my annulment, even while you were telling me it would be all right?'

'Of course not. The Pope would not be influenced.'

'Was the petition even sent, or is it still lying somewhere among David Beaton's papers, delayed while the two of you decide it is no longer needed?'

'Meg, Meg, you must be brave,' he said.

She would not be brave. At last her resolve broke and she started shouting incoherently, sobbing. He grasped

10

her by the shoulders and pulled her to him, almost crushing the breath from her.

'You are the one I love. Nothing changes that.'

She pulled back. 'Am I to continue as the royal whore after you are married?' She saw from his face that this was exactly what he had in mind. 'Will you set me up as your official mistress as I am told they do in France? Will your new French wife expect that?'

'I hoped...'

'What's in it for me?'

'I've arranged an income for you from the Edinburgh customs.'

'I don't want money.'

'You must have it.'

'Jamie. What about Jamie?'

'My love...'

'You promised he would be your heir.'

'You know I have provided for him. I'll do more. He'll have a good church living. The best. St Andrews. He will never want.'

'He will always be a bastard. Like all the others,' she spat out.

'He's the one of my sons I love best, nothing changes that. I love him as I love you.'

Did she believe him?

He slid his arm round her shoulder. 'Come to bed.'

She pushed him away. 'No.'

'No?' He slid his hand down her front, pulling at the laces of her stomacher. 'Please, Meg.'

She rose to her feet and looked down at him crouched there on the cushions by the fire. There he was, the King of Scots, begging her. But what she wanted most he would not give her.

'No,' she said, and turned and walked from the room without a backward glance.

She made her way through the deserted passages to the family quarters and her own room. Her younger sister who shared the room barely stirred as she entered, murmured something in her sleep and settled down again, her head under the quilt.

Margaret pushed open the shutters. She sat for a long time looking out into the night. There was a new moon and she thought of how the superstitious people would turn over the coins in their pocket, if they had any coins, and make a wish. She had no coins in her pocket and she did not make a wish.

Instead, as the first signs of light began to appear in the east, she undressed and put on her nightgown. She slipped from the room and padded silently up the stair.

She let herself into the room slept in by Robert Douglas. He had this to himself, a small plain room. It was all he had ever asked for. He was asleep and gently snoring. She sat on the edge of the pallet bed and shook him.

He was alert in an instant, a soldier's trick, his hand already reaching for a weapon, but of course in his bedroom in the house of his kin there was no weapon.

He sat up.

'What are you doing here?'

'Did you know the King is going to marry a Frenchwoman?'

He pulled up the bolster to support him while he sat up.

'She's not been chosen yet,' he said. 'But it will happen. Beaton has it in hand.'

'No one told me.'

'No one dared. He wanted to tell you himself.'

'That was brave of him, then. Does everyone know?'

He shrugged.

'Everyone?' she persisted. 'George Seton?'

So George Seton had only been sorry for her. And her father? What had he been afraid of that he wouldn't look her in the eye? A public display of hysterics?

They were all laughing at her. Or worse, pitying her. Poor deluded girl. Was that what they were thinking? She felt rage boiling inside her.

There was the faint light of dawn coming through the gaps in the shutters and she could see her husband's face, softened by sleep. They had been wed when they were both twelve years old. It had not been the wish of either of them, but they had no say in the matter. In time, there had been born their daughter Euphemia, but for the last few years, while she was loved by the King, Robert Douglas had been her husband in name only. Now he was all she had.

She pulled her nightgown over her head, and naked, climbed into the bed beside him. Afterwards, as he turned his back on her and pulled the quilt round himself he said, 'Tomorrow I'll arrange with your father for you to move to Lochleven. My home will be your home.'

13

Chapter Two

The cluster of buildings dominated by the keep and surrounded by a high defensive curtain wall occupied the whole of the small island in Loch Leven. It had been the seat of this branch of the Douglases for as long as anyone could remember. Sir Robert Douglas inherited it from his grandfather, for his father had died while the old man was still alive.

As the boat approached the island Margaret could see pale faces on the battlements of the tower, castle servants and guards anxious to catch a glimpse of their new mistress. There was a dead feeling in her heart: grey, she thought, a grey place to live a grey life, for that was all that was left to her now.

The men put up their oars as the boat swung under the shadow of the walls while the helmsman eased it alongside the landing stage. Robert Douglas was waiting. He held out his hand and helped her ashore.

'Welcome to Lochleven.'

He took her on a tour of her new home, past the guardroom, the servants' hall, the bakehouse, the brewhouse, the little chapel where the priest hovered at the door. There was a small garden outside the curtain wall where two women were already working. The spring planting was well under way.

Sir Robert pointed to the scaffolding inside the curtain wall opposite the keep where men were manoeuvring blocks of stone onto a hoist.

'I'm building new quarters there,' he said. 'When the children start coming we will be cramped for space.'

But it was the keep, the large square tower, which dominated all. Five storeys high, it was accessible only by a door in the second floor, reached by a wooden forestair, removable, Sir Robert told Margaret, if the castle were under attack.

'Though of course such has not happened for a long time and is not likely to happen, now that we are at peace.'

No, she thought. Who would be interested in an insignificant little castle? Any invading army would merely sweep past on the shore.

He led her through the rooms of the tower, up through the Hall, the air filled with the smells of cooking from the kitchen underneath, and then to the private chambers and on to the top floor and their bedchamber. At each level she could look from the windows down on the courtyard and raising her gaze, out over the water to the mainland, the marshlands to the south, dark hills to the north. Surrounding everything was the high wall. *We're all prisoners here,* she thought.

'You are tired,' he said.

'Yes.'

'You may do what you wish in the matter of furnishings. Make it comfortable for yourself. My grandfather cared little for such things, and I have been away constantly in the service of the King. You have a free hand. I know...' He stopped awkwardly. 'I know you have been accustomed to better. But there is no shortage of money. Do as you wish.'

'Thank you.'

What she wished was to take a boat and sail back to the mainland, take a horse from the stables, ride like the wind, no matter where, never to return.

'Thank you,' she said again.

He was doing his best to be kind.

That first year, she was cold all the time. Firewood had to be brought from the mainland and it was not grudged, but no matter how high the servants built the fires the air inside the tower she was never warm. But Robert Douglas was true to his word and never questioned her expenditure on wall hangings, tapestries and rugs, anything to cover the cold stone walls and keep out the draughts. There had been no woman in the house to care that the linen in the kists had grown mouldy with damp and the mice were breeding behind the wall panelling, or that some corners of the rooms were not safe because the floorboards were rotten with worm. She had all these things put right. She was young, she was energetic, she was angry.

If she were with a man she loved, would even here be bearable? But the question was meaningless and after a time she stopped thinking about it.

For these were years of living with a man who was unfailingly courteous but rarely showed her any affection. Why should he? He had no illusions about her feelings for him. She was there as a duty and she did her duty. It was not from love that he came to her bed, and it was not from passion she received him.

The duty brought compensations. Euphemia, already a lively five-year-old, was followed by more girls and then William, the son Sir Robert so desperately wanted, and more sons. With each child she expected to die, but there was some happiness to be had in them.

The child she loved most was the acknowledged son of the King. Lord James Stewart spent most of his time in the Erskine seat at Alloa, sometimes in the royal nursery with his half-brothers and sister, but at times he was brought to Lochleven to be with his mother and to learn to know his stepfather and siblings.

King James kept his promise. All the King's sons were given lucrative church livings, but the Priorship of St

Andrews went to James when he was seven years old. While the boy was a minor the income went to the King, but when he came into his manhood he would be a very wealthy man indeed.

'Must I take Holy Orders, Mother?' he had asked seriously as soon as he was old enough to understand this.

'There is no need,' she said. 'Cardinal Beaton himself never did until he was appointed a bishop and the rewards were sufficient for him to think of it.'

Her husband rose in the King's service. When his duties took him to Edinburgh or nearby St Andrews, she sometimes went with him, and there she would catch a glimpse of David Beaton. He was plump and florid, with a big nose which they said could sniff out heresy like a fox will scent a hen. His clothes were the richest of silks and satins and the finest of fine wool. His fingers glittered with gold and jewels. His horse was a magnificent thoroughbred caparisoned in flame-coloured silks as fine as his rider's. Even when Beaton was making the sign of the cross over the poor people who crowded round him, his eyes were elsewhere, raised up towards higher things, higher ambitions.

He was Chancellor of the kingdom, the King's right hand, friend of the Queen, the most powerful man in the country after James himself. He was raised to a rich See in France and then made Cardinal by the Pope, earthly rewards for organising the French marriage.

He was appointed Archbishop of St Andrews instead of his uncle who had died, an inevitable appointment but not necessarily a popular one. This gave him the ultimate authority over the Scottish church and he set about with a vengeance to stamp out the new religious heresies which were invading the country from the continent.

17

Watching his rise to power, Margaret never stopped hating him and blaming him for the King's decision not to marry her.

Chapter Three
1542

It had rained constantly since September. The chaplain mooned around muttering about the end times. When Margaret sharply told him to stop he sulked away into the chapel and knelt there, praying. He frightened the little skivvies with the tale of Noah's flood and there was nothing to reassure them, for the waters of the loch surged and frothed as the swollen rivers poured into it and the rain continued to fall. Outside everything squelched underfoot and the winter vegetables were rotting in the ground faster than they could be lifted.

Eventually Margaret had to send some of the younger ones away to their homes on the mainland. They were useless anyway as they would scoot up to the roof of the keep at the least excuse and cower there, watching the black waters of the loch. Useless to tell them the castle had never flooded, that the low-lying haughs on the shore to the west would always carry the water away.

Now there was more reason than ever to be thankful that the castle was so well protected by the waters of the loch. Despite the season, despite the weather, there was still fighting on the border with England. There had been some victories, some losses. Sir Robert had answered the King's call to muster all the men from his estates and had gone to join the armies.

They were restless in the castle. A servant, returning from carrying messages to the mainland, returned with garbled reports of a great battle in the south, but no one had been able to tell him where exactly or when, nor even if Sir Robert and his men had been involved in it.

'The reports came from deserters from the army.'

'They admit to being deserters?'

'No, my lady. That is what our people at the stables think they were. None stayed long enough to be questioned.'

Now today, thankfully, the rain had stopped. Fog was closing in round the castle. All was still.

Two-year-old William, sickly since birth, was having one of his difficult nights, when he could hardly breathe. Margaret prepared a basin of hot water scented with pungent spices and made him bend over it while she arranged a towel in a tent over his head to contain the steam.

'Breathe, William,' she commanded and the nurse holding him whispered *breathe*. He wheezed and gasped. Breathe, William. The scent of the basin was overlaid with the smell of the fog which seemed to penetrate every corner of the castle, though all the shutters had been closed.

He began to breathe more easily. The nurse rubbed his back and made soothing noises to him.

There was a movement at the door. 'My lady,' said the soft voice of a guard. 'A boat coming towards us.'

'How close?'

'Halfway. The fog is thick but we can hear it.'

'Just one? Stand by.'

William, still crouched over the scented steam, was calming down. This attack was nearly over but someone would have to sit with him all night. Margaret nodded to the nurse to stay and rose to her feet.

Down below the men were standing by, armed and ready, some at the landing stage, others posted round the island, while others waited on the wall walk, looking down, muskets ready. There were only old men here. The young ones had gone to war with Robert, but those that remained would fight to the death if they had to.

One boat they said, but one boat could be cover for many more silent boats with ill intent. Everyone living in the castle knew the different sounds boats made, those that were rowed confidently with nothing to hide and those that moved silently over the water at night. In these restless times it behoved the people to know the difference.

Faintly there came the soft swish of oars. They could see it now: one of their own boats carrying two people, the oarsman and one other. It drew into the landing stage.

With relief Margaret saw that it was her husband. As she moved towards him he stepped out of the boat and stumbled. Why, she thought, he has become an old man. What has happened? He swayed, nearly falling, till caught in the arms of a waiting man. He was carried, barely conscious, into the castle.

'What of our men?' Margaret asked the boatman.

'He was alone. He said he had sent all his men to their homes.'

'What else.'

'He said, it is over. That is all he said. It is over.'

Sir Robert slept while the servants stripped and washed him, scraped the mud from his legs and arms, picked the lice from his body hair. He slept for twelve hours during which all the occupants of the castle waited and watched.

No one else came.

Margaret moved quietly between his bedside and the nursery, where William and the other children, initially upset by the agitation caused by Sir Robert's return, had settled with their nurse.

When Robert drifted up from sleep he was disorientated and soon lapsed back into unconsciousness, but by the time it was daylight on the second day after his arrival he was able to sit up in bed and take some food.

His story came haltingly. There had been a battle on the border. Many of their commanders had been taken prisoner by the English.

21

'Unwillingly or not,' he added bitterly. It was well known that there were several magnates who would have preferred an alliance with England instead of with France.

'Were there many men lost?'

'Many threw down their arms and fled.'

'Yes,' she said. 'There was talk here of deserters.'

'Cowards, one and all'

'But you were not there?'

'No, I was with the King at Lochmaben. It was hellish. There was flux among our men, and worse. And rain, nothing but rain. After word of the battle came, he ordered that everyone stand down. We struck camp. He has gone to Linlithgow to be with the Queen. She is near her time. And by God, I am glad to be home.'

And he bent his head into his hands and wept.

She rose. 'We are glad to have you home.'

She called a girl to sit with Sir Robert. She felt overwhelming relief. The King was safe. He had not been in the fighting. She sent a silent prayer of thanks to God.

They waited. From time to time Margaret sent a man to the mainland to find out what was happening, if anything. Generally he came back to tell them there was no news.

One day he returned in great excitement. They were saying the Queen had been confined. A girl-child, unfortunately, but the King and Queen were still young and there would be many more babies in the royal nursery. It was little enough cause for rejoicing in this dark season but it was all Scotland had.

'Where is the King, does anyone say?'

'He is at Falkland.'

Not far away, but a different world. Margaret knew Falkland Palace well. It was a palace built for summer pleasure and she had spent many months there with the young King, hunting and hawking, dancing, dallying and loving. Her heart ached with longing to be there again with him, by his side, nursing him if he was ill, as the messenger was saying.

'Ill? He is ill?'

'That is what they say.'

She left them then, Sir Robert and the servant talking.

On the turn of the narrow stairwell she sank down on the step and leaned back against the cold stone wall. God preserve him, she prayed. God preserve him.

Then one day there was a signal from the shore and the boat which drew into the jetty carried a messenger from the Lyon King of Arms, bearing a letter for Sir Robert.

He came into Margaret's chamber with the letter in his hand.

'What is it?' She put down her sewing.

He told her baldly without preliminary. 'The King is dead.'

'Oh.'

'Wife,' he said. 'Do you understand me? The King is dead.'

'I hear you,' she said, and picked up her sewing.

He grabbed her arm, making her drop her work. He yanked her to her feet and shook her.

'Do you understand what I am saying? He is dead. James is dead. That is an end of it.'

He pushed her to the floor, and unlacing his breeches threw himself on top of her, pulling at her skirts. But when he had exposed her, scratching and bruising her, and pushed himself between her legs, he found that he could not penetrate her, try as he might, and he could only lie there, sobbing with anger.

Chapter Four

Lord James Stewart did his best to show no emotion when he was told of the death of his father. Inside he thought his heart would break.

At Falkland Palace he took his turn, along with the King's other sons, to watch over the body. In the stillness of the long night he resolved that his first loyalty would always be to the baby princess, queen-to-be, his new sister. He knew from the talk swirling round the palace, that there was going on a furious battle for control between my Lord Arran, heir to the throne should the baby princess die, and my Lord Cardinal. The other lords were taking one side or the other, or none, and it was not clear who would prevail should the baby princess die. Lord James resolved, in those dark hours, that for the sake of peace the baby princess must not die.

When the funeral was over and the body of the King laid to rest in the sepulchre at the Abbey of Holyrood beside his first wife, Queen Madeleine, Lord James went to the house in Edinburgh of his stepfather, Sir Robert Douglas. He needed to talk to his mother.

'Now that my Lord Arran has been appointed Governor, what should I do?'

'What would you wish to do? Do you wish to serve him?'

'No.'

'You're not yet old enough to take your place in the councils, but when you do you must be clear in your mind where your loyalties lie.'

'My loyalty is with the princess.'

'Then here is what you must do. You must ask to be taken into the service of the Queen Dowager.'

As he rose to go, she added, 'But, son, never forget that your first loyalty is to yourself.'

The household of the Queen Dowager at Linlithgow was much diminished. The Lord Governor, the Earl of Arran, presided over the royal household at Holyrood Palace and most of the courtiers were with him. Some of them, and some of the servants, preferred to remain in the service of the Dowager, but though recovering quickly from the birth of the princess, she no longer had any influence or power.

It became obvious to Lord James that she was being excluded from decisions, even those affecting herself and her daughter. No longer was there the constant stream of couriers, no longer the queue of petitioners waiting in the presence chamber. From time to time an order would come from Holyrood Palace.

She was to allow the English ambassador, Sir Ralph Sadler, to see the baby.

She was to deliver to the Governor the Crown Jewels.

She was to reduce her household further; the expense was becoming too great.

Messengers went from Linlithgow, as she wrote letter after letter to the new Lord Governor, to Chancellor Cardinal Beaton, to her family in France, but the responses were slow in coming and discouraging when they came. Her family, shaken by what had happened, could only counsel patience. And she, fretting, was convinced that all about her were spies.

Lord James, answering her summons, found her in a fury one day. She tossed a letter from the Governor onto her table.

'He wishes to form an alliance with England.'

'Is that how he will bring the war to an end?'

'Did my husband die for nothing?'

25

As the price of peace, King Henry wished to seal the alliance by the betrothal of his son Edward to the baby princess.

'Never,' said the Queen Dowager.

'Never,' said Cardinal Beaton, who had come in person from St Andrews to talk to her. The Queen Dowager stood up, the signal for the audience to be at an end.

'Never,' she repeated and swept from the room.

The Cardinal glanced round at the people standing around. He caught Lord James's eye and raised an eyebrow.

'Lord James,' he said, taking the boy aside and wrapping a fat arm round his shoulders. 'You here among all these women and old men? You could do better. I have need of bright young men in my household.'

'I thank you but I am settled here with the Queen.' And I am the son of a king, he thought, and you are but a laird's offspring no matter how high you have climbed.

That night there was a subdued banquet of sorts in honour of the Cardinal. Watching him seated beside the Queen Dowager, Lord James, from his position at the back of the Hall, thought of the words of the radical preachers. *The priests are venal and illiterate.* The Cardinal was certainly venal. His greed was reputed to know no bounds but he was not illiterate. *They take the pennies of the poor and give in return false promises of glory for their immortal souls.* There was, he thought, one thing that he might find himself in sympathy with the new governor, Arran. The man was said to be favourably disposed to those who called for reformation of the worst of the church's corruptions.

There was music but no dancing. The court was still in mourning. The Queen Dowager dismissed the company early and they all drifted off to bed.

Lord James was one of the squires whose turn it was to remain on duty outside her chamber, in case he was needed. He looked up to catch the signal of a waiting-woman beckoning him forward. The Queen wished to speak to him.

'What did the Cardinal have to say to you?'

'He was suggesting that perhaps I might like to join his household.'

'And would you like?'

'No, Your Grace.'

'Where does your loyalty lie, Jamie?'

'With you and the princess.'

She looked at him. 'You are very like your father. More than any of the others.'

She dismissed him with a smile.

In the weeks that followed Lord James watched and listened. He listened while the Queen Dowager fretted about the agreement of the Three Estates that Princess Mary should be married to Prince Edward of England.

Buy time, said the Cardinal. Dissimulate.

He listened while they thought they could counteract the power of Arran, by inviting the Earl of Lennox back into the country.

He has an equal claim to the throne, was the Cardinal's argument. 'Better, for he claims Arran's parents were not free to marry when he was born.'

The Queen Dowager: 'Lennox will be unwilling to leave France. He has lived there too long.'

'If Your Grace could perhaps suggest Your Grace's hand in marriage might be a possibility...?'

Dissimulate.

He listened to her assurances to Sir Ralph Sadler:

'Nothing would give me greater pleasure than to see my daughter married to the son of King Henry.' Even though Henry has laid our country waste and his invasion led to the death of my husband. Dissimulate.

To the Cardinal: You are the only one I trust. Even my servants have been sent by the Lord Governor to spy on me.

To the Lord Governor: The Cardinal's views are well known. If there is the treaty with England, he will remove himself to France. Scotland would be quit of him.

To Sir Ralph Sadler: Of course Lord Arran wishes to marry the princess to his own son whatever he might say.

Dissimulate.

To the Cardinal: I am writing to my family in France to support any appeal you may make for French aid.

To Sir Ralph Sadler: Had the Cardinal the organising of the negotiations for my daughter's hand with your prince, he would have handled the matter better.

To the Lord Governor: I would wish the Estates to hold firm to their course as long as they agree the princess must not be given up to the English until she is of an age to marry. Till then you must remain as her wise and capable Regent.

And if the Queen knew that he, Lord James, was listening to the preachers and that he had in his room books by Martin Luther smuggled in from Antwerp, he would quickly lose his place in her court.

Dissimulate.

Chapter Five
1543

Sir Robert Douglas received a summons to a meeting of the parliament, the Three Estates, to be held in Edinburgh on 3rd January. Grumbling at the need to travel at this time of year, in this weather (perhaps they are hoping no one would go, suggested Margaret), he mounted his horse and set off with a small group of retainers.

A week later Margaret received a letter from him to say he would have to remain in Edinburgh. If she wished to join him at their town house she was free to do so, provided she left Lochleven secure and the children well.

'Tell me,' she said on her arrival. 'What could you not say in your letters?'

'Some say the King did not leave a will. Others say he did but that it was destroyed. Others say he made certain requests on his death bed which are being honoured, others say they are being ignored. Who is to know where the truth lies? The proposed regency of five people would not work, so it is Lord Arran as Governor and Beaton as Chancellor. Don't ask me how it came about. I don't know. There was bargaining under the table. A small group made the decision and the rest of us could not gainsay it. We had no arguments against.'

'The Cardinal takes second place, then.'

'The Cardinal's reward for agreeing that Arran will be Governor is the Great Seal. He'll make the most of it to line his own pockets. Make no mistake, Arran may be Governor in name, but the Cardinal governs in practice.'

January gave way to February. The days were short, but the incessant rain of the previous few months had

29

stopped, giving way to clear skies and cold winds. There was tension in the air. They could all feel it. Margaret, out every day with her maid to the market to order supplies for their small household, could feel it. Sir Robert, like the other men attending the parliament, walked up to the Tolbooth and back in the middle of the road, with his servant close by and his hand resting on the pommel of his sword. Even the churchmen attending the parliament came with armed retainers, and wore armour under their cassocks and daggers at their belts.

By night no curfew had any effect. There could be heard voices raised in anger and occasionally the distant clash of steel. Too much drink taken in the taverns exacerbated the tensions, but drink was not needed for men to find cause to fight. The lords, in daily contact with the Governor and the Chancellor, divided into two factions. Those who favoured neither side watched both parties warily, waiting to see which way the wind blew. If the lords themselves were above actual physical violence their large, armed trains of followers were not.

'Jamie is at Holyrood with the Queen Dowager,' Margaret told her husband one day. 'I have had a message from him.'

'Do you want to go and see him?'

'Yes, if I may.'

The next day she made her way through the narrow streets of Edinburgh and down the hill to the palace. Although it was barely first light there were many people about and she was struck by how many of them seemed to have no business to go to, since they showed signs of merely lingering and watching everyone else.

She knew her way round the palace. Had she not been here many times with her parents and the King? But inside she hesitated. The King's quarters were now occupied by the Lord Governor, she had been told. The Queen would be in her own part of the building, but the Queen's chambers had not been in use in the days of her visits here, for at that time the King had no wife.

She asked a scurrying maidservant to direct her. The girl, laden with cleaning buckets in both hands, barely paused but merely indicated with a jerk backwards of her chin a flight of steps in the far corner of the courtyard.

Margaret made her way up the spiral stair. She paused when she heard quick footsteps above her and a lad in page's livery came tumbling down, still tying the tapes of his shirt.

'Whoa, lad,' she said. 'Where would I find Lord James Stewart?'

'Second door on the left at the very top,' he said, straightening up respectfully and pulling down his doublet.

'Will he have risen?'

'Don't know,' said the boy. 'He's not on duty today.'

She found the door and knocked. It was opened and there stood Jamie. She threw her arms round him and then when he wriggled free of her she realised he was still in his nightgown. He spoke over his shoulder to someone in the room and there was a masculine grunt and the sound of someone turning over in bed. Margaret could see the pallets lined up on the floor. She had forgotten that of course he would be sharing a room with the other squires. There came raucous wordless calls.

'I'll get dressed and come down,' he said. 'Wait.'

'I'm sorry. I did not mean to embarrass you.'

He shrugged. It was nothing. Soon he joined her.

'Which is the Queen's room?'

He indicated a corridor, at the far end of which two guards were standing outside a door. He led his mother down into the gardens. There was still a vestige of frost on the corners where the rising sun had not yet touched. At this time of year the trees were bare, only some blackened berries still clinging to the leafless branches.

'I came early because I thought you would be with the Queen all day.'

'So I would be. But as you had sent word you were coming I asked leave to meet you.'

'Does she treat her people well?'

'Very well. She is kindness itself.'

'She inspires great loyalty, does she?'

'Yes.'

'She has some advisers, does she not?'

'Some.'

'Who does she depend on?'

'No one, Mother. She trusts no one.'

'Not you? Surely she trusts you.'

'Perhaps.'

'That is good. You must stay loyal to her and serve her well. Who knows where it may lead.'

'I have sworn to do so.'

'Yes, of course. You don't need me to tell you. I suppose her principal adviser is the Cardinal?'

'Sometimes.'

'He is always full of ideas, the Cardinal. So Sir Robert tells me.'

He was silent at that and they paced up and down. But soon his pleasure in his position at court got the better of him and he began to tell her more about his life there, of the music, of the regular exercise at the butts, how they went out riding whenever possible, how he helped with the Queen's hunting birds.

Then he fell silent.

'Mother,' he said. Then hesitated.

'Yes?'

'What does it mean that the Earl of Lennox might return?'

She drew in her breath. 'The Earl of Lennox is the sworn enemy of Arran.'

'That is what I understood.'

'If he returns,' she found herself choosing her words carefully. 'If he returns there might be the possibility of civil war. He claims the throne you see.'

'So I understood.'

'Who has suggested he might return?'

'My Lord Cardinal.'

She took her leave of him at the door to the palace. He kissed her hand and then disappeared up the staircase to his quarters.

So he is learning to be secretive, she thought as she made her way home. That is a good thing because one day soon he would be old enough to take his place among the ruling lords. But he must not be secretive with his mother.

Meantime she could see a way where she might seek her revenge on the Cardinal.

'Will you take me to the next audience with the Governor?' she asked Sir Robert.

The room was crowded. Sir Robert was soon drawn aside by men he knew. Margaret stood by herself, unheeded. She stroked the new velvet gown which had been made for just such an occasion. She had been away from court for eight years. A generation of courtiers was growing up who did not know her. Once, this presence chamber had been as familiar to her as her own home. Now it looked different, for everyone was in black, still in mourning for the King. But as she recovered from the sudden panicky breathlessness which her entry into the room had instilled in her, she was able to look round and could see that there were degrees of blackness. Here on this laird it was drab, there on that lord it had the shimmer of silk. A lady nearby wore jet beads but the setting was gold. There a lord wore black velvet, but the sleeves were slashed in the English style to show snowy linen underneath.

Over the people's heads she could see the King's tapestries and the painted ceiling. Nothing here had changed. It was still the same room. Only the figure on the dais was different. She could not see the Governor. All she could see was the Cloth of Estate over the throne.

One day it would be Jamie sitting there.

She felt a surge of excitement as she breathed in the heady scent of the pomanders and perfumes with which people had doused themselves and the underlying sweat made more intense with the heat, while round her the murmur of voices rose and fell. Nearby two men were talking in low voices of the health of King Henry of England. A woman was explaining to anyone who would listen that she had a neighbour who was a witch. Another was rehearsing his arguments for a court case involving land, and everywhere men clutched sheaves of papers. If the Governor would not hear them, they would leave the papers with one of his clerks.

Whenever someone was called forward the crowd separated to form a channel for him to pass and then closed up again, grumbling that there was no sensible organisation and matters should be heard in order of merit. One by one the petitioners were dealt with. Some strode from the room angrily, others left smiling with their people round them to clear the way. And for everyone leaving, two more would arrive.

Now there was a movement up at the front. Arran rose, the session over. She had her chance.

As he walked down the room between the rows of men, some bowing, some looking over his head, Margaret moved to be in his path, apparently casually, and caught his eye. He stopped.

'Lady Margaret,' he said. 'It has been a long time.'

'It has,' she answered. 'I often think back to those days long ago when we were all young together, you and I and the King and so many other people now gone.'

He peered at her. Is he looking for the girl he once knew? Was he remembering that in the circle of young people surrounding the King he had often been treated with contempt? He had been younger than the rest of them, she remembered, and regarded as a nuisance. There had been a game when they were very young, when they pretended that the King's life was in danger whenever Arran came near, for was he not the heir presumptive, and therefore assumed to be looking for a chance to assassinate the King? It was nonsense of course. But children could be cruel.

And Arran was as likely as not the one who would run to an adult to report some misdemeanour; one who would be your friend one moment and the next would turn against you. Oh yes, it was a long time ago and they were all children then, but the boy becomes the man and from what she had overheard from her husband and others, my Lord Arran had not changed.

Without answering he took her arm and led her out. In the antechamber he signalled to his people to go on without him.

'We should see more of you,' he said. He kept his tight grip on her arm. Close up, she could see that the fleshy pouches under his eyes were speckled with black dots. 'That would please me,' she said softly.

'You must come to court more.' His wife was constantly pregnant. It was said he was trying to divorce her, alleging she was mad. 'I will tell Sir Robert to bring you more often.'

'That would be good.'

He was a head taller than she was. She had forgotten that, as she had forgotten what a greedy child he had been, and now his belly strained at the fine wool of his doublet.

The very finest, she noticed. And the jewels in his cap had belonged to the King. She recognised the setting.

'I often remember the old times,' she said. 'And I am happy that old feuds will be forgotten.'

'Yes, so much is in the past and should stay there.'

'Now that my Lord Lennox is to return,' she added.

'What?'

'When my Lord Lennox returns.'

He dropped her arm. 'Who says he is returning?'

'I understand the Cardinal has invited him back. No doubt you have in mind a suitable post for him in the new government.'

'No doubt,' said Arran. He straightened up and without a word strode out of the room.

Margaret watched him go and turned to find her husband standing in the doorway looking at her.

'Where did you hear that?' he asked.

'I overheard something.'

'Is it true?'

She shrugged.

'You should not repeat gossip.'

'I didn't mean to.'

He grunted and strode on, with Margaret following.

She was awakened early in the morning two days later.

'We're going home,' he said. 'Tell the servants and be ready to leave today.'

'What's happened?'

'The Cardinal has been arrested. He is in close custody. The court is in turmoil. This is no place for us.'

But Margaret, as she gave instructions and supervised the packing of their clothes, rejoiced. The Cardinal would have his desserts at last. She hoped he would hang.

But as they rode northwards towards the ferry she realised that the visit to the court had unsettled her. Somehow she must try and get herself a permanent place there. Her brief foray had set the blood tingling in her veins. She had mouldered at Lochleven for too long. If Jamie was to come into his own, he was still young enough to need her help, and for that she needed to be as close to the court as possible.

Meantime there was only the return to Lochleven and settling down to a quiet life once more.

Chapter Six

The Privy Council headed by an increasingly marginalised Governor agreed to the betrothal of the baby princess to Prince Edward of England. This in turn brought the promise of a treaty of peace with England.

'God willing it lasts,' said Sir Robert.

'Amen,' said Margaret

Her husband had spent the last week travelling round his estates collecting the Candlemas rents. He could report now that despite the Three Estates trying to tell everyone that the treaty with England was good there was an uneasiness in the country.

'The people don't like the idea of the babe wed into England.'

'I don't like it,' said Margaret.

'It is for the best. We don't want another war.'

He arrived back at Lochleven late one day. He had been in Edinburgh for the formal signing of the treaties with England. There were two: one to wed the baby princess to Prince Edward as soon as she came of age, the second a treaty of peace.

'I only stayed to see them signed. It gets worse all the time,' he told Margaret. 'It is hardly safe to walk abroad. Yesterday the mob destroyed the garden in Sadler's house.'

'The English ambassador?'

'Aye. And worse. He was shot at in the street. Dear God, Meg, can you imagine it. If he had been killed, would England have stood by and done nothing? These fools don't know the damage they do.'

'Was he injured?'

'No, thank God. Badly shaken. Not half as badly as the Governor. He's beginning to understand how unpopular this betrothal is. The Queen Mother has returned to Linlithgow.'

But Margaret had a proposal of her own.

'Robert, now that there is a truce with the English and there will be no more wars, I would like you to build a new house on the mainland.'

'We are comfortable here. And safe.'

'It is too cold and damp for the children. William's chest is bad again. I do not think he will survive another winter here.'

He heard her. His son's life was precious to him above all else.

'Where the stables are now. Where the children could have more freedom, and the air is healthier.'

He grunted. 'We shall see.'

And then somehow, by a mixture of friendship and bribery, some said, while others said it was the influence of the Queen (for had not her closest ally, my Lord Seton, been the jailer?) whatever had been arranged, the Cardinal was soon back in his own palace in St Andrews, protected by his own guards. He celebrated mass at Easter with maximum ostentation.

A few days later one of the boatmen, bringing over to the island letters for Sir Robert, told him that there were rumours of a French fleet off the coast.

'Near Dunbar, they say. So the French will come and save our little princess from the English.'

'Don't talk folly,' said Sir Robert.

'That's not all,' insisted the indignant boatman. 'They say that the English have seized two Scottish merchant ships. Taken the crews prisoner. That's piracy.' And he jabbed Sir Robert in the chest in case he did not understand.

'Piracy,' he repeated. 'Is this what we have to put up with now our princess is to marry into England? Is that what you agreed to in the parliament? We'll have nothing left. No princess, no ships and no manhood either.' And he went off to the kitchen to be fed, grumbling all the while.

Shortly after that Sir Robert sent word round the men of his estates to stand by in case of a muster, for it seemed to him that all sensible men should be preparing for the possibility of war.

Chapter Seven

After the arrest of the Cardinal the Queen returned to Linlithgow, the better to protect her daughter. Lord James went with her.

There, the small beleaguered court watched the machinations of the Governor. They rejoiced at the release of the Cardinal. Now almost daily, messengers came to the Queen with reports from her spies, for with her sojourn in Edinburgh bringing her back into contact with her friends, she now had people everywhere, watching and listening. But it was becoming obvious to all of her retinue that she and they were almost prisoners in the Palace of Linlithgow. Requests that she might travel round the country, as she had been in the habit of doing with her husband, were dismissed by the Governor, politely, it is true, but nonetheless dismissed. A request to travel to the summer palace at Falkland was ignored.

Then could not she and the princess go to Stirling Castle, which after all was her own property under her marriage settlement? Refused, even though some of her furniture and plenishings had already gone there.

Soldiers arrived to form an extra guard, ostensibly to protect the princess on the grounds that there was a rumour of a possible kidnap, but clear to everyone within the palace that the guard was there to prevent them from leaving.

And then, just as more rumours reached them of a French fleet off the coast of Scotland, Governor Arran himself arrived at Linlithgow, with more armed men.

'It is for the protection of the princess,' he told the Queen. 'The French will try and kidnap her.'

'They will do nothing of the sort without my consent, and I have not given it.'

'Did you invite them here?'

She turned her back on him.

They watched as additional artillery was hauled up the hill to the palace and moved onto the walls. As July gave way to August word came that the Cardinal was marching to Linlithgow at the head of an army. They began to prepare for a siege.

Lord James Stewart stood on the wall walk and watched the Cardinal's army amassing on the fields beyond the town. Beside him stood the Queen.

'How many?'

'Several thousand. At least five.'

'Your eyes are better than mine. Read the banners for me.'

He scanned the crowded field. 'The Cardinal of course. With the largest tent. They come ready to stay for some time. Other bishops' men. Dunblane. Galloway. My Lord Huntly from the north. Lennox. Argyll. They each have hundreds of men and horses, and a great deal of artillery.'

And still they came, in wave after wave. As he listed the banners of the lairds as well as the lords and churchmen, his sharp eyes picked out the Douglas banners, one of them his stepfather, Douglas of Lochleven, and others of his kin. He hoped for his mother's sake that there would not be much demanded in actual fighting.

'Everyone,' said the Queen with satisfaction. 'Everyone.'

'Almost,' he had to agree.

And then his heart leapt for into view came the Erskine standard. 'My Lord Erskine,' he said. His grandfather. And his uncle.

'Of course he would not let me down,' said the Queen. 'Lord Erskine was ever the most faithful of men.'

And she gripped Jamie's forearm and laughed.

'And the Cardinal at the head.'

They left the wall walk and went back into the palace where Arran, Lord Governor, was pacing up and down the Queen's presence chamber, waiting for her. Beside him, arms folded, looking at the floor, stood a messenger, and the Governor had in his hand the letter bearing the seal of the Cardinal.

'This is rebellion,' he said. 'But you will be safe here. My men will resist any attempt to attack the palace.'

'What does the Cardinal ask?'

'He pretends that I am holding you as a prisoner. This is nonsense.'

'Is it?'

'He demands, demands, mark you, he that was my prisoner not so long ago, demands that I hand the princess and yourself over to his care.'

'My lord, this would have been avoided had you allowed me to travel to Stirling as I wished.'

The next day the talks began in a hastily set up council chamber. Lord James, in his place behind the Queen's chair, listened intently.

Recriminations. Yes, that was to be expected. Each man had his own reading of the events of the past.

For Arran: he had been trying to bring peace between England and Scotland.

For the Cardinal: the Governor had betrayed Scottish sovereignty and endangered the life of the princess.

For Arran: was the Cardinal intending to invite foreign invaders, the French in fact, onto Scottish soil?

For the Cardinal: what then were the English, if not the invaders Scotland had resisted for centuries?

It became obvious the Cardinal had the upper hand.

He had more men.

He could claim to be impartial.

For was not the Earl of Arran heir presumptive to the throne? Was there not in all his actions the ambition to be not just governor, not just regent for the baby princess, but king?

If the church, wary of Lord Arran's new-found tolerance for the growing Protestant agitation in the country, was pushed too far, might the Pope not be persuaded to declare Arran illegitimate, for was there not doubt as to the validity of the marriage of his parents? And that would clear the way for my Lord Lennox, sitting at the end of the table without saying a word, he who also claimed to be heir presumptive to the throne and if the time came when he could act on that claim, would use force of arms.

Jamie was aware of these undercurrents and listening hard for the actual words, never heard these threats uttered, at least not in his hearing, but they were there. It could be seen in the way that as the days passed Arran's diminishment was almost physical.

The outcome of the negotiations was that my Lord Arran would rule with a council of advisers and that the princess and the Queen would move to Stirling Castle. From henceforth the guardianship of the princess would be in the hands of four nominated lords.

And who better to be one of those guardians than the man who held Edinburgh and Stirling Castles, the quiet grey-haired man who said little but the weight of whose presence had added common sense to the raucous discussions, who better than my Lord Erskine.

Chapter Eight

I had him longer than you did.

This was Margaret's thought as she waited to see the Queen. I had him longer than you did. She repeated it to herself. It gave her strength, for she could feel the butterflies fluttering in her belly. And he loved me. He loved *me*.

There were others waiting. Some of them clutched petitions. Others were men passing through Stirling who deemed it advisable to present themselves to the Queen, out of courtesy if not from particular loyalty, for this was where the power lay now. My Lord Arran might nominally preside over the council in Edinburgh, but the Cardinal, friend of the Queen, still held the Great Seal, and my Lord Erskine held Edinburgh and Stirling Castles and would hold them for the princess and her mother no matter what befell.

Here was where the power lay and here, Margaret had determined, was where she must be.

The door into the presence chamber opened and her name was called. Several attendant ladies stood behind the Queen Dowager's chair while round the dais there were a number of men and women.

She paced through the room and curtseyed. She was familiar with these rooms. They should have been hers, but they had been designed and built by the King in the French style for his French bride to remind her of home. In the years of his marriage, she sometimes visited her parents when the court was not in residence, and at these times she would slip in here and wander round, fingering the fine tapestries, tracing with her finger the carvings on the furniture. She would lie on her back in front of the fire gazing up at the carved portraits in the ceiling, portraits of kings and queens and heroes. One of them was of the Queen. It should have been of her. Sometimes she liked to imagine that the portrait of a woman in a yellow dress was of herself. She had once had such a dress. But she did not dare ask anyone. Draw attention and it might be taken down, but she believed King James had given this commission to the artist without explanation, his present to her.

In the years since Marie de Guise had come to Scotland Margaret had caught occasional glimpses of her. Now, waiting to be invited to speak she could study the woman and see that she had changed little, thinner perhaps, less rosy in her complexion but still a handsome woman.

Behind the Queen's back those of her ladies who knew Margaret whispered something of her history to those who did not. There were covert glances at Jamie, standing with the other lads over by the window. The women looked at her with curiosity. There was nothing friendly in their manner.

The Queen Dowager knew her of course. They had met only once before. It had been during one of the King's illnesses when it was thought he would die. Margaret had left Lochleven to travel to his side, certain that he needed her, but she was at a disadvantage and the Queen had routed her. Her time had passed and she was not wanted. She accused the Queen then of making the King ill. Harsh words which she herself did not completely believe. She had seen the King suffering in a similar fashion before the marriage.

The Queen stepped down from the dais and nodded to Margaret to follow her. In the privacy of her bedchamber, the Queen sat and gestured to a stool nearby.

She began without a greeting. 'I know your husband fought bravely alongside the King and for that I thank him. And I am grateful that your son,' she paused and then went on. 'Your son Lord James serves me well.'

'He is his father's son.'

There was silence. Perhaps that had been the wrong thing to say. She had practised this in her mind. She had thought to appeal to the woman's sentiment for her late husband.

The Queen Dowager's face was impassive, her hands folded in her lap. Margaret lowered her gaze.

'What do you wish to ask of me?'

'Your Grace. I would wish to serve you as one of your ladies.'

'I am already well served.'

'The Erskines have always been loyal to the crown. My father had the care of... of the late King when he was only a boy. The King never lost his love for my father.'

'I know. He often spoke of it.' Was there a softening in her voice?

'I would serve you loyally.'

There was a pause. Then the Queen Dowager rose. 'Thank you. But I have no need of more attendants.'

The audience was at an end.

The baby princess lay swaddled in the cradle in the nursery. The cradle-rocker's foot moved rhythmically on the bar, while she fiddled with a piece of crochet on her lap. She looked up at Margaret's approach.

'My lady.'

'I hope you are well, Johanna.'

'Yes, ma'am, thank you.'

Margaret pulled over a stool and sat down.

'I have just come from the Queen. It is sad to see her looking so tired.'

'Yes, ma'am. Everyone is concerned for her.'

'She has suffered so much and we can all feel for her. But you look tired too. When does Ruth come to relieve you?'

'I hope she comes soon.' Johanna shifted awkwardly.

'My dear, you don't look well.'

The girl blushed, embarrassed to be the focus of concern. 'My courses, ma'am,' she whispered.

'Cramps, is it?' asked Margaret sympathetically.

'I need to go to the privy.'

'Why don't you go? I'll rock the baby. She won't wake up.'

The girl hesitated but she was obviously in some discomfort. At Margaret's encouraging smile she rose and shrugging a shawl over her shoulders, left the room. Margaret sat down in the chair and placed her foot on the cradle to begin rocking. The little princess, tightly swaddled and sound asleep had not stirred.

Margaret looked closely at her. The eight-month-old child looked healthy enough. If anything she seemed slightly big for her age. She wondered if this was the same cradle in which this little girl's brother had been found dead all those years ago, even as his mother knelt in the chapel praying for the life of her other son, lying ill in St Andrews.

How awful it would be, she thought, if this child also died here. But babies did die.

The room was quiet. The other nursemaids were away having their meal. Indeed they had little to do here save stitch clothes for the baby. Much of the clothing would not remain in the nursery for the child would outgrow it, but would be distributed among the people of Stirling. That is, if the Queen did not remarry and bear more children. She was young enough and it was very likely that she would.

But if this child were to die the Queen would return to France, for there would be nothing to keep her in Scotland. She would return to France and marry some scion of the royal family there. She would be happier in that life. And Scotland would be rid of her.

48

So Margaret mused. The room was quiet save for the occasional shush as a log shifted in the fire. Faintly from outside came the murmur of the castle going about its business, the clatter of a maid's pattens as she hurried across the courtyard, the voice of the Master at Arms as the guard changed, the lilting whistle of a kitchen lad.

Outside the windows there were swallows nesting in the eaves, for the nursery was high up, and the twittering of the chicks calling for food created a soothing background sound. Occasionally there would be the sharp distant cry of a hunting buzzard. When the chicks fledged there would lie one of the dangers.

The child was lying so still in the cradle that Margaret felt a sudden fear and bent over. Yes, the child was still breathing. Relieved she sat back and resumed rocking. How long could a child stop breathing before anyone noticed?

There was always someone with the child, day and night, but if it was the middle of the night and the light was dim, and a girl perhaps dozed off, as they were wont to do, it would be easy for baby to die without a sound, without stirring.

Margaret stopped rocking and bent forward. Her fingers twitched at the pillow under the baby's head. She had seen in some other nurseries a baby, unswaddled, wriggling and twisting on its blanket and too easily tumbling onto its face, to be rescued by a mother before it suffocated itself.

A baby could be easily suffocated and could be thought to be still asleep.

If this baby died, then the squabbles among the lords would break out again. Might those of no particular loyalty not turn then to someone who was flesh and blood of the late King, his favourite son?

Jamie was too young yet. But he would not always be young. Dear God, she prayed, let this child live long enough for Jamie to come into his own.

She came to with a start. Had she fallen asleep? God help me, she thought. I was dreaming of the death of this child. She was already on her feet when Johanna returned. She did not stop to talk.

In the chapel she threw herself down on the floor before the altar. Her breath now came in short, sharp sobs. *God help me. What was I going to do?*

She lay on her face before the altar, trembling, for what seemed like hours. One of her father's chaplains found her there.

They assumed she was ill, and made her go to bed, where she was coddled as if she was fragile, but it was many hours before she could still the beating of her heart and the pounding in her brain.

It was because she refused me, she thought. I wanted revenge, God help me I was going to take it out on the baby. She would try again. She needed to be back at court. There she could help Jamie come into the power that was his right.

Chapter Nine

Stirling was *en fête*. Lord Erskine, as the princess's guardian and as Keeper of the Castle, was in charge. He had given the heralds free rein to prepare plays and farces, musical entertainments, displays of chivalry and archery, whatever would amuse the visiting lords and the common people alike. Several hundred people would be fed. The magnates who had come from all over Scotland, the baby's relatives who had travelled from France, the visiting ambassadors, all would be banqueted in the Great Hall, while everyone else would have their fill in less elaborate style.

In a gesture of defiance to an enraged King Henry of England, the baby princess, nine months old, was being crowned Queen.

Margaret, moving round the castle while the preparations were going on, overheard frequent comments on the perfidy of the Earl of Arran, my Lord Governor. My lord ditherer, some were calling him.

Two days earlier Arran had recanted of his Protestant beliefs. He did penance for his apostasy, was granted absolution by the Cardinal and received back into the Catholic Church. The Protestants who had enjoyed their brief few months of hope put away their Bibles.

Whatever their private differences, Arran and the Cardinal could at least unite on this great day. Two hours earlier Margaret had watched the procession as it left the Queen's quarters and walked slowly towards the already crowded Chapel Royal. Arran was leading, carrying the crown, with Lennox following with the sceptre, while the Earl of Argyll, whose son was married to Lady Jane Stewart, half-sister of the princess, carried the great Sword of State.

Of the others crowding behind, Margaret only had eyes for Lord James following the procession. He, along with the other half-siblings of the new Queen, had their parts to play in this great day of her coronation. As he passed his mother on the way out he doffed his pearl-decorated cap and bowed.

The baby was crowned Mary, Queen of Scots by a resplendent Cardinal Beaton. Arran was first to receive the wafer in the mass that followed.

Margaret was not the only one to know that all was not as united as it appeared to be. Those lords who had professed allegiance to the new Protestantism and who found the Catholic ritual offensive, stayed away.

Later, standing at the back of the Great Hall watching the festivities Jamie said to her, 'It seems to me, Mother, that no man's loyalty can be depended on.'

'No,' she said softly. 'Your father's skill as king was that he could balance one against the other, so that no one gained ascendancy.'

'It is a skill which Her Grace the Queen Dowager has learned. For, Mother, no man can be trusted. They flit hither and thither in the wind as their own selfish ambition takes them.'

The Earl of Arran at the top table was slumped in his chair and languidly waved away another of the lords who had approached to speak to him. He had already eaten and drunk too much. Also at the top table, Earl Lennox was bending forward smiling to his neighbour, the Queen Dowager, who was speaking earnestly to him. Even as they watched, her hand fell onto the Earl's sleeve and was as quickly withdrawn.

'What about Lennox. Does she trust him?'

'My Lord Lennox will not be in this country long.'

She was instantly alert. 'Why do you say so?'

'Because his ambition to replace my Lord Arran as governor will come to nothing. Because at the same time as he is wooing my lady the Queen Dowager, he is swearing allegiance to King Henry. He wants to marry Henry's niece.'

Margaret was silent while she absorbed this information.

'How do you know this?'

'No one pays much heed to boys coming and going. We overhear much. Most of them do not listen.'

'But you do.'

'Oh yes, Mother, I do.'

But, as Sir Robert said to her later when she returned to Lochleven after the festivities, what did it all mean in the end? The Queen was a baby not even a year old. The chances of her survival to womanhood were slim. A man had to look to the reality of the situation and the reality was the rapidly diminishing power of the Lord Governor, who could do nothing without the agreement of the Council of Regency. And the Council of Regency was controlled by the combined increased power of the Cardinal and the Queen Dowager, united in their religion and their adherence to France. There would be a Council of Regency for at least another fifteen years and much could happen in that time.

'Remember it is not much more than three years since the coronation of the Queen as was, and now she is a widow and all has changed.'

The summer had passed and autumn settled in. Building work had started on the construction of the New House on the shore of the loch. Sir Robert led her over the works, which were now at first-floor level. The stonework was in place and a team of carpenters was working on the window frames while the weather held.

She walked along the front of the building. It would be a good house, she could see that. Large, modern, comfortable. She turned and looked north to where the island lay in the loch, the keep stark against the sky.

'Pray God for continued peace with England,' said Sir Robert. 'Peace to finish this.'

'It may take more than prayers.'

'Meg.' He was at her shoulder.

'What?'

'I wish there was more kindness between us.'

She sighed. 'I have no complaints. I am sorry if you feel I have not been a good wife.'

'You have been a good wife. But...' He left it there and walked towards the jetty where the boatman was waiting to take them back to the island.

As they crossed the water she said, 'Thank you for the New House.'

'It is as you say. It will be healthier for the children.'

It could be said that the prayers of some were answered, for news came in January that a son had been born to the royal family of France, a child who would one day be king.

And to the pro-French faction of Scotland, this was a gift from God, a boy who could be betrothed to the Queen of Scots. By that time the Three Estates had ordered a widespread ceremonial book-burning of all religious tracts and Bibles in the English tongue and repudiated the treaties with England.

Chapter Ten
1546

Margaret and Robert were in St Andrews for the marriage of their daughter Euphemia to Patrick Lindsay of the Byres, a good match as far as family went, though Margaret had her reservations about the man himself.

'It's a good connection to have,' Sir Robert said as they settled themselves in their lodging.

'I don't like him.' Even as she said this they could hear his loud voice as he arrived in the house.

'Mother-in-law.' He took off his cap and bowed.

'You are welcome, Patrick,' said Sir Robert when his wife showed no sign other than a wordless inclination of her head in acknowledgment of his greeting. 'Man, man, you've been in the wars.'

Patrick Lindsay fingered the bruise which spread like an angry stain across his cheek and chin. One eye was almost closed.

'Nothing,' he said. 'The other man came off worse. The apothecaries are still trying to put him together.' His laugh was raucous and coarse.

'You will excuse me,' said Margaret. 'I must see to the girls.'

Hotheaded, ever ready for a fight, she fumed. At twenty-four he was old enough to know better. With the English troops almost on their doorstep there would be fighting enough to be done without aggression among themselves.

She ached at the thought of little Phemie, fifteen years old, wed to this man. When she'd tried to delay the betrothal Robert had shown uncharacteristic impatience. The girl herself was nothing loath. She saw the swaggering young man as a romantic figure, a soldier scarred in battle, an adventurer in the tradition of the stories of King Arthur's knights, Robert the Bruce, Hercules all the heroes of their childhood tales.

'She will have her babies and her house to manage, as you did. What does it matter to her what fights he gets into? It will not affect her.'

The young couple were to go in the train of Cardinal Beaton to Edinburgh where there was government business to be transacted. Margaret hated to think of her girl in the company of the Cardinal. It did not reconcile her to Patrick Lindsay that he was one of the Cardinal's men, but then who was not in this town?

Before he left, the Cardinal summoned all the men with property in Fife to a council. The war with England was intensifying. There was an English fleet being readied to sail up the east coast of Scotland, he told them. They would harry the coastal areas and intended to land at St Andrews. So their intelligence had it and he did not doubt the truth of it. The whole of Fife and beyond was threatened. He needed the counsel of the local men to organise a resistance to any possible invasion.

Sir Robert came back to the house with a grave face.

'We've to stand by with men and munitions, ready to ride at a day's notice.'

'Dear God, is this war ever to be over? Four years now and no end in sight.'

But despite the danger, Margaret persuaded Robert to let her stay on in St Andrews while he went home to muster his men. 'There will be plenty of warning if the English fleet is sighted. We can be ready to leave at a moment's notice.'

Robert gave in after only a little persuasion. He could see for himself that the coastal air was good for five-year-old William and his eldest son was dear to him. His mind was already working on the organisation of the men from his estates.

Not least of the reasons for her wish to remain in St Andrews was that Jamie was attending St Salvator's College. It was obvious that the life of the college suited him. He looked content. Did he miss the life of the court? No, he assured her. He was content here. Time enough to think of the future. He would like to take his place in the councils of state, but not yet. Time enough, he implied, when the old men had gone.

'But Mother, come and see this.'

They walked to the cathedral. He stopped on the road opposite.

'See here, Mother.'

She saw. A bare patch on the earth. A small heap of stones, the beginnings of a cairn. Even as they stood there one of the canons from the cathedral hurried past and with a kick, almost casually scattered the stones.

Jamie waited till the man was out of earshot.

'This is where they burned Master Wishart.'

'Were you there?'

'Aye. I was here.'

'I have heard something of it. We do not live totally out of the world at Lochleven.'

His expression was sombre. He turned and walked on, past the cathedral, down past the harbour and out onto the road which led south of the town. He paced along silently and Margaret hurried to keep up with him.

When they were clear of the town he stopped and stood looking out to sea. 'Master Wishart spoke sense. My fellow students have all heard him at one time or another, as he travelled, preaching. He brought new ideas, ideas from the learned men in Europe.'

'Lutheranism,' she breathed.

57

'Yes. It was more than the corruption in the church, no one argues with that any more. But he talked of the need to return to the teachings in the Bible. I was there when he argued with the professors here and I thought, this man has the right of it.

'Mother, the Cardinal feared that Master Wishart and the other preachers were being listened to by the common people. He fears what happened in the German states when the peasants rose in revolt. Out of fear the Cardinal has persecuted those who try to follow Luther's teachings. He has killed innocent men and women when all they want is to read the Bible for themselves. He fears what would happen if enough people begin to resist the authority of the church.'

'Be careful,' she told him. 'Be careful that no one hears you. Even though you are the son of a king, that will not protect you if the Cardinal turns against you.'

'I am learning,' he said with a grim laugh. 'I learn to express myself obscurely as one discussing the most abstract of philosophies.'

Despite the threatened invasion the life of St Andrews went on as usual, save that here and there along the coast camps of soldiers sprang up in readiness. Beltane came and went, with less celebration here than elsewhere, for the church authorities frowned on it as a pagan festival. Out in the country round about, to be sure, could be seen on the skyline the orange of bonfires as the people celebrated in the old way, jumping their cattle through the flames. Torches flickered and swirled on the headland up above the town like so many fireflies performing a tortuous dance. In the town raucous shouts broke the night as drunks hammered at the gates to be let in. Even in Margaret's own household the younger maids were giggling in corners and more than one crept out on May morning to wash their faces in the dew.

Margaret had a letter from Robert to say they had celebrated Beltane at the New House, but they would soon move back to the island for safety.

The Cardinal returned. He made a ceremonial journey through the streets to the cathedral. Watching from her window Margaret knew that it was time to go back to Lochleven. She did not want to stay on here. She did not want to breathe the same air as the Cardinal.

The next day, a Saturday, she rose early, before dawn. No one else in the household was stirring but she wanted to prepare for the journey home. She moved quietly so as not to wake William, still sleeping in his cot. Her room overlooked South Street. As she opened the shutters to let in air she saw a young man come out of a side lane onto the street. She recognised him. He was Norman Leslie, son of the Earl of Rothes. Roistering all night, presumably, and now on his stumbling way home. But he wasn't stumbling. He was standing quietly as if waiting, half in shadow. As she watched, another figure emerged from the shadows and joined him.

Within a minute there were a number of others gathered. There was no sound. From the way they had wrapped cloaks round their faces and the way they were moving silently, they were up to no good. It was none of her business, whatever mischief they might be intending.

Curiosity got the better of her. She swiftly drew on her cloak and thrust her feet into outdoor shoes. In the street she almost caught up with the men. They were making their way along South Street towards the cathedral, but she doubted that they would be thinking of early mass.

She stood hidden in the door of the Dean's house and watched young Leslie and his companions waiting. More men joined them, until there were nearly twenty there. They were all cloaked and all had their faces hidden by hoods.

They were not speaking. Whatever they intended to do had been planned and each knew his role. There was the faint rumble of carts as the first of the market traders approached the gates of the town, and a hesitant sound of music from the cathedral as the choir began exercising their voices ready for the mass.

The group of men padded up the hill towards the Archbishop's castle. Margaret, following, had no doubt they meant mischief. The Leslies were no friends of the Cardinal. There had been a dispute recently over some land. Robert, friendly with the boy's father, had told her something of it.

Then she saw one of the men take a pistol from under his cloak and show it to the others. It was swiftly put back. A rush of coldness swept over her as she suddenly understood what was happening. These men were bent on murder. She was not tempted to raise the alarm. There could be no doubt of the intended victim. No one else was important enough in this town, or hated enough, to have prompted this level of planning, of conspiracy. She found herself praying, but it was not a prayer that their victim would be spared. She prayed that the assassins, if such they were, would succeed.

The castle was already stirring. The Cardinal had started years before to fortify the castle, but the building work seemed never-ending. The drawbridge was down for a wagonload of stone standing ready to enter.

As she watched, Leslie and his companions pushed forward past the wagon onto the drawbridge. She heard raised voices and next moment a body in the Cardinal's livery tumbled into the moat. It was the porter at the gate, who had tried to stop the men. It all happened in a matter of seconds.

Then all was noise and chaos. The men wheeling the cart abandoned it and ran for their lives. Builder's men inside the castle were massed under the gatehouse,

60

struggling to escape. One castle guard attempted to lower the portcullis and died for his pains with the swift flash of a dagger. Shouts echoed from the castle and someone leapt out of one of the lower floor windows into the moat and swam to the town side. There was desperation in his face. He crawled out and lay on the grass, gasping.

The drawbridge creaked and began to rise but the mechanism must have jammed for it stopped half up, half down. It was doubtful if anyone in the crowd forming outside would have been willing to cross it. Even the constables, now arriving in response to the shouting, hesitated. The castle, church property, was outside their jurisdiction.

A burgess pushed his way to the front and began to shout orders. Where are the guards? Rescue the Cardinal. Fetch ladders. Now the crowd was joined by increasing numbers of churchmen, friars, monks, priests, a few nuns.

Several men appeared on the battlements, some waving pistols. One of them, young Leslie, shouted something but his words were carried away on the wind. Then there was a stillness in the crowd as the men heaved something that looked like a crimson sack over the wall. The crimson covering fluttered briefly in the wind and then slipped off, down into the water, leaving the naked body of a man hanging upside down from the battlements. The body was still twitching.

There was a groan from the crowd. Beside Margaret a black-robed priest sank to his knees and began to wail. Others of the church crossed themselves. A few looked desperately round and began to ease themselves backwards, out of the crowd.

The body of Archbishop Cardinal Beaton, anchored to the battlements by some method that none could see, twisted gently. His grotesquely fat belly hung over his bloodied chest and they could all see his private parts exposed. As they watched, one of the murderers heaved himself up onto the parapet, opened his breeches and urinated over the Cardinal's body, sending gobbets of blood splashing into the air. There was a sound from the watchers, something between a groan and a sigh.

And then Margaret bethought herself of her own safety and of William. She must get away from St Andrews, take William and go home. She freed herself from the crowd, which was growing every minute. Already churchmen were scurrying past her towards the cathedral, perhaps thinking to protect themselves with numbers inside a sacred place.

Who knew how many other murderers might there be in the crowd? Who knew whether it was the signal for a general uprising against the church?

She felt a hand grip her arm. It was Jamie, white and, for him, almost dishevelled. He had obviously come out without shaving or caring much about the way he was dressed.

'Get out of this,' he hissed at her and half pushed, half dragged her away.

'William?' he asked.

'Safe with his nurse.'

They stood aside to avoid some people running towards the castle, late sleepers who had just heard the news.

'I'll see you safe on the road,' he said. 'The sooner you are clear of the town the better. There is no saying what might happen now.'

Chapter Eleven

When Lord James spotted his mother in the crowd outside the castle he was shocked by the look of exultation on her upturned face as she watched the body of the Cardinal perform its obscene twisting dance.

When he had seen her safely on her way with William and the servants he returned to St Salvator's College. The people were drifting about the streets, talking in low voices of what had happened, but every now and again there was a movement back towards the castle, as if no one could quite believe what had happened and needed to see it again. The streets were filling up with pilgrims arriving in pious mood, to be met with the story of what had happened. They diverted from the cathedral towards the castle.

In the days that followed, the town resumed almost its normal business. The Cardinal's body was removed inside the castle. The assassins issued a proclamation. Calling themselves the Castillians, they proclaimed a Protestant State of Scotland.

Governor Arran came himself at the head of troops intending to storm the castle and take the murderers prisoner. They brought two large cannon, named Cruik Mow and Deafe Meg. But after a few preliminary sorties they discovered what everyone knew, that the castle, protected as it was on three sides by the sea and with only a narrow land access, was impregnable.

The Governor retreated and the soldiers relaxed. In the next few weeks and months supporters came from all over Scotland to join the men inside the castle. The soldiers had instructions to arrest anyone leaving the castle, but not anyone entering. It was all one to them how many people were inside the castle. Some day it would be stormed and taken, whether there were twenty or a hundred and twenty rebels inside and in the meantime the summer weather continued and it was pleasant in the town. The alternative, for them was to return to the front and fight against the English. St Andrews was the better option. They were in no hurry to end the siege.

Lord James watched and listened. Who are these people willing to align themselves with assassins? As the siege relaxed and people started to come and go, he found there were many reasons to be there. Some were Protestants who genuinely saw this as a chance to establish a new promised land. Others were relatives of the Castillians who felt vulnerable to persecution if they stayed at home. They felt safer inside the castle. And there were those who were just troublemakers, out for a fight, any fight.

As commendator of the Priory of St Andrews, he attended conferences of churchmen and councillors alike, while they pondered how to end the siege. It was evident to Lord James, as to others, that Governor Arran, after the initial attempt, was not willing to press too hard.

Why? Because his son was in the castle. Young Hamilton had been in the Cardinal's retinue, held, it was said, as a guarantee of the Governor's compliant behaviour. The boy was still there and could be said to be now a prisoner of the Castillians.

In the meantime all continued as normal in the town. The pilgrims, after they had been to the cathedral to worship the remains of Saint Andrew, now walked northwards to stand and gaze at the castle where the atrocity had taken place. Such a holy place, they would murmur, to suffer such abomination and they would hear the whole story all over again from the beggars who always seemed to be hanging about, grateful for a few coins in return for their tales, some of which grew wilder and wilder as the weeks passed.

There were noticeably fewer churchmen in the town. Those who had other charges to go to left, anxious to be clear of a place where they felt more lives might be in danger. When they gathered in the cathedral for mass they clustered together in front of the altar, bishops and deans, canons and brothers alike, constantly looking over their shoulders at the congregation grouped behind them, as if fearing sudden attack.

The children of the town had long since given up wandering along the beaches for miles hoping to find the body of the Cardinal, and with it a reward. Ask them how they would know it was his and they would assure you it would be dressed in red silk and wearing a cross.

David Beaton had been more important to the Scottish church as Archbishop than as Cardinal, for as Archbishop he was head of the whole church in Scotland. Without him the church was leaderless. It was the task of the Pope to appoint another Archbishop, but this right had long ago been granted to the Scottish Crown to choose the appointment. The churchmen held their breath to see whom Arran would choose.

It was no surprise when he appointed his illegitimate half-brother Alexander Hamilton. It was no more nor less than was expected of the nepotism in church and state, but it gave the Protestants more ammunition with which to criticise the church and the propaganda issuing from the castle was strident in condemnation.

The winter passed, an uneasy winter of stalemate, not only in St Andrews but in the war with the English. There were English ships in Scottish waters, but there had not yet been the threatened invasion. It was known their troops were poised on the border, waiting for the spring offensive to begin.

Plague was sweeping through both countries. Families were too busy burying their dead to care much about the future. Yuletide came and went barely noticed. With the colleges of St Andrews emptied by the plague, Lord James went to Lochleven to spend the Yuletide with his mother and stepfather.

'We are sick of this war,' said Margaret. 'How many long years? Five years since the birth of the Queen. How much longer?'

'There is no sign the English will give up. King Henry is said to be so angry that he has lost all sanity. And now that they have signed a peace treaty with France they have nought else to do but to attack Scotland.'

'And the Queen Dowager? What says she to the situation?'

'I believe she constantly presses her family in France and the King there to send help.'

'Is he likely to?'

'The new King is said to be favourably inclined to her. There is talk of little Mary being betrothed to the Dauphin when they are both old enough.'

Margaret leaned back in her chair. She glanced over to Sir Robert. Seated near the blazing fire, he had taken little part in the conversation. Now his chin rested on his chest and he would give an occasional *harrumph*.

'Why cannot we be left in peace?'

The table behind them was still littered with the remains of their meal. Jamie lifted a small wooden horse from the floor where it had been dropped by William, and turned it over and over in his hand. The children had been allowed to spend some time with their parents. Now, the adults were alone; the children, fretful with the excitement, had been taken off to bed.

They were silent. Margaret was covertly watching her son. Now sixteen, he had the easy manners of a courtier, but she was conscious of a stillness about him. He was watching all the time. Yes, that was it, he was alert to everything that was happening round about him. When they entertained the people of the village, Jamie had circulated and talked to everyone, missing nobody and seeming aware of their names and history without having to be told.

Since none of them were his tenants, he would have been entitled to be a mere onlooker; indeed he did not need to be there. But, he had told her, it is as well to be aware what the common people are saying.

In these days of unrest, yes, it would be as well to know. The talk turned to the situation in St Andrews.

'Why does not the Queen Dowager intervene?' Margaret asked him. 'Surely she could summon enough loyal men to take the castle. Surely she wishes to avenge the murder of the Cardinal?'

'It is not a royal castle. She has no interest in it. And though she is angry and would willingly burn all the Protestants there, murderers or not, she has more to concern her.'

'How have they attempted to take the castle?' asked his stepfather.

'Various ways. They tried mining underground, under the moat, but the men inside heard the noise and blocked the tunnel. They have tried taking it from the seaward side, but there is no way of approaching it. And there are English ships patrolling the waters. They prevent any of our ships from approaching.'

'They favour the Castillians, I expect.'

'Yes, they have King Henry's support.'

'So, stalemate. And what is my Lord Arran doing?'

Lord James hesitated. 'I cannot judge, for I am not privy to all of the discussions. Only those that take place in St Andrews and concern the church.'

Sir Robert pressed him. 'You must know what orders are coming from Edinburgh.'

'Well, none.'

'That doesn't surprise me. He never could maintain a true course. Pray God we never have to serve under him in the field.'

'His son is a prisoner in the castle,' Margaret reminded them.

'Even so.' Sir Robert grunted and rose to his feet.

'I bid you goodnight,' he said, and stumbled from the room.

Jamie watched him go. 'Is he well? He looks so much older than the last time I saw him.'

'He has never fully recovered from the illness that seized him four years ago when he was with the army near Solway. He has shivering fits and cannot rise from his bed for the ache in his limbs. Then he is well again and as vigorous as ever. But I hope he will not be called on to fight again.'

He looked at her soberly. 'When the English invade in the spring, we may all be called on to fight.'

But as the month of January ended and February began, a courier came from the Queen Dowager. Jamie was to return to court. Word had come from England that King Henry was dead.

Chapter Twelve
1547

St Andrews was crowded. The threat of the sickness past, the town had returned to itself and now in late August was as busy as ever with people determined to enjoy themselves. There was a truce between the Castillians and the authorities. It was obvious that the contamination, as the Privy Council saw it, had not spread wholesale to the rest of the country; to make sure, more stringent legislation against contaminating books was passed. Besides they had more than enough to do with the war with England. It was expedient to let the situation in St Andrews be and await developments.

There were rumours that negotiations were under way for a peace treaty with England, but equally there were other rumours that the talks had reached stalemate and fighting in the borderlands was as fierce and deadly as ever it had been. What was known was that the Governor, the Earl himself, had gone to lead the troops in defending Annandale and Nithsdale.

But the harvest was promising to be a good one and people were in high spirits. The sun was shining and the people had money in their pockets.

The Lammas Fair was in full swing. The stalls carried hens and ducks, cheeses and bread, vegetables and fruits, fleeces and woven cloth, pottery bowls and wooden platters. Among them moved the tinkers crying to the women of the town to bring out their knives for sharpening, and the fortune tellers, and jugglers and clowns, and the dancing bears, and the fattest woman in the world, and the smallest man, and the gamblers and cheats, and the dancers and minstrels and everything that made this the highlight of the year.

The cathedral was constantly full. With the passing in the spring of the fresh legislation against heresy, the churchmen had recovered their confidence and the town was once more crowded with pilgrims, come for the Feast of the Transfiguration of Christ and the additional indulgences which would accrue to them.

A priest was leading pilgrims round the town, reciting to them with tears in his voice the story of the Cardinal's martyrdom. Nearby a woman was proclaiming to anyone who would listen that she prayed to the Cardinal and he appeared to her in a dream and cured her palsy.

Jamie, walking into Margaret's lodgings soon after she arrived with the children, was almost incoherent with excitement.

'There has never been anything like it,' he told her, while ruffling William's hair and giving him a handful of marzipan sweets. 'Every day there are disputations between the church and the reformers. Come with me tomorrow. Master Annand will be preaching on the true church. Then we will go to the Mercat Cross and we will hear Master Knox preach in opposition.'

'I remember Master Annand from last summer. But who is Master Knox?'

'He's the priest elected by the people to preach at the parish church. He's also the garrison chaplain for the Castillians. He speaks sense. He has to preach out of doors or in people's houses. He has been forbidden entry to the church.'

It seemed that the whole town was taking part in the debates. Margaret squeezed after Jamie and two of his fellow students into the Church of the Holy Trinity.

'That's Master Annand,' Jamie murmured to her. 'The tall man at the altar beside the priest. He is the Principal of one of the colleges here, one of our greatest scholars.'

The mass wound its way slowly to its conclusion. When it was time for the congregation to go forward to accept the wafer – *This is the body of Christ* – it was noticeable that many people stayed where they were and those who wished to go to the front had to shoulder their way past them.

The disputation began.

Margaret, stifled by the crush of bodies round her, had some difficulty following his arguments, but others in the congregation occasionally raised their voices. Some shouted agreement, there were others raised against. He was saying that the church was the final arbiter on all things spiritual and that men must obey. The church on earth is the church in heaven. Who could interpret the wishes of God better than those who were learned in such matters? Who else but those who had been handed the keys of the Kingdom by Jesus Christ himself and who were his only successors? Who but the Holy Father and his ordained brethren?

It was a relief to her when the talk came to an end and she was swept out into the street by the crowd. She stood gasping for breath and waiting for Jamie and his friends to catch up with her.

They were whooping with delight. 'Master Knox will demolish his arguments,' one of them said, and he and Jamie each took an arm to escort Margaret back to her lodgings. They both were talking at once; she stopped listening, just thankful that Jamie's friend in front was clearing a way through the crowd for them, for it would appear no one wanted to go home, but gathered in groups in the street, arguing, poking one another in the chest to emphasise a point, voices rising and faces reddening. From behind came the sound of a physical fight breaking out, and a cry for the constable.

There were similar scenes two days later when it was Master Knox's turn to be helped up onto a mounting block outside the gate of St Salvator's college. Without any preliminary he launched into his arguments against Dean Annand and all the priests.

'Priests!' He was sneering. 'Priests who can barely read or write. Men ostensibly of God who never have read the Bible, the Word of God, in their lives, who pretend to be able to save your souls when their own are in jeopardy.' He waved a book above his head. 'This is the Word of God. This is the Word, not what a man in Rome says it is. This is where we find our salvation. Read the Word of God as it is written, not what they say it is.'

If that is a Bible, thought Margaret, then it is illegal and he can be thrown into jail for heresy just by owning it. But this was clearly a town where no one was going to be punished for what was said. Not yet.

Now every day on every corner there seemed to be a man proclaiming his faith to a crowd of jeering or supportive listeners. And meantime people crowded into the cathedral and received the wafer and prayed at the feet of the Virgin Mary and St Andrew and gladly bought the token that would comfort them when they thought of their immortal souls. And then they went out into the streets and were told by the preachers their immortal souls were in danger anyway, because they had placed their faith in men's promises and not in Jesus Christ alone.

'No wonder,' Margaret said later to Master Knox, 'people are bewildered.'

She had spent a quiet morning sitting at the back of the room in which Master Knox was teaching the children their catechism. Persuaded by Jamie to take William, she listened while Knox led the children through a story from the Bible, the story of Noah and the Ark. The children listened enthralled. Then he tested them on the lines of the catechism which they had been learning the day before. He taught them a few more lines, then with a piece of chalk on a slate he led them through a few more letters of the alphabet. He called one of the older boys forward and the boy read haltingly from the Bible.

Later Margaret, taking William out for a walk along past the harbour to the south beach, came across Master Knox standing on the dunes looking out to sea. She would have passed behind him without a word. There was something of desolation in the expression on his face, but William squealed at the sight of him, a squeal of delight for the man who told such enthralling stories.

'Shush,' said Margaret. But Master Knox heard and turned.

'Lady Margaret.'

'I am sorry. We did not mean to disturb you.'

'I am glad. I was falling into melancholy. It does not do to be too much alone.'

He fell into step beside her. With a nod, Margaret indicated to the maid that she should take William and go on ahead. William obediently slipped his hand into that of the maid and they hurried on.

'You are very good with the children.'

'The children are the future.'

'You have the skill of a good dominie.'

'That is what I am. A dominie. That is how I come to be here. I am tutor to the sons of a laird who is now one of the Castillians. Not, of course, one of the assassins, but one who had long supported the cause of the reformation of religion in this country. He joined them after. He wanted his boys with him and I could not desert the boys. Besides, I betrayed my dear friend, Master Wishart. Anything I can do to make amends I will do.'

73

'You betrayed Master Wishart?'

'Perhaps not quite in the way that Judas Iscariot betrayed Jesus Christ, but in the way the disciples fell asleep in the garden when he needed them. When Master Wishart needed me, I failed him.'

There seemed no answer to that and they walked on in silence.

'Knowledge,' said Knox. 'Education. That is the way forward. I teach the children to read, they can read the Bible to their parents and soon all will know the Word. Not the word as disseminated by unlettered priests in a language that none but they speak, but the Word as it is written. Let all read it for themselves, they will understand God's mysteries.'

They climbed the well-worn path up to the clifftop. This was the route taken by the people living all along the coast when on their way to St Andrews. Now, nearly at the top, they paused and looked back on the town and its spires.

'They point to heaven,' said Knox. 'But underneath there is ignorance and superstition. It is our task to blow away all that nonsense.'

'The Castillians claim they are Scotland's first Protestant kingdom.'

He laughed. 'That is what they say.'

'Do you think they will succeed?'

'Of course not. The government will eventually find the time and the will to overcome them. Who knows what may happen then.'

'Bloodshed?'

'Perhaps.'

The clifftop path was becoming busier and the afternoon was wearing on.

'I must go back,' said Margaret.

'Thank you for your company.'

74

Margaret called to the nurse and with a final farewell they left Master Knox, who strode onwards along the path, leaning forward into the wind as if he would defeat it as he would defeat ignorance and superstition.

But Margaret found that John Knox was not the only person given to brooding and puzzlement. When Jamie came to visit her these days in breaks from his studies he tended to sit silently, absorbed in his own thoughts. He had always been a quiet boy but now there was something else. She knew better than to ask. Besides, she suspected that what was troubling him, immersed as he was in the arguments for and against the church, would be too deep for her to deal with. So she waited.

Part of the trouble was revealed when he suddenly said to her, 'I wonder whether Master Knox speaks truth.'

'He speaks as he sees it.'

'He attacks the church and what he says is reasonable and sensible. But...'

'But?'

'But my living comes from the church. I am Prior of St Andrews. I do not do anything to fulfil that task. Others do the work.'

'It was in the gift of your father, the King. It is the way in which he provided for you.'

'And for my brothers. And for the sons of his favourites. Mother, the money comes from the pilgrims' pence. From the sale of pilgrim tokens.'

He left then, still troubled, and from time to time Margaret saw him in earnest conversation with John Knox.

Only a week after her conversation with John Knox on the clifftop, word flew round the town that a fleet of warships had sailed into the bay. There was a quick muster of the soldiers garrisoned in the town and a call to the citizens to arm, for the invasion from the sea had been long expected. It became obvious on their approach that these ships were not carrying the dreaded Cross of St George, but the French lily at their mastheads.

As the people crowding the shore watched, the two warships dropped their anchors in the bay. The six galleys which escorted them continued towards the shore and slid up onto the west beach. They unloaded a contingent of armed men. Someone had the idea of closing the town's gates against them, but as the gates began to move the soldiers pushed their way through.

Swiftly they spread themselves out round the landward side of the castle out of reach of a bombardment of slingshot and arrows from the castle, where the drawbridge had been drawn up and the portcullis dropped. Soon the castle was completely surrounded: soldiers on the landward side, ships on the seaward side. No one could leave.

As the people watched and waited there was nothing more. The bombardment, unanswered by the soldiers, ceased. Warily the street market and the fair made a half-hearted attempt to keep going, but fear got the better of them. If there was to be serious fighting then it were better to be away from here. Some housewives quickly bought up the produce which was reduced in price to almost nothing.

It was early the next morning on the turn of the tide when several of the merchant ships berthed alongside the harbour wall hoisted sail and left, making way whether reluctantly or not for one of the warships to come alongside.

Two large cannon were unloaded. These were hauled up the road by a structure of pulleys, so that no men were exposed to the bombardment which had resumed from the castle walls. The French captain strode forward and stood on the edge of the moat. He called up to the Castillians.

'Surrender. Defend yourselves for you are now dealing with men of war.'

76

Defiantly the shout came back, 'We're holding the castle for Scotland, England and France, all three. What quarrel do you have with us?'

But while the men were shouting insults the people in the streets had to scrabble clear, for now squads of soldiers were pulling two more cannon through the streets away from the castle. There were many men in the crowd who later expressed admiration for the ingenious way they used a system of hoists and pulleys to heave the cannon up onto the highest points of the town's buildings, one to the top of St Rule's Tower and the other up onto the steeple of St Salvator's college chapel.

And finally, at the end of the day when all was in place to begin the bombardment, Governor Arran rode into the town at the head of his men, dusty and exhausted. They had ridden, they told the people, from the borders where the Governor had been leading the fight against the English.

There were some jeers in the crowd at that. Had the Governor waited until the French were here to do his job for him?

The bombardment of the castle began. The height of the cannon over the castle was all it took. In a matter of six hours the cannonballs from sea and land reduced the walls of the castle to rubble. There was nothing the men inside could do to defend themselves.

They marched out of the castle, heads high, shouting defiantly. They were quickly seized and with oaths and blows pushed into a line. Chains were brought and fastened to the ankles of some chosen at random whether those who shouted loudest, whether ringleaders or not. Arran sat on his horse and watched as they were marched past him.

Suddenly Margaret, watching among the crowd, gave a cry.

'It's Master Knox.'

True enough, one of those taken prisoner was John Knox. He walked quietly in line with the others.

The cry was taken up by the people round her. She pushed her way to the front of the crowd and grabbed Knox's arm. Two soldiers pulled her away, swearing. Then Jamie was by her side, the people willingly making way for him.

'My Lord,' he shouted to Arran over the heads of the people. 'This man is the parish priest. He should not be taken a prisoner. He had nothing to do with the assassination.'

Arran looked at him coldly. 'He's a heretic.'

'So were you at one time.' But this was said softly so that only Margaret by his side could hear him.

'You are Prior here,' said the Governor. 'Do you so forget your duties that you will not defend the church?'

The voice of Knox broke in, raised over the racket. 'Lord James, it's all right. These are my friends. I will go with them and succour them as a priest should. I will not be found wanting in their hour of need.'

The prisoners were marched over the dunes to the west sands where the galleys waited. They filed on board and the galleys put out to sea. While this was happening the cannon were being lowered from St Rule's Tower and the college chapel roof and carefully wheeled back to the ships in the harbour.

Then, as the people stood helplessly by, the French soldiers entered the castle and looted it of gold, silver, tapestries, clothing, chapel ornaments, stores of food and wine, everything they could take; they destroyed what they could not carry. A soldier passing with a silver chalice cradled in his arms was spat at by one of the townswomen and received a blow across her face for her pains. Soon all that was left of the castle, within a day of its surrender, were piles of stone.

The oarsmen pulled the ship clear of the harbour, the sails were hoisted, the ship in the bay raised anchor, they wheeled and, accompanied by the galleys, in no time disappeared over the horizon.

Chapter Thirteen

The fiery cross had been sent round Scotland. All men between the ages of sixteen and sixty, fathers and sons, spiritual and temporal, lord and commoner, all were to muster at Roslyn to the south of Edinburgh, bringing with them weapons and one month's food.

A major assault from England, determined once and for all to subdue the Scots, had begun. They were already north of St Abbs and moving fast. Word was that they had not even paused to harry the borderers as usual, but had swept through without skaith to the Scots. Much of the east coast was already in English hands, the seas were patrolled by English warships.

The men answered the call in their thousands.

Margaret stood beside her husband in the stables. She did not ask him if he had to go: she knew he must.

'Come back safe, husband.'

He nodded to his squire who made a cradle for his master's foot and flung him up into the saddle. Time was when he would not have needed such help. She watched him ride out to where his contingent of fighting men was gathered, some mounted, the pikemen on foot, all carrying what weapons they could afford and all subdued. Like Sir Robert, they were tired of warfare. It had gone on too long to look for glory or heroics.

In the nursery the two younger children were squabbling, with the nursemaid trying vainly to distract them. In the schoolroom the two older boys were bent over their books. Their tutor stood up as she entered the room and she signalled to him to sit again. William looked up at her anxiously.

'Mother, why may I not go with Father?'

'You are not old enough.'

'I'll go when I'm old enough?'

'There will be peace by then. Recite to me some of the Latin verses you are learning.'

As he stumbled his way through, with anxious glances at his tutor, she could hear the very faintest of wheezes in his chest. Sir Robert had wanted them to move to the castle on the island for safety, but she had pleaded William's health as a reason to go instead to the greater safety of Stirling Castle. At least when he was grown, if he achieved his manhood, he would never have the health to be able to soldier like his father. It was comfort of a sort.

She gave orders that the household was to be packed up. The family with their immediate retainers would travel to Stirling Castle. The remainder of their people would move over the island. It had already been provisioned for a siege, just in case.

When she arrived at Stirling Castle to a relieved welcome from her father and mother, she learned that her brother had gone to fight. Her father of course was exempted. As guardian of the Queen his first duty was to protect her, with his life if necessary.

'Jamie?' she asked.

'Still in St Andrews. They've formed a militia to protect the Fife coast. They're ready for when the invasion comes.'

Margaret hardly saw Lord Erskine. He was closeted every day with the Queen Dowager while a stream of messengers brought them news of the armies.

The English, under the Lord Protector my Lord Somerset, were encamped at Tranent. The Earl of Arran had taken up his position north of the River Esk, with the sea on his left flank and his right protected by the great expanse of boggy land known as Pinkie Cleugh.

81

'The Earl of Lennox is fighting with the English,' Lord Erskine told the Queen Dowager.

'That traitor.'

'On our side Huntly has ten thousand men, Arran himself has twenty thousand. The English army is not so large but they have mercenaries from Germany and Spanish and Italian cavalry, all professional soldiers.'

'And warships.'

'Including the ships they stole from us, *Salamander* and *Great Neptune*.'

'*Salamander* came with me from France,' said the Dowager sadly. 'It was a wedding gift to us from King Francois.'

'I could wish for a commander in the field with more grey hairs,' said Lord Erskine but he said this privately to his wife and Margaret.

Messengers continued to arrive at Stirling hourly.

'My spies are telling me that the English are under-victualled,' said the Queen Dowager.

'I receive the same information. There seems to be a suggestion that the English may go home without fighting. I have intelligence that they want to parley.'

'Send word to my Lord Arran. If there is parleying to be done then the council must be involved.'

'Amen,' said Lord Erskine.

Margaret, quietly tending to their refreshments along with Lady Erskine, for no one else was allowed into the room, murmured 'Amen.'

The Queen Dowager heard her and looked up. She had not up till then noticed that it was Margaret in attendance.

'Amen, indeed,' she said. 'Lord James is one we would be happy to see spared fighting.'

'My grandson will do his duty,' said Lord Erskine. And they were silent, remembering that his son was also with the army.

'Your Grace,' he said. 'I think we should send the little Queen to a place of greater safety. It is not so long since an English army came within six miles of here.'

The Dowager agreed. Secretly that night a small party of women, trusted men and the baby Queen slipped out of the castle into the night, making for the Lake of Menteith and the secluded priory on the island, which was in the care of Lord Erskine's kin.

On Friday word came that the Earl of Home had engaged with Lord Grey's cavalry troops but hard on the heels of that messenger came another to say that Home's men had been heavily defeated and were fleeing, pursued by the English.

'Why?' demanded Lord Erskine. 'How did this happen? Has Arran lost control of his commanders?' But the messenger, exhausted with hard riding, could add no more information, except to mutter that borderers were notoriously unreliable.

The next day, Saturday, all at Stirling Castle went about their duties silently. They were aware that something serious was happening not so very far to the south, that this day would be decisive. All the fighting men of Scotland were facing an English army better equipped and better trained, which also had the advantage of a fleet of ships with guns trained on the shore.

A messenger came to say the armies had engaged. He was followed by others who attempted to describe what was happening, but who broke down in tears. At the end of the day came the final word.

The Scots army had been routed. Thousands lay dead over a long swathe of country from Inveresk northwards and the English army was within sight of Leith and almost at the gates of Edinburgh itself.

And then came more messengers carrying in their heads memorised lists of those killed. Many in the castle wept as they heard of the deaths of their kinsmen: McDowalls, Vans and Agnews from the far south-west; Gordon of Lochinvar in the far north-west; the eldest sons of Ogilvy, Methven, Ruthven and Livingstone, men of substance from Ayrshire, from Aberdeen, from every part of the country, along with all the nameless men from the villages and farms who had answered the summons to protect their country.

And soon after my Lord Arran himself galloped into the castle with a small contingent of his men. He brought the worst news of all for the family there. Lord Erskine's eldest son and heir had died. Lady Erskine closed herself up in her room and refused to come out.

Margaret tried to comfort her brother John. He was a devout man, training for the priesthood and looking to the day when the church would be reformed. Now he would have to step into the title and inheritance that should have been his brother's and the responsibilities that went with it. His grief for his brother was bound up with sorrow for himself.

Lord Erskine continued quietly about his duties, but he had little to say to the Lord Governor, who had survived the fighting when so many men had died.

And included in the list of dead which Arran brought was the name of Sir Robert Douglas, laird of Lochleven.

Chapter Fourteen
1558

The September winds whistled through the closes and pends and round the gable ends of Edinburgh, finding chinks in window frames and gaps in walls, whipped up wavelets on the Nor'loch and caused the flags flying above the castle to twist round their poles and then whip out with a crack. Round St Giles' Cathedral the beggars, scarred with leprosy or war wounds, missing a limb, or simple-minded, huddled in the shelter of buttresses, darting out to beg alms, meanwhile dreaming of travelling to warmer lands.

'I wish Jamie was home,' Margaret Erskine said to her brother as she parted from him at the castle gate. John was now Earl of Erskine since the death of their father, and Keeper of Edinburgh Castle.

'He is as well to remain in Paris.' And he added, with bitterness in his voice, 'After all, since the French now seem to rule Scotland, that is where he will do himself the most good.'

But Margaret, walking down the High Street from the castle, contemplated whether she should write to her son to beg him to come home. Lord James had been away for over six months, one of the commissioners sent to negotiate the detail of his sister's marriage to the Dauphin; he stayed on in Paris for the wedding celebrations. But that was in April and there was still no sign of him returning home.

Edinburgh had celebrated the wedding with days of festivities and the signs could still be seen: the remnants of a banner here and there hanging over a window sill, a sodden angel drooping from a gate, overlooked in the tidying up afterwards. Still occasionally children could be seen reenacting in their play childish parodies of the masques which had been held in Holyrood Palace. Not that any of the children had been present at the banquets, but the serving-men and women regaled their families with descriptions of the celebrations.

Jamie was needed here, for his level head and his influence with the Queen Dowager who, sharing her council's exasperation with my Lord Arran, had taken the regency into her own hands. The Scots lords had been shouldered aside. Too many of her advisers were French, and Catholic. People were wondering to whom the Queen Regent owed the most loyalty. To Scotland, or to France.

The religious reformers were becoming more vocal and regularly presented petitions to the Privy Council for greater freedom of worship, but every request was met with total rebuff. Each day that passed saw the church even more intransigent.

No, said the bishops, you may not read and interpret the Bible among yourselves. There can be no controversy on the Word of God. There is Purgatory after this life and you must continue to pray to the Saints for the souls of the Dead. A mild concession: if you grant the right of all that, then you may pray and baptise in your own tongue, as long as you do it secretly and not openly.

It was a pity that Archbishop Hamilton within days of the marriage of the Queen, while the country was still celebrating, had burned an old priest in St Andrews for heresy. One bonfire more or less, was that how the church viewed it? It incensed the people. They were saying the Queen Regent had authorised the burning.

Deep in her own thoughts Margaret, picking her way over the cobbles, had not noticed an agitation in the people round her. She was roused by sudden raucous voices. A mob was surging towards her. She backed away in fear, but they were not heading for the castle. They halted at the cathedral.

There was not usually a crowd around at this time for it was not the hour of a mass. The cathedral was being decked out inside for the Feast of St Giles tomorrow. She relaxed. It was people going in to help. But she looked again. They were not carrying garlands of flowers. The noise rose and more strident voices joined in the outcry.

She turned aside. Whatever was happening, she would avoid it. She began to descend the steps towards the Grassmarket, but there were people coming up and she was pushed back. She turned and tried to fight her way clear, intending to head back to the castle and safety, but the mob was too strong for her. Turning with them, she allowed herself to be swept along, scurrying with them for fear of being knocked down and trampled on.

'They've got the saint.' The roar was one of triumph.

Men stood on the steps at the door of the cathedral and raised above themselves the statue of St Giles. His carved robes had been newly touched up with blue and in his wooden arms a wooden deer was cradled. The statue was tossed into the crowd and bounced along from hand to hand. Once he disappeared, only to be hoisted up again, mud-smeared. Women were leaning out of windows above them, shouting encouragement.

How were the constables allowing it? Even as Margaret thought this she saw one of them sitting in the entrance to a close with his head in his hand, over which there poured blood.

Now the crowd surged down the hill to the crag that overhung the Nor'loch.

Heave. The cry was taken up. Heave, heave. There was a roar as the statue flew through the air and landed with a loud splash in the water. Everyone cheered. Everyone, save many people who were intent on extracting themselves

87

from the crowd. They wanted nothing to do with this. This was sacrilege. This was senseless destruction. The dishonour done to the saint's image was dishonour done to the church and who knew what punishment might follow?

But the mob wasn't finished. Not content with attempting to drown the image, which, light as it was, could be seen floating, it would seem the perpetrators must do more. Two men down on the shore had found a boat and were now out on the loch with grappling hooks. They seized the floating statue and pulled it into the boat to be rowed to shore, urged on by the watchers above.

By this time some of the others had dragged together branches and rubbish and built it into a pile with a stake in the middle of it. The idol was dried off by hard rubbing with a ragged cloak and lashed to the stake. The kindling was set ablaze. It went up with a whoosh and the idol burned with it. The wind whipped at the flames, driving the people back as sparks flew up and settled on clothing, to be beaten out.

Then, as the flames died down and as if no more could be done, the crowd began to quieten down and disperse. They had not been violent, save to the image and no one had been hurt except the constable, who was now safely in a tavern downing a beaker of ale with his friends, his head wrapped in a bloodied cloth but seemingly suffering no real damage.

Margaret, frightened for her own safety and the safety of her children, hurried back to her town house in the West Bow and ordered that the doors be barred. But there was no more violence that day.

Next day, the first day of September, was the saint's day and the procession went on as usual by orders of the Queen Regent. The canons of the cathedral borrowed a small statue of St Giles from the Grey Friars. It was smaller and less impressive and the deer cradled in his arms looked more like a little monkey and the portable shrine carried on the shoulders of worshippers was much too big for it, so that it looked lost in its bed of autumn flowers, but it was the saint's image, it was there and that was enough.

The churchmen assembled: bishop, priests, friars, canons and the rest. They would not be intimidated. In front was the Queen Regent herself, followed by a piper and others with tabours and shawms. They processed peaceably from the cathedral along the High Street and down the hill to the Abbey Cross. The trouble only started on their return, when the Regent left them at the Nether Bow to dine at the house of the merchant Sandy Carpenter. No sooner was she out of sight than the troublemakers of the day before elbowed aside the bearers and began to shake the idol loose from its perch. As it fell several hands grabbed at it and swung it against the nearest wall. The head broke off amidst jeers and shouts of encouragement. Most of the priests and friars fled but some who were braver fought the mob for possession of the saint. They succeeded in wresting it from the hands of a young drunk and fled with it into the cathedral. One of the Grey Friars was seen weeping as he recovered the broken head and ran to safety with it caressed in his arms.

'Come home, Jamie,' thought Margaret. 'Come home. You are needed here.'

Chapter Fifteen

'No doubt you deem it cowardly that the lords refused to lead their men over the border into England.'

Lord James thought it best to remain silent.

'We all know why they refused. Because we are sick of war with England. Why should they risk their lives merely to aid France?'

The merchant stood beside his passenger on the deck of the *Heron*. The ship had already entered the estuary and passed St Adrian's Isle to starboard. Now the east wind was driving them hard towards their destination, Leith. The voyage had been rough with high winds and heavy seas. Heavy weather this early, the captain said, bad winter ahead.

His father, recalled Lord James, would have found these conditions exhilarating. He had a love of the sea. For himself he was only impatient to be home.

Above them the captain had mounted the rear castle and was giving orders to the helmsman as they tacked their way landward. Above them the seamen were scrambling up the nets to the topmost masts, ready to reduce sail as soon as the order came.

Lord James had been ill when he boarded the ship at Dieppe and spent most of the voyage in his cabin. Today he was feeling better and ventured onto deck, huddled up in warm clothes. The owner of the vessel had seized him.

'I've a valuable cargo on this ship. Claret, some fine porcelain and glass from Italy. And where is the Scottish navy to protect us? I can tell you. Nowhere. In the old King's day, your father, begging your lordship's pardon, we had some fine warships. Where are they? Captured by the

English. My syndicate has lost three ships to English pirates in as many years. How can we trade safely? Tell me that.'

'Our treaty with France protects us.'

'Does it? Does it? What have we lost when we had France's so-called protection? My father died at Flodden. For what? To protect French interests. I tell you, Lord James, this French marriage is not as popular in Scotland as some would have you believe.'

Lord James reflected that William Knox, though having chosen to trade in men's goods instead of men's souls, had much in common with his brother John. He sought to steer the man away from his grievances.

'Do you return to France as soon as you have loaded up your holds again?'

'Not France. I expect to take on a cargo for Antwerp.'

'Are you in contact with your brother?'

'Of course. Every week there are letters passing.'

'I hope he is well.'

'Thriving. He is very happy in Geneva. His wife has just given birth to their second boy.'

'I am glad. I would like to send him information on the situation in Scotland.'

'He has that. He has many correspondents here.'

'He shall have my own thoughts, once I have been home long enough to understand what is happening here.'

'Send letters to my warehouse in Prestonpans. They will be safe with me,' said William Knox.

As he took his leave of Lord James at Leith he said, 'You mustn't mind my rant. I'm sorry you have been ill and we can only thank God you survived when the others didn't.'

Lord James was glad to be home, but he wondered how much of what the merchant said was the common feeling in Scotland. It was true the lords had refused to pursue the English troops over the border though ordered to do so by the Queen Regent. They would protect Scotland, they said, but they would not make war. He had himself taken arms against the English in the past as wave upon wave of invasion had destroyed so much of his country and killed his people. He knew from his visit to England to the court of the late King Edward how rich that country was. And wed to the King of Spain, Queen Mary Tudor now had unlimited resources for mercenaries and weapons and what was as important, unlimited credit with the merchant bankers of Europe. Scotland had no such resources. France did, and for that reason, for her own protection, Scotland must maintain her alliance with France and he must continue to work for it.

Whatever his own feelings.

There was the welcome home. He had expected that. He wished he could have gone first to the Queen Regent to report, not on the detail of the wedding, there were people enough to do that, but on the diplomacy that accompanied it. But the Queen Regent was at Falkland and courtesy demanded that he could not ride past Edinburgh without calling in at the Douglas town house in the West Bow.

There they were. He submitted to the embrace of the Dowager of Lochleven and the sharp sweep of her gaze over him. Nothing escaped Lady Margaret. She would see at a glance he had been ill. Six months had wrought a change in her, or was it his eye was more objective? The hair peeking out from the edge of her coif was grey.

Half-brother Sir William Douglas, looking well, though round-shouldered. That was the result of his weakness in the chest. But marriage must agree with him. And by his side his bride, Lady Agnes Leslie, daughter of the Earl of Rothes. A good match, now that the Earl had earned forgiveness on the battlefield for his family's involvement in the assassination of Cardinal Beaton.

92

'There has come news before you of poisonings...' began William.

'Later,' he said.

And half-sister Euphemia, stout, pregnant again.

'Well brother, living it up in the fleshpots of Paris while we mouldered here.' White-faced, snapping lips, grown shrewish. Not surprising married to Patrick Lindsay, who had already taken too much drink if his moist eye was anything to judge by.

'Brother-in-law!' Lord James slapped Patrick on the shoulder in false camaraderie. There was no knowing when he might need this man in the future.

Lady Margaret was pulling him to one side. 'I thought you would like some of the family to welcome you, but if you are not well enough, I can send them away.'

'Nonsense, Mother, I would like nothing better than to see my kin after so many months spent with strangers.'

Inside the house, already eyeing the board piled with food was his other brother-in-law, the Earl of Argyll, with his wife, Jane, hovering by his side.

She ran forward when she saw Lord James. 'Jamie, I am so glad to have you back.' And she began to gabble questions about the wedding. He answered these as best he could.

'And our sister Mary. Is she pretty?'

'Almost as pretty as you.'

The meal began. Lord James made an effort but was aware of his mother watching him while he picked at his food.

'So,' said Argyll, 'What about these deaths?'

'It was as we were preparing to return. We dined together just ourselves for we had an early start in the morning. We were all taken ill and after a few hours the others died. I left Cassillis in Dieppe. He was very ill but I left him in good hands, I thought. And now, when I landed today I learn that he died. I was the only one who felt well enough to travel and God knows that was not very well, but I was eager to get home. I'm well now. Orkney, Rothes and Fleming were ill and decided to return to Paris. As far as I know there has been no word of their condition.'

'What were the symptoms?' asked Margaret.

'Vomiting, purging. Sweat.'

'Poison then,' said Lindsay. 'By Christ's blood, why did the French not want you to come home?'

'It may have been some bad meat.'

'And you, Jamie,' said his mother quietly. 'How did you survive?' he shrugged, but all there knew his abstemious habits. He would not have gorged on the food, nor on the wine.

'I ate next to nothing.'

'But you've been ill.' She clearly did not believe him when he made light of it. He chose not to elaborate. He had been very ill indeed, but he was younger than the others.

'Who poisoned you? And by whose orders? That's the question. Did you have French cooks and French servers?' Lindsay could not leave it be.

'Some. Some of our own. I do not think it was deliberate.'

He could see they were not convinced. But he had his own reasons for not wishing further enquiry into the matter. He would continue to make light of it.

'The three who died? Are they being brought home?'

'Not on the ship I was on. King Henri is arranging for one of his warships to bring the bodies home.'

They began to talk then of the terms of the treaty, which were already known and been agreed by the parliament of the Three Estates. They marvelled at the size of Mary's jointure, 600,000 *livres*.

94

'The King of France must be very rich,' wondered Jane.

'And so Frenchmen are citizens of Scotland and we are now citizens of France. And,' said Lord James, 'the Frenchmen think we have the better deal. They cannot conceive we might not want to be Frenchmen.'

'Or Frenchwomen,' said Agnes.

And the talk round the table, now fuelled by some of his very fine claret he had brought with him, was scathing on the new title of my Lord Arran.

'Chatelherault. A dukedom. Substantial French estates.'

'Maybe he will make up his mind to live permanently in France.'

'There is no permanent with him. He will be back here before he is missed.'

At the end of the meal he excused himself and went to the privy. When he came out he found his mother waiting.

'Are you all right? I sent the others home. William and Agnes have gone to bed. Now, son, tell me how things stand.'

She settled him by the fire with a shawl round him, for he was shivering slightly.

'What can I tell you? I cannot say I totally enjoyed the last six months, though I was glad to see Mary safely married. The star of the Guise family is in the ascendant. Ever since our Regent's brother took Calais from the English the family can do no wrong. Their ambition knows no bounds and my sister is their best asset. King Henri is delighted with the match, though he struck a hard bargain.'

He sipped at the hot drink which Margaret handed him and made a face. 'What is in this?'

'Never mind. It will settle your guts and help you sleep.'

95

'I mustn't sleep late. I'll ride tomorrow to report to the Queen Regent.'

'Did the French agree the terms you wanted?'

'More or less. Their first son will inherit both crowns. If only daughters, then Scotland only. A woman cannot reign in France. As long as Mary lives in France then Scotland will be governed by a regent and till she has a child, Arran remains next in succession, or Chatelherault as it seems we must now call him. The Dauphin will be known as King of Scots.'

'So she will always live in France?'

'She has become more French than Scottish. We may very likely never see her here except for a summer visit now and again between childbearing. She has been brought up to know that she is Queen of Scotland and will be Queen of France in due course. There is no reason to suppose she will neglect Scotland but I doubt she would want to live here.'

'That would be the best that can be hoped for. But Jamie, the health of the Queen Regent is not good. It's not generally known. Just to her immediate circle.'

'And you with your spies.'

'We have mutual friends.'

'She is getting old.'

'She's the same age as I am! And I am in excellent health.'

'What do they say is wrong?'

'Heart weakness. But, Jamie, if she was to die, who would be regent instead? Arran? Again?'

'Presumably.'

They were silent.

'No, Jamie,' whispered Margaret. 'He was a poor useless regent before. Scotland would be better to have someone stronger, someone of true royal blood.'

He looked at her and nodded. 'You will let me know if you hear more of this.' He threw off the shawl and heaved himself to his feet. 'I'm going to bed. Have the man wake me early. '

She spoke as he lifted his candle and made his way to the door. 'Of the Dauphin,' she asked. 'What of him? What kind of man is he?'

Without turning round he said, 'If he were a puppy whelped by a bitch of mine I would have had him drowned at birth.' He paused on the threshold. 'And we had to bow the knee and swear fealty to him.'

He could not sleep. When he closed his eyes he could still feel the movement of the ship under him. Eventually he turned onto his back and lay staring into the darkness and tried to order his thoughts.

There was sorrow at the deaths of his fellow commissioners. He had hardly had time to grieve. They were his companions for the last six months and they died, and he had not.

There had been the six months of celebration, banqueting, hunting, masques and dancing and everything that went with a marriage of a queen and king-to-be. Why then was he left with the uneasy feeling that all along the Scots had been merely tholed as a necessary adjunct? He was offended by the evident disdain, insufficiently hidden behind the chivalry, for a small country which should be grateful for the honour given it by a wealthier one.

If it were true there was the undercurrent of resentment here in Scotland against the French which William Knox had talked about, then it did not augur well for peaceful relations. There was no doubt he was expressing the sentiment of most of the merchants.

There was the business of the St Giles riots barely two weeks ago which his mother had described to him. There was an indiscipline in the reformers which boded ill for the future. They were losing sight of their purpose and criminality was not in their best interests. John Knox had been able to instil discipline into the Castillians more than ten years ago. On his brief visit four years ago he had put new heart into the growing band of Protestants. His preaching tour of Scotland, before he was forced to leave, had strengthened the petty churches where the people met to read the Bible and study. All that was now forbidden.

But it would be good if they could persuade him to return. Another such preaching tour would calm down the more hotheaded of the evangelicals and perhaps demonstrate to the Queen Regent that the church need not fear them, for were they not worshipping the same God?

And underneath all these worries, there was another, that touched on by his mother. With Queen Mary in France for the rest of her life, Scotland would be under the control of regents. At present the Queen Dowager acted as regent. What would happen when she died, which might not be all that long if Lady Margaret's intelligence was correct? The man still with the greatest claim to be regent was Chatelherault and events in the past proved he had been a disaster. No, it could not be him again. Who else was there who would be acceptable to the lords, who hated to see one of their own raised above them? If there were a vacuum the French would impose someone and it would be one of their own people. Scotland ruled by a Frenchman? It could not be. He knew that it was his mother's ambition that he himself should take the role.

And the more he thought about it, the more he knew that she was right.

Chapter Sixteen

'Do you really believe that these,' the Queen Regent pushed the papers in front of her aside with one finger. 'These are genuinely the requests of reformers?'

'They are, Your Grace,' said Lord James.

'They are not. This is the work of Englishmen bent on stirring up opposition to me and my daughter, and yes, to the church also. Have the English not been smuggling Bibles into Scotland for years? And heretical literature. Pamphlets that purport to teach the ignorant what the Bible means. Why? In order that they can destroy my daughter's rule and defeat Scotland once and for all.'

The men standing round the table stirred uneasily. They knew the preachers who had written the petition. Some, like Lord James, had been aware of its contents even as it was being drafted out.

'The English had no hand in this, Your Grace,' said Lord James.

'I believe,' said Argyll, 'that the petitions are just what they say they are.'

'And what is that, my Lord?'

'A reasoned argument for the reform of the church. A plea for more tolerance. The people only want to be able to meet publicly, or even just in private, to worship in our own tongue. Their own tongue.'

'I read that,' snapped back the Queen Regent. 'And to take the wine as well as the bread. Only a priest, consecrated by his bishop, may taste the wine, which is the blood of Our Lord. All else is heresy.'

She rose. 'I will discuss this no more. I say again, my lords, that these misguided people are mere pawns in the pay of the English.'

When the door had closed behind her Lord James bent down to pick up the petition from the floor where it had fallen.

'Now what?' asked Argyll.

'Try again,' said Lord James. 'Another petition. Keep working at it until we find a form of wording she will accept. She will, in time. When she sees that there is no threat to herself or the Queen.'

'You believe she can still see reason?'

'Of course she will,' said Lord James, hoping he sounded more certain than he felt.

He left the palace and walked up to the castle to dine with Lord Erskine. He found his mother there.

'What progress?' she asked.

'Very little. But she just needs to be persuaded that it is genuine religious belief that informs all the reformers. She is not blind to the abuses of the churchmen.'

'There is more unrest in the town.'

'I know. I could feel it, just walking here.'

'The town council are complaining the church does not even fulfil a fundamental duty, looking after the poor.' Lord Erskine moved hastily away from the fire when his wife, Annabella, glared at him. Ostentatiously she pulled her shawl round herself. She hated living in Edinburgh Castle.

'The whole country is restless. Even from the north Huntly has been reporting trouble. We are drafting out another petition,' said Lord James. 'We try again.'

'She won't listen, as long as she has all those Frenchmen advising her,' said Erskine.

'Don't say that,' pleaded Lord James. 'If she hears one word of criticism of the French she will be certain she has read the matter aright, that it is for political reasons that the reformers want change.'

As he escorted his mother home she asked, 'What did you decide to do about Master Knox?'

'We will invite him to come back. A preaching tour will put new heart into the people.'

He walked on to Holyrood Palace where he had quarters so as to be near to the Queen Regent, one of whose principal advisers he had now become. As he bade goodnight to the halberdiers at the door he could not help but reflect that the palace had become a dreary place.

There were no longer elaborate banquets for visiting ambassadors and little time for evening leisure. The musicians were silenced, enough retained only to play in church; the Queen Regent herself claimed to have no time now to play on the virginals, as she had been eager to do in happier times. The instrument stood idle.

The furnishings were looking neglected. From time to time there would be brought from one of the Queen's other palaces, from Doune or Falkland or Stirling, silver plate to replace much that had been sold off. Already when dining alone the Queen Regent ate off pewter. She needed money to pay off the debts incurred by the cost of the war against England. The French soldiers stationed in Scotland had to be paid, and so much ordnance had been expended that she had resorted to borrowing. Now it all had to be repaid and the palaces were shabby in consequence. The tapestries were beginning to look dirty and threadbare. The few *tapissers* who were now employed could not cope with the constant running repairs needed.

'The money wasn't there. The Queen Regent looked to France for financial aid. Lord James was not the only one who thought this unwise but what else could she do? The people were already too heavily burdened with taxation.

With the French, against the judgement of the Scots, the Queen Regent had imposed new taxes, not only on the merchants and towns but on the church itself. Even this was not enough to stem the outward flow of money and caused further unrest.

On the day the Three Estates passed the legislation which naturalised all Scotsmen to be Frenchmen and all Frenchmen to be Scotsmen, Lord James stood beside the Queen Regent and Lady Seton at the open window listening to the distant rioters. The night was cold and the women shivered.

'Come inside, Your Grace. The night air is not good for you.'

The Queen ignored him.

'I cannot understand it. Are they not happy to be French?'

There was a distant crash. It sounded as if a building was falling down. Perhaps it was. There was a sudden flare in the sky as the rioters set something ablaze.

Round the periphery of the palace the guards stood shoulder to shoulder, ready to fend off any who came to threaten, but the rioters were taking their anger out on the Frenchmen and Englishmen who lived in Edinburgh and Canongate.

'To them France means only that we have been drawn into wars we did not want.'

'It is a man's duty to protect his country.'

'A man will look to his own first,' said Lady Seton.

'Here they do.' The Queen's voice was bitter. 'A Frenchman knows that his first duty is to protect his country.'

Lady Seton glanced at Lord James in the dim light. She had come to Scotland as one of Mary of Guise's ladies-in-waiting and had married the widowed Lord Seton. As she said later to Lord James, 'Even married to a Scotsman it is difficult to understand you. You do not think as Frenchmen do.'

'France and Scotland will be one,' said the Queen Regent resolutely, 'and Scotland will be the beneficiary. They will know it soon. Close the window, James. Come play a game of chess with me.'

But it was only a few days later that the Queen Regent sent for him again. He knew why. He hurried through the palace corridors to her quarters. No doubt she had received the news which he had just heard from his own courier.

When he was admitted she turned to him with tears in her eyes.

'The Queen of England is dead.'

'Dead, Your Grace?' He moved quickly forward and took her arm. She looked ready to faint. He eased a chair forward and sat her in it.

'My dear sister Mary,' she said and burst into tears. 'Her country and mine were at enmity but we were sisters in the faith, holding the church true and steady in the face of her enemies.'

He could hear distant running steps as the news was carried throughout Holyrood Palace. Queen Mary of England was dead. The latest courier, he who had been with him when the Queen Regent's summons came, had further word that the English lost no time in asking Mary Tudor's half-sister Elizabeth to be their queen.

It was obvious the Queen Regent had this same news. Now she was reading again through the letter.

'It cannot be,' she said. 'They cannot have the Boleyn bastard as their queen.'

'She is Henry's daughter. They will see it as an obvious choice.'

'It is not an obvious choice,' she spat out. 'Conceived in sin and born in sin, while her father was married to

103

another. My daughter has the right to the throne of England. Born of royal blood, her grandfather the first Tudor king, who else has the right?'

Dear God, he thought, is there no end to the Guise ambition? This would only cause more trouble when they were on the verge of peace with England.

It was two days later that another messenger came. He was admitted, knelt, and showed his credentials: an emissary from the King of France.

Eagerly the Regent tore at the seal and read the letter.

'Ah,' she said triumphantly. 'King Henri has proclaimed my daughter Queen of England, Ireland and Scotland.'

'That is perhaps not so wise...' But Lord James was speaking in vain. She did not hear him. 'Send for the Archbishop, Jamie. We must have special requiem masses. And the Three Estates must proclaim my daughter Queen of England.'

With a nod she dismissed him and he bowed himself from the room. The Three Estates would do no such thing. If she persisted she would be on a collision course with them.

But then on the first day of January there was an event that overshadowed for the people of Edinburgh any interest they might have in the ambitions of their Queen.

Chapter Seventeen
1559

The court was at Holyrood Palace for the Yuletide celebration. Towards evening on 1st January, Archbishop Hamilton asked for an audience with the Queen Regent. Her women were dressing her for the banquet but he was admitted as soon as she was decent.

He held a crumpled document in his hand.

'My Lord Archbishop, what is the trouble?'

'This.' He thrust it at the Queen. It was taken from his hand by one of the ladies-in-waiting who handed it to the Queen.

'What is it? My Lord, it is wet.' She held it gently by one corner as it hung limply down.

'Forgive me, Your Grace, it came from the Grey Friars.'

She looked at him, waiting for him to speak.

'This document was nailed to their gate. I have been receiving people all day who tell me similar notices are being found on the doors and gates of all the priories and monasteries in Edinburgh. This evening I had a messenger from Haddington. The Cistercian Monastery there has received one and there is another from Linlithgow from the Augustinians. These abominations may have spread even further afield. Even to St Andrews itself. I fear, Your Grace, that this... this thing, is being disseminated widely.'

The Queen Regent handed it to another of the ladies, who stood looking at it foolishly, uncertain what to do with it. She attempted to hand it back to the Archbishop but he shook his head and refused to take it. It was taken from her by Canon McKendrick from St Giles', who had accompanied the Archbishop and now stood quietly behind him.

'What does it say, my Lord?'

'It purports to be a letter from beggars addressed to the friars accusing my people,' he spluttered, 'demanding they give up their holy vows. It is iniquitous.'

'And from widows and orphans,' muttered Canon McKendrick who was now balancing the wet paper in his spread hands.

'Yes, yes. It is a heresy, Your Grace. They threaten us, the church, to enter our Houses, eject us and take over possession.'

'Not us,' said the Canon. 'Just the friars.'

'But what does it *say*?'

The Canon began to read.

'*Zealous brethren, we call upon all of you to attach this warning upon the gates and ports of all the friars' places within this realm...*'

'Yes, yes,' said the Archbishop. 'They've done that. Go on to the next bit.'

'*The blind, crooked, lame, widows and orphans and all other poor, so visited by the hand of God that they may not work, to the flocks of friars within this realm, we wish the restitution of wrongs past and reformation in time coming, greetings.* It goes on to say that since they can now read the Word of God for themselves, they know that offerings and alms should belong to them, and the friars being sturdy and healthy do not need the alms which they beg under pretence of poverty.'

'Never mind that, go on to the next bit. The threat. Read the threat.'

'*We think it right, before we enter with you in conflict, to warn you, in the name of the great God, by this public writing fixed to your gates that you remove from our said Houses...*'

'Their Houses! Their Houses! The nerve.'

106

'Your Grace,' Canon McKendrick looked up from his reading. 'There is a bit here which says that since the Houses were built with alms properly belonging to the poor, then the Houses properly belong to the poor.'

'Go on,' said the Queen Regent.

'...remove from our said Houses, between this and the Feast of Whitsunday next so that we, the only lawful proprietors thereof may enter thereto, and afterwards enjoy those commodities of the church which you have hitherto wrongly held back from us.'

'And what do they say will happen?'

The Archbishop was almost howling. 'They threaten violence. They threaten to take possession with force of arms and eject the friars.'

'From the whole cities, towns and villages of Scotland the first day of January.'

'This is what happens when you allow ignorant people to read the Bible,' shouted the Archbishop.

There was silence. The Archbishop, perhaps conscious that he had raised his voice in the presence of the Queen Regent, stood, breathing heavily.

'All of them, you say? The Grey Friars, the Black Friars?'

'And the Greenside White Friars.'

'The women... What of the nuns?'

'Even them. The Sciennes Priory had one. Now they are frightened. As well they might be.'

'The Feast of Whitsun.'

'That is the normal day for changing tenants,' said the Canon.

'Four months. You have four months to find out who perpetrated this. Arrest them.'

'Your Grace,' the Archbishop shrugged helplessly.

'You do not think that this was really written by beggars and orphans, do you? This was written by educated men. Find them. Find the printers.'

107

She rose. 'My Lord, you will stay and dine? And please, let us not discuss this further today. We have guests.'

The word spread round the city and every day for the few short hours of daylight people clustered round one or other of the gates of the friaries to read the notice posted there. As soon as one was torn down by the authorities, another would appear. Whoever was distributing these seemed to have an unending supply. As well as those affixed to walls and gates, other copies were circulating by hand.

The printers in the city were questioned and their premises searched but the galleys of type that must have been kept permanently set up could not be found. The individual compositors whose job it was to set up type found themselves being followed when they left work for the day. One of them, challenging a man lurking in his path, received a mouthful of abuse, accusing him of being an insurgent, bent on rebellion. He knocked the man down and found himself in the Tolbooth for his trouble. It was clear they were all being spied on, in the hope that one of them would lead the authorities to wherever the printing press was hidden. The printers complained to their guild and the guild complained to the city fathers about the disruption to their businesses and the damage done to their equipment during the search.

The merchant ships lying at Leith and the other ports were subjected to extra searches of every cargo offloaded, in case the notices were being printed elsewhere and brought in, hidden in cargos. One constable, more imaginative than the rest, sniffed at all the notices that came his way; a smell of spices would give a clue, he said. But chests of spices were searched as well as bales of cloth and boxes of other luxury goods. Nothing was found.

The town council met in session in the week following the first appearance of the notices. Who were the people who were publishing these notices? The idea that the beggars, the poor, the widowed and the orphaned could have united sufficiently to be able to organise this was, they all agreed, a ludicrous notion. But none could throw any light on the real perpetrators.

They were less inclined to worry about who had done it, as what effect it would have on the city and more particularly on business. Those whose premises were situated close to the various religious Houses quietly began organising extra protection, physical in the way of heavier doors and shutters, and in manpower, arranging for employees to sleep there to be ready at a moment's notice to fight whatever hazard presented itself.

On the other hand, they were all agreed, the problem of feeding the city's poor would undoubtedly be easier if they, the council, could have access to the wealth of the friaries.

The friaries themselves were laying in extra provisions in anticipation of a siege. The price of grain, always higher in the winter, rose still higher and there was a near riot of housewives at the market.

At the Privy Council meeting Lord James Stewart counselled dialogue.

'I think the situation could be calmed if Your Grace would ask the Council of Bishops to rethink their situation. Their total rejection last year of the petitions for more freedom of worship has made matters worse.'

M. D'Oysel, the French ambassador, broke in, 'Lord James is known for his sympathy with rebels.'

'Not rebels, no,' replied Lord James.

The Frenchman ignored him. 'Rebels, Your Grace. They threaten the peace of our kingdom. They will threaten even France itself.'

'Not a bad idea,' muttered Argyll.

'My lord, you said something?' The Queen Regent looked round the room but no one would meet her eye. She went on, 'this is what I have decided. There are garrisons on the border with England no longer needed, now that we are at peace. I will recall those men and they will defend the Houses against the rabble.'

'Madam, would you have Scotsmen firing on Scotsmen?'

'If necessary.'

'Or worse. Frenchmen firing on Scotsmen.'

M. D'Oysel thumped the table. 'Do you too sympathise with these rebels, my Lord of Argyll.'

Lord James nudged Argyll, who growled something under his breath and subsided.

'There is no money to pay the soldiers,' said the treasurer.

'We know that,' snapped Argyll.

'The money will be found,' said the Regent.

'The men who have fought on the border will have served longer than their sixty days. They will not be willing to stay in the army without compulsion.'

'Then compulsion must be used.'

'Your Grace, they will go home. They will be needed for the spring sowing and other work on the farms if we are to have a harvest this year.'

'The matter is closed.' The Regent signalled to Secretary of State Maitland, who placed more papers in front of her.

'My lords, we touch on another matter. We are still grieving for the death of our stepson.'

There were murmurs of agreement round the table and nods towards Lord James, whose half-brother, another son of the late King, had died suddenly some weeks earlier.

'Since he was commendator of the Abbeys of Melrose and Kelso, it is necessary to make a new appointment. The abbots have been pressing me to do so.'

Even the members of the council who hitherto had sat silent at the far end of the table stirred at that. The benefices of Kelso and Melrose Abbeys, their lands spread over the fertile wooded plains of the south-east, were among the richest in the country. It was a desirable appointment. Whoever was commendator could expect unlimited wealth to find its way into his pocket. There had been some speculation as to which of the lords could expect it to be awarded to one in his family.

'I appoint my brother, the Cardinal of Lorraine.'

There was silence. No one looked at the Regent. Lord Erskine opened his mouth as if to say something, then at a glance from Lord James, closed it again, whatever protest he was about to voice left unsaid. In everyone's mind was the vision of the wealth of these great abbeys draining away to France and Frenchmen.

Maitland leaned forward and murmured in the Regent's ear.

She rose. 'Gentlemen, I had intended to lay before you the legislation I plan to pass when the Three Estates next meet. But we have wasted too much time today. Those matters can wait.' She left, followed by Maitland.

Lord Seton slipped out after her. The gentlest and quietest of the Regent's friends, he would not stay to hear words spoken against her.

After that the meeting broke up in acrimony, the Frenchmen and the Scotsmen leaving the council chamber separately, not speaking to one another.

Lord James sought an audience later that day with the Regent. She admitted him, though she had shed her court dress and was swathed in a dressing-gown. One of her women attendants was kneeling at her feet, rubbing balm into her ankles. The room was filled with the overpowering scent of lilies.

'Your Grace, we are trying to advise you as best we can,' he said gently.

'Are you? When I am opposed at every turn? God knows what a life I lead. It is no small thing to bring a young nation to a state of perfection. For twenty years past I have not had one month of rest. I have tried to teach these people the ways of France, of standards of honour and courage and justice, and I have failed. I do not understand your people, Jamie.'

She began to weep, and with an agonised look of apology to the waiting-women, he withdrew, regretting his impulse to try and talk to her again. He had caught a glimpse of the Queen's swollen ankles. He knew such swelling to be a sign of dropsy, and dropsy, he mused, augured ill.

Archbishop Hamilton preached in St Giles', threateningly, and in the parish churches the priests repeated his words, to jeers. What punishment could they threaten? Was every beggar, orphan, widow and cripple to be arrested and imprisoned? Were they all to be excommunicated?

There were fewer friars now on the streets and any seen begging was seized and beaten up. Many left the city, hoping to find refuge in a brother House somewhere in the country, but there were stories coming from all round about and from as far away as Dundee and Glasgow and even Aberdeen, that similar notices had appeared on the monasteries and friaries there.

A weeping Mother Superior from the Dominican priory of nuns was promised by the Queen Regent that some of the royal guards would be there to protect her House.

The beggars themselves had become more aggressive, swaggering round the town, frequently drunk, and shouting abuse at any churchman who strayed into their path, throwing clods of earth and worse. One scarred veteran of the wars, a Cornishman with no love of either English or French, drew on a folk memory and led the chanting from a rising long ago in the south.

> *When Adam delved and Eve span,*
> *Who was then the gentleman?*

The sound of this sent a shiver of fear through the court at Holyrood.

'Wash the feet of the beggars?' hissed the Queen Regent.

It was Maundy Thursday. The churchmen had set in motion the usual ceremonial to celebrate this. The monarch had always washed the feet of twelve beggars, in emulation of the washing of the disciples' feet by Jesus on the eve of his crucifixion.

'Your Grace, it is written...'

'I know it is written, my Lord, but do you seriously expect me to kneel at the feet of...' she spat out the word 'rebels who threaten the very existence of my government?'

'Your Grace.'

'And of the church. The very existence of the church is at stake.'

'Our Lord washed the feet of...'

'Then let you do it.'

Easter fell on 5th April, six weeks before the deadline for the threatened takeover of the religious Houses. The tension in the city was rising. When the word was let out that the Queen Regent was unable to attend the Easter ceremonial in the abbey and that therefore the Bishop would perform the customary ceremony of washing the feet of the poor, crowds gathered round the gates of the palace. There were rumours that the Queen Regent was seriously ill. There were other rumours that she was not in the palace at all, but had already left for France to join her daughter there.

The Queen Regent was served mass that night in her private oratory within the palace, accompanied by her confessor and several of her ladies-in-waiting.

The churchmen attached to the Abbey of Holyrood spent the whole of Good Friday on their knees, or crouched on their misericords, holding a vigil, while the choir chanted the names of those involved in the saga of Christ's crucifixion: Judas, Annas, Pilate, Barabbas, Simon of Cyrene. The chanting droned on, audible to the restless crowd outside.

Holy Saturday dragged on till night came and the church porches were all suddenly ablaze with light as the fire was lit. At the door of St Giles' the Bishop lit the Paschal candle at the flames and led the way into the church, the churchmen processing behind, then the town council, the deans of all the guilds, the burgesses and merchants, each with his candle lit from the fire. The people crowded in behind.

Lumen Christi, cried the Bishop and they all took up the call.

The people left outside, shivering in the cold, fell silent and some wept, for this ceremony had been part of their lives since their birth. Unsettled by all the disturbances since January they felt that not only was the church under threat but their own security. It was all very well for the Protestants to say that the church was corrupt and greedy, but without it, what had they?

Just before midnight all the church bells throughout the city began to ring and as if this were a signal, the Queen Regent emerged from the palace and led her courtiers across to the Abbey of Holyrood where they entered, ignoring the silent people outside. The door closed and the mass began.

114

After the ceremonial, ordinary life was resumed and the days passed.

The city was tense, waiting for Whitsunday, 15th May.

Chapter Eighteen

For most of the winter Margaret had been staying with William and his family in their Edinburgh town house.

There had sprung up throughout the city meetings of like-minded protestants. Margaret, and William, both sympathetic to the new teaching occasionally attended one of these. Thus it was that she was present when the momentous news came through.

It was the beginning of May. At this meeting the preacher Master John Willock was to read a passage from the New Testament and lecture on it. When the twenty or so congregation was gathered and were waiting for him to begin, he rose slowly to his feet and looked round the room.

'My friends, this may be the last occasion on which I will be preaching to you for some time. I have to tell you that I and three of my fellows have been summoned to appear before the Privy Council at Stirling. The charge is sedition.'

He held up his hand as murmurs ran round the room. 'I do not know what has caused this. Do they suspect we wrote the Beggars' Summons? I did not, and as far as I know nor did any of the other preachers of the true gospel. Let us pray that common sense will prevail and the council will see we mean no harm to the authority of the Queen or her Regent.'

He opened his Bible at the text from the Gospel of Mark: *You will be handed over to the courts; you will be beaten in synagogues; you will be summoned to appear before governors and kings on my account to testify in their presence. Before the end the gospel must be proclaimed to all nations.* He read it in a firm voice, almost with relish, and began calmly to expound on it.

He wound up his sermon and had begun to lead the congregation in prayer when the door burst open. Master Willock ignored this and continued to pray but he had lost the attention of his listeners.

He stopped speaking and watched as the man pushed his way to the front of the room.

'I come from Fife. I have news.' He paused for breath. 'John Knox is come. My friends, John Knox is come.'

Lord James travelled in the party of the Queen Regent and the Privy Council to Stirling Castle. As soon as he arrived he made his way to Lord Erskine's room.

'Are you to be on the panel to try the preachers for sedition?' asked Lord Erskine.

'No, I've been able to avoid that. I would not willingly sit in judgment on them.'

'You know she intends to include Master Knox in the summons now that he has arrived?'

'No, I did not. I haven't been given details. The Queen ploughs her own furrow on this.'

'Talk to her, try to persuade her not to do this.'

'Where is Knox?'

'Last I heard he was in Dundee. I understand the preachers will come here as commanded. The risk is that they come with a crowd of supporters.'

'Then they must be stopped.' Lord James was vehement. 'It will look like a rebellion. God knows we can't have that.'

'You would have me fire on them? On a crowd probably unarmed?'

'I'll talk to her. Try to persuade her to withdraw the summons. But she has not been listening to me lately.'

'No,' Lord Erskine sank his head in his hands. 'She will not listen to reason. I tried to explain that her authority is not at stake here, that the people are genuinely only interested in freedom of religion, but she does not believe me.'

They looked at one another in despair. Then, hearing the voice of his wife calling from the next room, Lord Erskine rose. 'Do your best, Jamie. I bid you goodnight.'

'It was he,' spat out the Queen Regent. 'This man Knox, did he not write a book condemning the rule by women? He said we were not fit. I, who have ruled this country for near twenty years am to be told I am not fit? Is that not sedition? What has that to do with freedom to read the Bible, or freedom to baptise in your own tongue?'

The Privy Council were silent. A few looked with some compassion on the Queen. Her face was white and lined. Some wondered if she were ill. Every now and then she would pause and those beside her would see her hands clenched in her lap as if she was intent on subduing some pain.

'It is only because he is newly come,' said Argyll. 'He has a reputation built on hearsay. Mind, he has been away from this country for several years. People are only curious. When they find he is just a preacher like the others, they will soon drift away again.'

'No. This man will lead the people to rebellion. And I tell you, my lords, if there is rebellion and I am lost, then you will be lost to France and you will fall into the hands of England. And what will happen to your freedom then?'

The Privy Council meeting continued, with occasional interruptions from messengers. The Queen Regent had given orders that all who brought news of the mob were to be admitted. Now they were told the people had stopped at Perth. The leaders feared reprisals if they continued on to Stirling.

They were still in session when a message came asking if John Erskine, Laird of Dun, could be heard, for he came as the envoy of the preachers. He was admitted.

He bowed to the Queen and the assembled councillors.

'What message do you bring?'

'Your Grace, we come in peace. We respectfully ask that you withdraw the summons to the preachers. They have no will to oppose your authority in any matter save that of the right to peaceful worship.'

'I do not believe you.'

'Your Grace, as God is my witness I speak the truth.'

'Where are they now?'

'On the outskirts of Perth.'

'Tell them to stop at Perth. They must come no further. We will think the matter over.'

The laird undertook to deliver the message and bowed his way out.

'You see,' reasoned Lord James. 'Let them rest awhile at Perth. Let them listen to the sermons of the preachers. Many must already be yearning to return to the comfort of their homes. And their farms are being neglected. They will soon disperse.'

He was ignored. The Queen Regent sent an usher to fetch the heralds. She called a scribe. 'Here are my instructions.' The council listened with only the occasional mild protest quickly suppressed as she dictated a proclamation.

The heralds left.

With a nod to the aghast councillors the Queen Regent rose and swept out of the room.

Lord James went quickly to Lord Erskine's room. Erskine of Dun was still there, taking the chance of some talk with his kinsman before returning to Perth.

119

'I am glad I am in time.' Lord James found the laird shrugging into his doublet ready to leave. He told them both what the proclamation said, the proclamation that was even now on its way to Perth.

'The Queen Regent has said that despite stopping at Perth, your preachers are condemned as outlaws. They are put to the horn.'

Dun sat down heavily. 'On what grounds?'

'A day's delay. Yesterday was the day for appearing here.'

'We would have been here, save that we thought it wise to hold the mass of people back. You cannot halt a march as easily as reining in one horse. And I came to explain. Am I not here to tell her the preachers will come, tomorrow, or the next day or whenever she wishes?'

'Go back and tell your people there must be no trouble. Hurry man, the heralds will be there before you.'

But when he saw Dun to the stables and mounted on his horse, there was nothing he could say further. One look at the angry face of the man told him all. He stood by the gate and looked down at the faint plume of dust which was Erskine riding north, fast, to Perth. It was thirty-five miles from Stirling to Perth and a fast rider could accomplish the journey in not much more than an hour.

God help us, I hope she has not unleashed the whirlwind.

Throughout the day the people in Stirling Castle, who by now all knew the situation in Perth, went about their business quietly. Even the youngest of the kitchen lads was aware that something was afoot. The people from the town who came about the castle brought gossip as well as provisions.

The privy councillors waited tensely for news. The Queen Regent, serene in the confidence that what she was doing was right and supported by her French advisers as well as by messages of support from the Archbishops of Glasgow and St Andrews, ate her dinner and rested in the afternoon. She spent two hours closeted with her secretary going over the papers for the parliament which she proposed to call at the end of May.

It was as if she had forgotten the Beggars' Summons. It was now 11th May, four days before Whitsunday.

It was late and the sun had almost set when the herald returned, galloping through the castle gates and almost falling from his horse. There was dried blood on his face. Lord James, watching out for him, was beside him as soon as he dismounted. Seeing the man's shaking hands, he gripped them between his own.

'Tell me,' he said.

'Riots. In Perth. They've gone mad.'

'Come with me to the Queen.'

As darkness fell more messengers followed. As report followed report it became obvious that the situation was worse than they thought. The rioters had gutted St John's Kirk in the centre of the town and then moved on to the monasteries. The Carthusian Abbey was sacked and the Grey Friars and Black Friars turned out of their Houses. Their buildings had been desecrated, their contents taken or destroyed, with many of their most precious statues tossed in the river to sink or float away.

'It was John Knox who did it. He inflamed them with a sermon against idolatry. They were intent on destroying what they called idols.'

The councillors gathered in silence to listen to the reports while the castle servants passed the information in whispered exchanges.

The Regent left the council to receive the reports and retreated to her oratory, where she spent hours on her knees, weeping. Before dawn she was back in command, ordering levies of all the fighting men in the shires round about to report for duty. Lord James and Argyll sent for men of their own.

'Send word to Lord Chatelherault to report here.'

Lord James protested. 'What can he do that we cannot?'

'He has Protestant sympathies,' said Argyll.

'So do you,' said the Regent.

'But I have been consistently loyal to you.'

'My Lord of Argyll is right,' said Lord Erskine. 'There have been rumours that Chatelherault may join in the Protestant cause.'

Nonetheless she sent for the Duke. She was closeted with him for two hours. There was no one of the Privy Council there, but her secretary was sitting quietly at the back of the room taking notes. He was a man who found it useful to be on good terms with everyone and as a result enough of the conversation found its way back to Lord James.

The Regent had begun by grieving that since she was only a woman she could not lead the troops in the field herself. She had need of a man to do that. Unfortunately, Scotsmen would not follow a French commander.

Chatelherault agreed.

'I do not understand it,' she went on. 'Are we not all French, are we not all Scots?'

'Not many look at it like that.'

'But we do, my lord, do we not? And since you are the second person in Scotland after my daughter, who else will have the authority? You and your brother the Archbishop should unite to defend Scotland against this danger. One the head of the church, the other the heir to the throne. Alas,' she was warming to her theme now and had her hand resting on his arm. 'Alas, I am but a woman and cannot judge whether men be false or true. And my authority goes for nothing when men are angered or roused.

It needs the strength of another man to see Scotland through this dire danger which presents itself.'

She paused. It could almost be said that the Duke's mind, racing, was clear to anyone who knew him. If the Stewarts were truly to be overthrown, then so might the Hamiltons along with them. His old enemy the Earl of Lennox, lurking in England, was not the only man descended from earlier kings who with force of arms would assert a right to the throne.

'You are right of course, Your Grace.'

'So you will lead an army to arrest these men who threaten the peace of Scotland?'

'It is not such a senseless idea,' said Lord James later to Lord Erskine. 'It would be wise to keep Chatelherault loyal. God help us if he were to take it into his head to lead the rebellion.'

Lord Erskine looked at him. 'Is it such a good idea? I do not forget, Jamie, that my brother, whose shoes I now wear, and your stepfather, that good man Robert Douglas, died at Pinkie Cleugh, when Chatelherault was leading the Scots army. Leading them into defeat. And,' he added softly. 'Fled the field.'

Chapter Nineteen

When word came to Edinburgh of the rioting in Perth, William Douglas decided he had better return to Lochleven and evacuate the family, for who knew how far the disturbances would spread and Perth was uncomfortably close. Margaret returned with him.

The kitchen of the New House had always fed wandering mendicant friars, given them a few coins and sent on their way, but now Margaret learned that since January the friars who came were lost souls, men who'd left their Houses for fear of what was to come and were trying to find safety.

Men and women who had been at Perth on the day of the riots, returning south to their homes, carried tales of stirring sermons from the preachers and destruction of the idols of the Jezebel, the Church of Rome. Some were still exhilarated from the experience, others subdued. But all agreed things could never be the same again. Meantime there was farm work pressing and they were anxious to return home.

'What do you think will happen now?' Margaret asked one.

He shrugged. 'I suppose the bishops will pay for more idols and put them back. Who knows? But you should have heard Master Knox! His preaching would stir the soul of my old stick here.'

'But what do they want?' cried William in despair.

One of the men, pausing on his journey to rest, told him. 'We want the right of our own religion and we want the Frenchmen to go home.'

William decided that for the safety of the family they should move across to the island, to put the waters of the loch between themselves and any rioters. It was becoming evident as the days passed that this was likely to be more than just an isolated riot by a few hotheads. The whole country was stirring. Already some of their own people had disappeared, gone to join the growing band supporting the protestants against the Queen Regent. They began to fear all-out civil war. The accommodation at the old castle would be tight and perhaps uncomfortable, but they would be safer there.

Soon word reached them of clashes between the armies of the Regent and the armies, if by such a name they could call the thousands who had rallied to their cause, of the Congregations of Christ, as the protestants were now calling themselves.

Lord James came to the island quietly, rowed over by one of his own men. Margaret, making her rounds to settle the castle for the night, was alerted by the barking of the dogs and the sudden illumination of flares as the guards moved to the jetty.

He leapt ashore. 'It's all right, Mother, it's only me. No, don't disturb William. It's you I want to talk to.'

In her chamber she stirred the embers of the fire while he pulled off his boots. He leaned back in his chair and closed his eyes.

'Tired?'

'Weary of it all.'

The room was quiet. After the initial flurry of his arrival the guards returned to their allotted places and outside nothing stirred. Around them the castle slept.

'I don't know what to do.'

She said nothing. It was a long time since she had seen her confident son at a loss. Now he tried to speak and hesitated. Where to begin?

125

'I have been a good and loyal servant to the Queen Regent. She was the wife of my father, she is the mother of my sister. I could not do other than admire and support her. I believe she has sincerely and honestly done her best for this country.'

He stopped. He bowed his head in his hands. His next words were muffled.

'I think I can no longer support her.'

Moving closer to lay her hand on his arm she could feel that he was trembling.

'What has happened?'

'Wait. Let me collect myself.'

'Wine? Have you eaten?'

He waved this aside. 'No need. No need.'

Soon he was able to go on.

'My father...'

'Yes,' encouragingly. 'Your father?'

'My father the King often talked to me when I was a boy. He would allow me into his chamber when he was bathing and dressing and we would talk of many things. He would talk often about the difficulties of being king. That was when the servants were dismissed and we were alone.'

'You were always his favourite.'

'Sometimes I thought I was going to be king after him. But of course it coud never be.'

She did not dare interrupt him. He was pursuing some line of thought of his own and expressing it randomly.

'She has been a good ruler. None can deny that. She has kept the English at bay and kept the protection of France. There has been much she has done that is commendable.'

He was arguing with himself.

'It has gone too far.'

He had risen now and was pacing the room. Suddenly he stopped and dropped back into the chair.

'The negotiations went well with the Congregations. Argyll and I represented the Queen. Glencairn, their spokesman, is a reasonable man. So is Erskine of Dun. We agreed that all the fighting men would leave Perth. No one in Perth would suffer punishment and there would be no punishment for adherence to the protestant cause. It was also agreed that no Frenchman would come within three miles of the town. That was sensible and enough to bring peace. It *would* have brought peace, I am sure of it.

'She entered the town. That was agreed. But she could not stay calm when she saw the damage done. We had described it to her and the people were already beginning to put matters right. But she was angered by the destruction. I could not fault her for that. I was angry myself. But she should have kept better control of her feelings. She dismissed Provost Ruthven. He is a supporter of the Congregations. I thought it unwise and I said so. He is well respected and he could have returned law and order to the town.

'She ordered up a troop of soldiers. We argued with her. We advised her not to. It was in breach of the agreement. There was to be no garrison there. She brought in a division of mercenaries, Scots mercenaries in the pay of France. They are recently returned from fighting on the continent. They have French commanders. It was a clear violation of the terms of the agreement. The terms I had negotiated. There were to be no French military in the town.

'I challenged her with this for in men's eyes I have been made to look untrustworthy but she said... oh, Mother, would that I had not heard her. She said that she regarded a promise made to heretics as no promise. Heretics! She still regards all these people, these people with a genuine grievance against the excesses of the church, these people who only want to worship in their own tongue, she brands them heretics and does not feel herself bound by a promise to them. A promise made by a regent on behalf of a queen to her people.'

He paused. He was almost weeping in his outrage.

'They had calmed down. There would have been no further trouble. I am sure of it. She has lost all judgement. But I am to blame.'

'How are you to blame?'

'I invited John Knox here.'

'It might have happened without him.'

'No, it would not. He is the most eloquent of the preachers. None can stir the people like him.'

'But you are not responsible for that. Jamie, it is not your fault.'

'I signed the letter that brought him. If he had not come, there would have been none of this.'

'The Beggars' Summons...'

He gave a harsh laugh. 'Would that I knew who had done that. But we could have kept them under control. A scattering of largesse. A few bribes to the worst of the ruffians. A show of strength. And in time, a demonstration that the churchmen would mend their ways.'

'But the Queen Regent did none of that.'

'She did not listen. What am I to do? There are two armies out there, facing one another, thousands of men. Oh, dear God, what am I to do?'

'Can you withdraw from the court and take no further part in this?'

'No, I cannot.'

'Plead illness.'

'That would be cowardly.'

Her mind was working furiously. What to advise?

'My son, there is only one road for you to take.'

He waited.

'You must join the Congregations.'

He looked at her with despair.

'Betray the Queen Regent?'

'Yes.'

She left him alone to gather himself, while she fetched up from the kitchen a glass of wine and some bread and ham.

She watched him as he ate. He had grown like his father. He was now twenty-eight years old. He had the reddish tinge to his hair that all the Stewarts had. With his broad shoulders and lean torso, despite the mud-splashed trews and the linen at his neck grubby from too many days without washing, nonetheless he was every inch a king's son.

'Civil war,' she said, almost to herself.

'Not against the Queen herself. I will always be loyal to my sister. I have sworn it.'

'The Regent will call you a traitor.'

'She may call me what she will.'

He rose. 'I must go.'

She put her arms round him. 'It is the just side,' she said.

Chapter Twenty
1560

Margaret stood on the ramparts of Edinburgh Castle and watched the smoke of cannon drifting down from the crags above Holyrood Palace. They had been firing on Leith for days past. Faintly, as the noise of the cannon ceased she could hear the clop of hooves. The horsemen admitted at the Netherbow Port were now making their way up the High Street: two riders, one bearing the royal standard, then a litter and another half-dozen riders at its back. Beside the litter there walked Archbishop Hamilton of St Andrews, behind him, three other bishops. A few ladies-in-waiting followed and the small procession ended with several plodding men with halberds.

'If he expects me to go down and welcome her, he can think again,' said Lady Annabella at her side. 'I won't do it. You can if you like. Yes, go on. The sight of you here might turn her stomach. Hasten her end.'

Lord Erskine had taken up his position inside the gate to welcome the Queen Dowager. He had moved here some months earlier, leaving Stirling Castle in the care of his deputy. Edinburgh Castle housed the armaments manufactury and the royal mint. In the ongoing conflict he was keeping the castle neutral.

The portcullis was raised, the small procession entered and the portcullis slammed down again. There was something final in that heavy rattling thud.

Lord Erskine knelt; a word or two and then he rose and led the way into the palace.

It was not until that evening that Margaret caught her first sight of the Queen Dowager. Ignoring her brother's instructions to stay away, she slipped into the Hall where the Queen was dining. She counted on the rumour that the Queen's eyesight was failing, misted over, and that she would not recognise people at the far end of the Hall. She need not have worried. The Queen was surrounded by her small band of people and ignored all others.

Lord Erskine had offered the Dowager the privacy of dining in her own chamber, but she refused this. 'I am the Queen Regent,' she said. 'The people must see me.'

No one contradicted her. She had been deposed from her position as regent by parliamentary decree some months earlier. There was now a Council of Regency, headed by Chatelherault. She chose to ignore this, still signing documents as regent, still communicating as far as she was able with her French allies.

Margaret was shocked, despite herself, at the deterioration in the woman. She looked much older than her forty-five years. Her wrists, glimpsed as she stepped forward on the arm of Lord Erskine, were swollen and the flesh of her ankles hung over the tops of her slippers.

'I would have her arrested and hanged.' Margaret's sister-in-law had slipped into the seat beside her. She reached for some fish. 'Erskine is too soft. If I were in his place I would have refused to let her in. He supports the reformers. Why should he allow her refuge here?'

'Compassion for a sick woman, perhaps,' said Margaret.

'She should be with her army in Leith, live there and suffer the consequences.'

'Let her have what comfort she can,' said Margaret. 'It will not be long.'

Lady Annabella shrugged. 'Let us hope. Till then he would do well to hold her prisoner.'

She will be virtually that here, thought Margaret but said nothing. She did not think the Queen Dowager would leave Edinburgh Castle again.

In the past year law and order had completely broken down. There were indecisive battles between the armies of the Queen Dowager and the Congregations, and long periods of attrition. The Dowager pleaded for more help from France and the Congregations negotiated reluctant aid from the new Queen of England, Elizabeth. The Congregations briefly occupied Edinburgh, pulling down images of the saints in the friaries and abbeys and taking all the gold and silver vessels they could find. These would be melted down and sold, for money was desperately lacking on both sides. Soldiers had to be paid. But they were not strong enough to hold the capital and Edinburgh was once more in royal hands.

They talked: every week there were delegations. The leaders of the Protestants insisted they only wanted to establish a reformed religion. They had no interest in overturning the Queen's rule. M. D'Oysel, the French ambassador, had no doubt that they were rebelling against his sovereigns, King Francis and Queen Mary.

Now Leith was under siege. It was occupied by the French and they were holding it in the hope that fresh troops would arrive. English ships supporting the Congregations patrolled the River Forth but the Scotsmen, despite holding the Crags and setting their cannon on the heights, were not strong enough to take the town. But Leith was the port for Edinburgh and without free access, food supplies would soon suffer.

While the Dowager could count on the loyalty of Chatelherault she remained optimistic, but the day came when the Duke joined the rebels. Lord James, Argyll and the Duke's own son, the Earl of Arran, had persuaded him. And many of the other Lords had slipped away from her side as well; whether for religious or political reasons, perhaps they themselves could not distinguish. There were many who saw an alliance with Protestant England as more attractive than a continued alliance with Catholic France.

Now, with the Queen Dowager in residence at the castle security was tightened even further. Lord Erskine gave instructions that no one was to be allowed to enter without her express permission. He interpreted this in his own way. He ordered searches of all those leaving the castle in case they carried messages from the Dowager to her troops and indeed intercepted many of these, but he also considered that he could use his discretion as to who entered the castle. The prohibition did not cover his own kin. When Lord James came one night he was admitted.

James shook off his cloak in Margaret's apartment. 'I will speak to Erskine. The Lords wish to send a delegation to parley with the Queen,' he said. 'The English are considering giving up on the siege of Leith.'

'Surely not. Pull out, now, how can they desert us?'

He held up his hand. 'They are not deserting. What they propose is to attack this castle instead.'

'Attack Edinburgh castle? That's madness. Would they?'

'We managed to dissuade them. They had the illusion that it might be easily taken. We assured them otherwise.'

'It doesn't bear thinking about. What would happen to the Queen if the castle were taken? She would be in danger.'

He looked at her shrewdly. 'Do you care?'

She was taken aback by his sharp tone. 'She is a sick woman.'

'It won't happen anyway. Elizabeth would never sanction such an act of aggression against a fellow Queen.

Besides, it would lead to war with France. No, what we can do is talk.'

'She has no power left.'

'Yes, she has, Mother. She is the only spokesman for her daughter.'

The next day the castle labourers erected a large tent in the outer bailey. This would be deemed to be neutral ground for the purposes of the negotiations.

A few days later a silent crowd lined the High Street to watch the English delegation make their way towards the castle. The Englishmen walked in tight formation and eyed the people warily. It was not so long since they had been fighting the Scots, and here they were, come to save them, but not sure of their welcome.

By the time they had been admitted, the Queen Dowager was already seated on a comfortable chair behind a table draped with cloth to hide her swollen body. She had been carried there earlier; she did not want anyone to see she could not walk easily. It would be a sign of weakness and the Dowager never showed any weakness.

With her was Lord Seton, ever faithful, and Archbishop Hamilton, still loyal to her for the church's sake despite the defection of his brother Chatelherault.

Margaret slipped in after the English delegation and sat in the anteroom of the tent with the Queen's ladies. They scowled at her and made great play of stitching at the linen cloths they had on their laps. They would not eavesdrop on the proceedings, but they could not prevent Margaret from doing so.

The envoys were Sir George Howard, son of Lord Norfolk, and Sir James Croft, Warden of the Eastern Marches. They presented their demands to the Queen Regent, who read them and laid them on the table.

'*Non.*'

Sir George began to recite their demands: that the French soldiers be sent home; that the Protestants be allowed to appeal to Queen Mary in France.

'*Non.*'

'Your Grace,' said Sir James Croft, more diplomatically than Sir George, 'these requests are simply a basis for negotiation. Perhaps there are some lesser matters we can agree on.'

'No sovereign will take orders from any other and the King and Queen of France and Scotland will not take orders from the so-called Queen of England. Nor from their own subjects. I am the Regent and I will deal with all these matters. Have I not done so up until now according to the laws of the land?'

There was a pause. No one felt able to put her right.

'Furthermore,' she continued, 'why should there not be French soldiers in Scotland? Scotland is a French country, is it not? Why should they not be here to defend us against an uprising of the rabble?'

As dusk fell Lord Seton signalled for torches to be lit. The sudden flaring made them realise how dark the evening had become. One of the Queen's ladies whispered to another, 'She must be exhausted.'

'It will kill her.'

Sir James Croft became more conciliatory in tone. 'Madam, you have done so well in your governing and have always been for peace. Everything lies in your hands. Can there not be some appeasement? Both parties in this may be able to reach a compromise.'

'How can I compromise when a troop of English soldiers passed immediately under my castle walls yesterday? Am I supposed to ask for appeasement in the face of such aggression?'

Eventually, when the midges and other insects were beginning to make the tent unbearable with their buzzing

135

and nipping, the delegation was dismissed and when it had left the castle and all was quiet, the Dowager was helped painfully back to her own quarters.

Chapter Twenty-One

The Queen Dowager was dying. She was now unable to rise from her bed in the hushed and darkened palace. The guns on the Crags had fallen silent. As word went out from the castle, Scots, English and French paused in their battle, with some relief, for it was obvious to all that there was now stalemate.

Margaret, as the sister of the Keeper of the Castle, was not refused entry to the sick woman's bedchamber. Often now she would take up a position behind the bed where the Dowager could not see her.

The chamber-women did their best not to weep as they tended to their mistress, turning her swollen body over in the bed and rubbing balm into her flaking skin. It took two of them now to turn her.

From time to time the Queen's mind wandered. Sometimes she thought she was back in France. Then she would weep and call for Louis, and the younger attendants, those who were not allowed to handle the Queen, had to be reminded that she had been married twice and Louis was her first, French, husband. Sometimes she would call for James and plead with him, but what she wanted was lost in gasping tears. Once in the silent dawn a cock could be heard to crow and the women looked at one another superstitiously, but the woman on the bed began to mutter the Office of Lauds, the first office of the convent day. Where had she learnt that? Whether this was rational memory or hallucinatory dream they could not tell.

But there were days when she refused to take the medicine prescribed and on these days her mind was lucid. She asked that the Bishop of Amiens, attending on the

French troops, should come to her. She wished to make her confession. When Lord Erskine let it be known that he was sending for the Bishop, they the Council gave their consent, except for Chatelherault.

'What for?' he spluttered. 'We'll have no bishops and no confessions here.'

'My lord, she is dying.' But he would not be persuaded and without his agreement nothing was done. She made no reproaches.

'My body will not trouble me long,' she said. 'But I still have work to do.'

She asked that the lords should come and see her. Lord Erskine hesitated. 'The lords, Your Grace?'

'Lord James, Chatelherault, the Earl Marischal.'

They arrived, Chatelherault in front, eager and conciliating, perhaps already regretting his harshness over the matter of the Bishop, the Earl Marischal and Lord James Stewart following.

'I am very cold,' said the Dowager. One of her women leaned forward with a mug of warmed wine and she managed to sip some of it.

She made a visible effort to gather her strength and looked straight at the men kneeling round her couch.

'I leave the care of Scotland in your hands and I trust you to be loyal to my daughter, the Queen. Maintain the alliance with France. France is your greatest strength in the troubled times that lie ahead. Put not your trust in England.

'I have had the honour to be Queen and Regent of Scotland and no woman ever had a greater or finer responsibility thrust upon her. I have always favoured the welfare of this realm as much as that of France. There was goodwill...'

Here her voice faded and there was only a gasping for breath before she was able to continue.

'There was always goodwill on my part. If I have made mistakes it was through lack of wisdom and want of judgement. I urge you, obey the Queen. Come to a peaceful agreement with M. D'Oysel who only has the interests of Scotland at heart. It would be best for Scotland if they all went home, French and English alike. Beware in case the English remain and never go home.'

Her cheeks were wet.

'Forgive me, my lords, if I have offended any of you.'

There was nothing any of them could say.

Chatelherault, always easily moved to tears, was weeping also. If there were an opportunity, thought Margaret, listening to this from the shadows, he would switch sides again and support the Dowager.

The Earl Marischal looked stonily at the wall above the bed.

Lord James, nearest to her, was now holding her hand. His head was bent. Margaret, watching him, saw a tear fall onto his sleeve. It would leave a mark, she thought absently.

She was done, her strength gone. One by one they kissed her hand and backed out of the room.

They paused in the antechamber as if they did not know what to do. Should they stay till the end?

'I remember her coronation,' said Chatelherault to no one in particular, his voice breaking.

'So do we all,' said the Earl Marischal, 'and much else besides.'

The men round him waited for him to say something else, but he thrust his cap on his head and stomped from the room.

Lord James spoke softly to his mother who had followed them.

'Let me know if her condition deteriorates.'

She nodded. She would keep him informed. But, she thought, it would not be for a few days yet.

The Dowager was sufficiently recovered the next day to dictate her will. She asked that Lord James and the Earl Marischal be there to witness it.

They did so. The Earl left and Lord James sat by her bedside for another half-hour and they talked quietly. When she dismissed him she squeezed his hand.

He was weeping openly when he left the room.

Margaret, waiting for him, was exasperated. Was it not to everyone's benefit that the Queen Dowager would soon be dead? She herself would be glad to see the back of the woman who had deposed her in the affections of the King.

'I loved her,' said Jamie. 'She was like a mother to me.'

He stumbled from the room.

The dying woman sent for Chatelherault's son, the Earl of Arran. He was not liked, but he could not be ignored. As Chatelherault's son he was next in line to the throne after his father, should the young Queen Mary die childless. There were already rumours that he had inherited the madness of his mother.

He could hardly hide his excitement at being in the centre of all this drama. 'Is she really going then? Really? Will they stop fighting for the funeral? I've ordered up a suit of black clothes ready. Do you think she will want the body taken back to France? What do you think she wants me for?'

Whatever she wanted him for was between the two of them. She spoke softly to him and was not overheard and when he left he was frowning and muttering to himself.

He was the last of the requested visitors. It was clear to all the ladies and the doctors that her strength was finally gone. The Archbishop moved forward and slowly and with great dignity administered the Viaticum.

140

She dozed, occasionally moaning. Her breathing became more laboured. In the shadows of the room her women knelt, heads bowed in prayer.

'I think,' said the doctor, 'that the end is coming.'

Margaret sent a boy to fetch her son, and he and the Earl Marischal, who had been waiting in the quarters of Lord Erskine for just such a call, were there quickly. They stood in a window embrasure out of her sight and waited.

Margaret, by the head of the bed, gripped the dying woman's hand. The Dowager was now too far gone to know who was beside her.

The doctor leaned over and listened. Then he stepped back and nodded. Margaret eased the dead woman's fingers one by one from her hand.

Chapter Twenty-Two
Winter 1560

Lord James Stewart added some marginal notes to the draft legislation which he had been studying for the last two hours. As he threw down the quill, now too worn for further use, he glanced over to where his mother was sitting by the fire.

A book lay on her lap but she had not turned a page for some time. Her favourite, *The Golden Targe*, the book which had belonged to his father. She must surely know it by heart by now. He thought she had fallen asleep but with the noise of the falling quill she raised her head.

'Finished?'

'For today. I must go. Chatelherault will fret if I am late.'

After he'd left, Margaret continued to sit idle. The streets round Jamie's town house were generally quiet, but more so now that a heavy snowfall had driven the citizens of Edinburgh inside early in the day. Now this evening there were few reasons for the citizens to venture beyond the comfort of their firesides. By day the city was crowded with revellers celebrating the Yuletide early, while the country people crowded round the luckenbooths on Castle Hill, buying trinkets for their lovers. But now all was quiet.

Jamie himself would not have gone out save that he was dining with Chatelherault at the new Hamilton mansion house at Kirk o'Field. The two chief members of the Protestant Council now governing Scotland had much to discuss.

But Chatelherault, mused Margaret, was not to be trusted. He had changed sides too often in the late

142

disturbances. He was now no more than a figurehead. The power lay with Jamie. The Privy Council were content to follow him, for had he not led them decisively to this victory? Jamie was king in all but name and would continue to be so for many years.

Since the death of the Queen Dowager in June all had changed. The resistance to the Protestant army seemed to have lost all purpose and a peace treaty soon followed.

Now the French had gone. The English had gone. Scotland was in control of her own destiny and Jamie was in charge of Scotland. All was as it should be.

Those glorious summer days had been full of rejoicing. Even William, who had fought bravely by Jamie's side, had exultantly forgiven the English for killing his father, now that Queen Elizabeth had sent more soldiers to aid them in their fight.

He had been among the lairds taking part in the Reformation parliament. His fellow lairds came from all over the country clamouring to be allowed to represent the Third Estate. There was scarcely a bed to be found in Edinburgh that July as people crowded into the capital. Those churchmen of the old religion who had taken the new Confession of Faith and had become Protestants were there. And the church was in the hands of the people.

John Knox was adamant about this. He and the other preachers who had worked hard to convince the people of the justice of their rights were thrashing out a new Confession of Faith and a new structure. There would be no more bishops.

'It is a pity you do not have a voice in the parliament,' Margaret said to him as they stood in the crowded gallery listening to the arguments. She had grown fond of him in the last few months.

'My voice will be heard.' And indeed for a great deal of the time he looked like a contented man. The first item of business, the organisation of the new Church of Scotland, the abolition of both the Pope's power in Scotland and the mass itself, was passed with such enthusiasm that none dared vote against it. If some of the lords still called themselves Catholic they kept it to themselves and after all who knew what rich pickings there might be once the old church was made to give up its wealth? Look what had happened in England.

Now several months later, the arguments about money were breaking out. The preachers wanted the riches of the old church to be handed over to the new church, but the problem was that the revenues from the church had for many years been paid to the lords or their sons and they refused to give this up.

Now there was a coolness between Lord James and Knox. Margaret was sorry for it. Knox had been harsh in his criticism. Jamie was still drawing his income from the priory of St Andrews, though the priory itself was now an empty shell. The extensive estates it owned could not be so easily destroyed and rents continued to be collected.

She rose now and snuffed out the candles on Jamie's desk. They were not needed. Her single candle and the firelight were enough. She threw another log on the fire and stretched out in her chair. How could she resolve the tension between Jamie and Knox? They had to work together. And her brother Erskine had fallen out with Knox for the same reason, refusing to give up his income from the church. He needed all his income, he said, to maintain his position as Keeper of both Edinburgh and Stirling Castles.

But perhaps the arguments would soon pass. There was too much work to be done in rebuilding Scotland for such disagreement to last.

And perhaps the sorrow which this December brought would do much to unite the men again. For in these short dark days, John Knox's wife died. Marjorie, who had sustained him through exile and danger, who had been his scribe and letter writer when arthritis crippled his hands, who had borne his two beloved children and had rejoiced with them all in Edinburgh in July, was gone.

Margaret, remembering the happy young mother, the kind friend, now found herself weeping gently once more. She had been one of those who stood only a week ago in the semi-darkness of the December day on the edge of the quiet Greyfriars graveyard when they lowered Marjorie's body into the ground while the tolling of the Great Bell of St Giles' could be heard throughout the city. She would never forget the wracking sobs which the man had made no attempt to suppress.

Margaret roused herself. She had sat for too long when she should be in bed, for tomorrow would be another busy day. Jamie was to sleep at Hamilton House overnight.

She was mounting the stairs when she heard the clatter of hooves in the pend which led through to the stables at the back of the house. She called to the watchman who guarded the rear of the property.

'It's my lord back,' he told her. 'He has someone else with him.'

Jamie burst into the house. He had not paused to take off his boots and his cloak was rimed with frost. At his back was John Knox. Hastily Margaret led them back into Jamie's room and kicked the fire into life.

'Jamie?'

'News,' he said, tossing off his cloak. 'You tell her, John.'

Master Knox bent his head in a cursory bow to Margaret. He looked so careworn that Margaret had to resist the temptation to give him a hug.

'The King of France is dead.'

Margaret felt her heart gave a plunge.

'Mary's husband?'

145

'I had a message tonight that he was dying,' Knox continued. 'I knew Jamie was dining at Hamilton House so I hastened round there. They would have to be the first to know.'

'And while we were there word came from Lord Grey at Berwick that Francis has died. My own spies have not yet sent me word. Your people, Knox, are sharper than mine.'

'Dead?' said Margaret. 'The Queen is a widow? What will happen now?'

'God knows.' Lord James helped himself to some wine from the flagon that was standing on the table and poured one for Knox.

At a gesture from Margaret they both sat. 'What does Chatelherault think of this?'

'He is all a-quiver.'

'She won't want to come back here, surely,' said Margaret. 'She is settled in France. Jamie, you know her. You're the only one who has met her. Will she want to return?'

He shrugged.

'Might there be a bairn?'

'Oh no,' said Lord James. 'No bairn.'

'That's in the hands of God,' said Knox.

'Rest assured,' said Lord James with a short laugh. 'There will be no bairn.'

'If she comes back here she will bring papists with her. And all her Guise relations,' said Knox. 'We'll never be free of them.'

'If she wants to come back we can't stop her,' said Lord James. 'I had best be the one to go to see her. She knows me and trusts me. If she needs to be advised what best to do, then it is as well to come from me.'

'You must keep her away,' said Knox. 'We don't want her here.'

No, thought Margaret. If the Queen comes home, then Jamie will lose some of his power. That should never be allowed to happen. No, they did not want Mary back.

Chapter Twenty-Three
1561

The leftover banquet meats had been taken to be distributed amongst the poor, the players cleaned off their paint and the cleaners moved in to sweep up the litter and wash the floors, sticky with spilled wine and trampled food.

The young girl sank down on a cushion on the floor of her bedchamber and spread her arms out above her head. 'I do not want to go to bed,' she said. 'I want this day never to end.'

'My dear,' said Margaret Erskine. 'There will be another day tomorrow and another after that. And after that many more glorious days such as this.'

'I will be happy here?'

'The people love you already.'

'*Ma chère amie,*' said Mary. 'My brother told me you were a friend of my mother.'

'I was with her when she died. I held her hand.'

The girl was sobered for a moment. 'They told me she did not suffer.'

'It was a very peaceful death.'

'You were her friend and you will be my friend also.'

'I hope so, Your Grace.'

The Queen took her hand out of Margaret's and sprang to her feet. Such energy, thought Margaret. It had been a long day. The procession from Leith had begun to form in the early morning and the Queen had travelled on horseback at a slow pace from there to Canongate and then up the long hill to the castle, pausing regularly to speak to people in the crowd who were giving her a tumultuous welcome. Then there had been gathered at the castle all the people she had to meet and then the journey back to Holyrood Palace and the celebrations which followed at which she had entertained charmingly all the various ambassadors who made a point of being in Edinburgh for the occasion.

As Mary Seton unpinned the Queen's hood her long auburn hair, imperfectly restrained in its coif, sprang free and tumbled down over her shoulders. One of the chamberwomen tutted and carefully released the strands where they became caught up in the pearls which studded the sleeves of her gown.

Margaret stood by, watching. The Queen's clothes, French made, French style, were beautiful. She had thought the clothes of the Queen Dowager were sumptuous but these went beyond that. The old Queen's clothing had become shabby in the last few years as the money which should have replaced them went instead on ordnance and mercenaries, first to pay for the wars between Scotland and England and then the war against the Congregations. After her death, what was left of the royal wardrobes had been gradually and quietly raided for anything that would be of use.

Margaret was not the only woman who would in the next few days find an excuse to be in the royal wardrobe while the new Queen's many gowns were being unpacked: rich velvet and silks in crimson and blue, underwear of the finest lawn, fur-lined cloaks, rich brocades, and sleeves embroidered with gold and silver. No expense had been spared to provide this girl with everything worthy of a queen.

Mary Livingstone lifted the long rope of black pearls from the Queen's neck, then unfastened the emerald bracelets at her wrists. There had not been so many jewels seen in the palace for a long time.

Margaret saw that the women fussing round the Queen were absorbing her whole attention. She curtseyed unseen, and slipped from the room.

As she passed the Hall she could hear the raucous laughter of men still drinking. Some of the Queen's Guise relatives had come to Scotland with her to see her settled, with no word of when they would go home. Already in the first few days, suspicious of the Scots, they were forming a protective group round her, but some of the courtiers were beginning to align themselves with the French.

There was a sudden braying laugh and she recognised the voice of her son-in-law, Patrick Lindsay. Boasting, she was sure. Impatient, forceful, by no means stupid, but always ready for physical action, he had fought against the French as hard as anyone in the late wars and now he seemed ready to make friends with them.

She could make out the voice of the Earl of Bothwell. As Lord High Admiral he commanded the fleet which brought Mary back from France. He was a staunch supporter of the Dowager in the late conflicts, but the council were doing their best to let bygones be bygones and embrace in their midst as many of the lords as possible.

She found Lord James alone. He had taken a major part in the day's welcoming festivities. Now he was working, studying papers which he laid aside when she entered.

'Shouldn't you be in the Hall?' she asked.

'I have no wish to spend the night with drunken sots.'

'The day went well.'

'Yes, she plays the part to perfection. Good training. She seems docile. We'll keep her busy with the celebrations for a while. As soon as the weather improves she can go on a progress round the country.'

'The Guise will want to involve themselves in government.'

'We'll make sure they don't have the chance. They will find this country uncongenial. They will dislike the weather and the people will be unfriendly. They'll go home. Now, in the matter of her household, it is as well her closest companions have been our own people.'

Mary Seton, Mary Beaton, Mary Fleming and Mary Livingston, the girls who had been sent to France as children with their Queen, were the daughters of the families closest to the Stewarts by blood. They would remain as her ladies.

'She'll need more. What preferences do you have?'

'Anyas of course, as Earl Marischal's daughter she is an obvious choice.'

'As your betrothed, even more obvious.'

He nodded with a smile. 'To keep the families who favour the old church happy I thought one of Huntly's girls.'

'Catholic. Is that wise?'

'We have to strike a balance. But they are still a bit too young so that's for the future. But I've mentioned it to Huntly. It should keep him happy. He's been subdued since Mary turned down his offer to raise an army to restore the old religion, but I don't trust him.'

'Shall you include him in the Privy Council?'

'Perhaps. We'll not change it, not just yet.''

'With you as her principal adviser.'

'Of course. Chatelherault can be brought into line.' He laughed. 'He is already plotting to marry Mary to his son.'

'Impossible.'

'Of course it's impossible, but when did that ever stop a Hamilton?'

'Watch your back,' she said.

'I always do that.'

151

Suddenly he raised his head and listened. From outside there came the faint sound of singing.

'Are they serenading her?' asked Margaret wonderingly.

He pushed open the shutters. It was wet and cold outside, the unseasonal haar which had settled over the River Forth not having lifted even for the arrival of the Queen. Now the mist drifted into the room, bringing with it a blast of chill air.

More loudly came the sound of pipes and drums and a sudden roar of voices raised in song.

'It's a psalm. They're singing a psalm.'

'To show her,' he said grimly.

'Why are they doing that?'

'In France it is the habit of the Protestants to march through the streets singing the psalms. It's a way of asserting themselves, making themselves heard. In Paris it caused riots. Knox might have had something to do with it.'

'Will she understand that?'

'Maybe not. But if she does she might be frightened. I'll send her word that it is nothing.'

'Should you turn out the constables?'

'I don't want to cause more trouble. Anyway, it's too cold for them to stay out there long.'

Even as he spoke, the noise lessened and they could hear the fading sound of the pipes as the singers went off in the direction of the town.

She rose to go. 'Get some sleep, son. It will be a busy day tomorrow. Soon we must look at the next question.'

'What is that?'

'A husband for her. Get her wed and pregnant and she'll be too busy to interfere with your plans.'

Chapter Twenty-Four

From an early hour there had been activity at the Chapel Royal of Holyrood Palace. People were seen entering and the windows glowed as candles were lit inside. The crowd of idlers who seemed to spend all their time round the kitchens of the palace, stirred themselves. The word passed quickly. The chapel, which had only last year been stripped of all its popish idols, was being prepared for a mass.

A crowd began to gather to block the way of the scurrying servants. A boy approached, faltered and turned to run, but a heavy hand gripped his shoulder. The candlestick he was carrying was seized and held aloft.

'Where'd you get this, lad?'

'From the Bishop.'

There was a growl from the crowd. Someone hit the boy, bursting his nose. He struggled to free himself from the hand gripping his shoulder, but others grabbed at him and pulled off his jerkin. Blood and snot dribbled down his face. He was kicked and fell.

Two of the palace guards hearing his wails came running up and pulled the angry men and women away from the boy. The candlestick was dropped and in the scuffle was seized and disappeared under the cloak of a man who hastily ran off, unhindered.

But the guards fell back. They would not argue with the men who now approached, men known to be of the Queen's court.

'Are we to suffer the idol again in our midst?' one of these new arrivals shouted.

'Put the priest to death,' shouted another.

The mob gathered round them, chanting. *Death, death.*

Margaret, who had finished dressing, heard the noise and looked from her window on the opposite side of the courtyard. As she leaned out to hear better, she recognised the voice of the man who was shouting about idolatry.

Her son-in-law Patrick Lindsay.

'Stop this idolatry,' he shouted again, and at his words the crowd surged towards the door of the Chapel Royal.

Here they were halted. Margaret could not see what had stopped them. She pulled a shawl round her shoulders and hurried downstairs.

The door to the Chapel was closed and before it Lord James stood with his arms folded across his chest.

'I gave my word to the Queen,' he shouted to make himself heard. 'Did we not fight for freedom and tolerance of our religion? Does anyone now prevent you from worshipping God in the way you want? Allow Her Grace the same courtesy.'

'Was it all for nothing,' yelled back Lindsay. 'Did we fight so the Pope can sneak back in?'

Lord James set his face and held his stance.

Some in the crowd, seeing that there would be no more excitement, began to drift away but Patrick Lindsay was clearly out for trouble. He pushed forward till he was almost touching Lord James and looked in his face.

'Let us in. We'll stop this.'

Lord James stood unmoving. Lindsay raised his arm as if he would strike. Lord James took a step back and drew his sword.

There was an indrawn breath from the mob. Lindsay backed off and turned to encourage them, but the people knew Lord James. He was a hero to many of them. He was the man who had led the Congregations to success. They were none of them going to threaten him.

There was a movement in the crowd and the Queen's other half-brother, Lord John Stewart, stepped forward and took up his position beside Lord James. He looked rough. Last night he had been celebrating too late and too long with his cronies. But today he was there to protect his sister.

Patrick Lindsay turned his back and swaggered away.

Margaret went back up the way she had come and ran through the passages to the Queen's rooms. She found the Queen dressed and ready with the women she had brought from France forming into a line behind her.

Seeing Margaret the Queen smiled. 'You will accompany us?' she asked.

'No, Your Grace.'

The Queen looked beyond Margaret to the small group of women who, drawn by the noise outside, were already gathering. 'You will?' Eyes respectfully lowered, they shook their heads.

'We cannot,' said Margaret.

The Queen shrugged and led the way to the private stair that led to the Chapel Royal. Margaret abandoned her plan to worship at St Giles', but waited to see what would happen.

When the mass was over Lord James and Lord John and some of their men formed a guard round the priest and the other servers and saw them safely clear of the palace and out of sight of the mob.

The Queen returned to her quarters, passing through the presence chamber, nodding and smiling serenely at the people waiting there, and entered the privy chamber where Margaret was waiting for her.

Out of the gaze of others, with only her friends by her side, Mary's face crumpled and she looked near to tears. She seemed not to hear the platitudes murmured by her personal chaplain behind her.

'Do they hate me so?' she whispered.

'They hate your religion,' said Margaret.

The Queen was trembling. She was only a young frightened girl. It was as if she had never faced a mob. Perhaps she hadn't. Perhaps she had been so protected in France that she was barely aware of hostile elements out there in the world.

'I do not understand,' she said.

Margaret put her arm round the girl's shoulders. 'You must stick to what you know to be true and good,' she whispered. 'Do not listen to those who would try to undermine your faith.'

When she saw the Queen's lower lip tighten in a determined line she removed her arm. Yes, let the girl stick to her religion.

'I'm sorry,' said Lord James, when he arrived later. 'I should have anticipated it. We will try and make sure it doesn't happen again.'

'Who were they?'

'Some hotheads. No one of any account.'

'I am glad you were there, Jamie,' whispered the Queen.

'We'll keep you safe,' said Margaret.

But the Queen kept her chaplain by her side for the rest of the day and saw no one.

Chapter Twenty-Five

There were those on the council who complained about the power which Lord James exercised over his sister. Some said he was still acting as if he were regent. Well, the girl was young and had a lot to learn. She had to be guided by older and wiser heads and who better than her brother? And better Lord James than the Guise family, some of whom were still in Scotland, with others in France sending a stream of letters giving advice and instruction.

There was no question that the court was a livelier and happier place under its young ruler. All the dreariness and austerity of the Dowager's rule had given way to gaiety and laughter, as the Queen and her young companions frolicked and danced and sang round the old Palace of Holyrood. Every evening was a banquet and at every excuse there was poetry and plays and always, always music.

Frivolity and licentiousness, roared John Knox from his pulpit in St Giles' Cathedral. Since, still taking advice in such matters from her French uncles, she refused to ratify the Acts of the Reformation Parliament setting up the new reformed church, he was constantly accusing her of wanting to return Scotland to the Catholic religion.

'I do not have such an intention,' protested Mary to Margaret, who repeted this to Master Knox.

'That's what she says,' she added. 'But I know from the clerks that she is in regular communication with Rome.'

'I know,' Knox said. 'My people there tell me she assures the Pope of her loyalty.'

It was pointless for Mary to issue a proclamation within weeks of her arrival undertaking not to interfere with the established religion. It was pointless for her to provide financial support for the new church from her personal resources. The Protestants, who had fought so long and so hard for their freedoms, and at great cost, were more wary than ever of her intentions. They could only point to Mary's country of nurture, France, where the Protestant Huguenots were being hounded and massacred.

But the differences could be put aside and Mary and her council, headed by Lord James, with Secretary Maitland in complete agreement with him, could continue the work which had begun before her arrival to restore law and order to the country after the anarchy of the wars of religion.

And there were always the joyous occasions when it would appear they were almost united.

Lord James was marrying Lady Anyas Keith. The Earl Marischal spared no expense in the wedding of his daughter. She might be marrying a bastard, but he was a king's son and the Earl thought highly of James personally. He had favoured the new religion from its earliest days and had been one of the main supporters of the Protestant preacher George Wishart, martyred so many years ago. The two men were of the same mind.

The couple were married by John Knox in a crowded St Giles' Cathedral with virtually every noble of Scotland in attendance. If Knox's marriage sermon, in which he cautioned Lord James against being softened in his approach to reform by the influence of his new wife, sounded somewhat sour to the ears of his more attentive listeners, they could attribute it to his own sad want of a wife.

Relations between himself and Lord James continued cool. For some weeks back Knox had been even more vociferous in the pulpit against the Queen's religious practices. He feared that the legislation for the setting up of the new church and its finances was being watered down.

'We'll soon have the English version, neither fish nor fowl nor good red meat but an abominable compromise. Before we know it the mass will be back and God knows I fear the mass more than a legion of soldiers.'

'Why, John? Why do you fear the mass so much?' asked Margaret.

'Because it appeals to the senses and not the mind. Because the ignorant and the ill-informed become intoxicated and the brain stops to think. The whole ritual has moved so far from the simple Word of our Lord that people have forgotten the purpose of it. We would take that back.'

At the three-day celebrations which followed the wedding John Knox strode up to Margaret and growled, 'Madam, when so many are starving it ill becomes any of us to flaunt our wealth and such vanity is ungodly.'

He turned and walked away without waiting for an answer, while the girls round Margaret did their best to suppress their giggles until he was out of earshot.

The Queen at the top table had Lord James on one side of her and Anyas on the other. They were talking animatedly. The Queen liked the girl, known for her common sense, and she was already one of the Queen's favourite ladies-in-waiting. She would be a good wife for James. A frivolous girl would never have done.

And thinking of frivolous girls Margaret looked over at the Queen's companion, young Mary Fleming, whose mother, still in France, was notorious for licentiousness. The Queen's secretary, Maitland, was leaning over the back of the girl's chair, whispering in her ear. She could only hope the girl would not take it seriously.

There was a stir as the Queen's herald raised his voice to silence the company. The Queen had an announcement to make.

'My lords,' the Queen's voice rang out. 'On this happy day, on the occasion of the marriage of my dear

159

brother James to my dear companion Anyas, I wish to reward him for his services to me, his sister, and to our beloved country Scotland. It pleases me to announce that I have yesterday created Lord James the Earl of Mar.'

The cheers that followed this were hesitant.

Mar was one of the most ancient earldoms of Scotland and one of the most disputed. It was a substantial gift, carrying as it did large estates in the north and the fealty of the men who lived on them. But all present knew that the revenues from those estates had been enjoyed by Lord Huntly these last ten years or more. How would he take this? Did the Queen realise what she had done?

Lord James himself, standing beside the Queen and his new bride, looked unmoved. For Margaret, who had also known in advance, this was a proud moment. Raised to an earldom, James could now take his rightful place among the nobility of Scotland. He was no longer merely the prior of St Andrews, but a peer of the realm. He was equal to all of them.

There was a growl of fury at her side. She turned to see her brother glowering at Lord James.

'The Mar title should be mine. It has always been held by an Erskine. What right did the Queen have to give it away while it was still in dispute?'

'James is an Erskine too. Why not him?'

'Your son,' hissed Lady Annabella, 'will not rest until he has everything.'

Lord Erskine turned and stalked out of the room, followed by his wife. Margaret started after them ready to defend her son, but was suddenly conscious that the people nearby had fallen silent and were avidly listening. She stopped and smiled and made her way back to her seat.

The Queen gave a signal, the boards were cleared and the dancing started.

Lord Erskine could not leave the matter there. His fury expressed at the next Privy Council meeting could be heard even through the closed doors of the council chamber. In support of his case he called on his known loyalty to the Queen's mother and his family's generations of service to the crown. The other council members declined to take sides. For them it was a matter of indifference what title Lord James carried. His was the main voice on the council and as long as the Queen trusted him nothing would change that.

'How could you let the Queen do this?' Erskine asked Maitland. 'I assume she was in ignorance that the title has been long disputed.'

'It belongs to the crown as right,' said Maitland. 'It was hers to bestow as she would.'

'You should have advised her differently.'

Maitland, a close ally of Lord James, shrugged.

The Queen sat quietly, badly shaken by the row.

'What am I to do?' she asked Margaret, later recounting the events in the council. 'Am I to be defied already?'

'It is not defiance,' said Margaret gently. 'My brother feels strongly about it. The title did belong to the Erskines for so many years and they were cheated out of it. It was a long time ago, but my family still claim it.'

'I can't take it back. How could I?'

'Perhaps,' said Margaret. 'You could find another earldom for Jamie and afterwards bestow the title of Mar on my brother. That would right an ancient wrong.'

'Yes, perhaps I could do that. But not yet. I will not be defied.'

Chapter Twenty-Six
1562

'I want to trust him,' said the Queen. 'He is my cousin. He was my father's friend.' What she did not say was that Lord Huntly was a Catholic. She found herself with few friends of her own religion. She could ill afford to lose one, especially one as influential as George Gordon. 'But surely, it is not right that he never attends our council meetings.'

'Lord Huntly disapproves of the negotiations for you to meet Queen Elizabeth. This is how he shows his displeasure.'

'All my councillors should be eager to do what is best for Scotland.'

'My Lord Huntly will do what is best for my Lord Huntly,' said James. 'He rules the north for his own interests, not yours and certainly not Scotland's.'

'He is more than a king in his own lands,' said Maitland. 'And he talks of establishing the mass in all of the north. Your Grace cannot permit that. Not if you want Scotland to remain at peace with itself.'

It was early afternoon. They were in the Queen's small private parlour in the tower room. They had dined, the Queen, Lord James and Secretary Maitland, with Mary Seton in attendance. Mary had left when, with a nod, the Queen had indicated she had private business to discuss with her two councillors before the Privy Council meeting.

Maitland coughed and said gently, 'You should know, Your Grace, that Lord Huntly's son John Gordon is swaggering around town claiming that Your Grace wishes to marry him.'

She burst into a peal of laughter.

'That arrogant young man? How silly he is. Surely no one will believe him?'

'There is talk that you encouraged him in his courtship of you.'

She stopped laughing. 'I did not encourage him.'

'You smiled kindly upon him and danced with him.'

'Is it now a sin to smile at one's people? Am I to walk around with a scowl on my face? Am I to refuse to dance with any man unless I intend to wed him?'

'It's just what people are saying. There will always be foolish people who believe everything. It could do Your Grace's reputation harm. Bear in mind how the liaison with Robert Dudley has damaged your cousin Elizabeth's reputation throughout Europe.'

'I will not have such talk. John Gordon must be restrained from such nonsense.'

The Queen lingered by the window for a moment, looking out on to the green parks with their beech trees already turning from delicate green to the darker green of summer. It was clear she would rather be out riding than sitting in a council chamber.

Lord James reflected that only a year into her personal reign and already she was becoming more confident. But the confidence would have to be channelled in the right direction. And Huntly would have to be put in his place. He held all the power in the north, but he held it at the Queen's command and an opportunity would come to put the Earl in the wrong and turn the Queen against him.

Lord James was a patient man. He could wait.

The opportunity came sooner than he expected.

Huntly's son Lord John Gordon, he who boasted that the Queen would marry him, fell into a dispute with Lord Ogilvy and seriously wounded him in a brawl in the street. He was arrested and committed to prison, escaped and was now on the run in the north, protected, it had to be assumed, by his father.

The council ordered Lord Huntly to give up his son. He refused. The council, conscious that Lord James was attempting to recover the revenue of the Mar estates from Huntly, agreed unanimously that none was better placed to pursue the errant young man and bring him to justice than Lord James himself. There were some who were not displeased to think of Huntly's tail being tweaked but were disinclined to attempt it themselves.

'Mary, my dear,' her brother said to her some days later. 'Perhaps it is time for a journey north. Make it clear to all that you are the Queen of the whole of Scotland. And make it clear that no one is above the law.'

August was chosen for the Queen's northern progress. It was a large cavalcade. The Queen's normal household was augmented by a large contingent of fighting men under the command of Lord James.

The weather could generally be expected to be fine at this time of year, but when they left Edinburgh heavy rain was falling and continued to fall as they made their way north, through roads that became quagmires, slowing the heavy carts carrying their supplies almost to a standstill.

The houses and castles where the royal party stayed on their way were cold and everything felt damp. Several of the Queen's ladies were sneezing and coughing and though they had been banished from her side, they were not ill enough to be sent home. The civic welcomes were wet, half-hearted, sulky affairs. The weather was too poor for any of the normal outdoor amusements which might have entertained the Queen and no one was in the mood for dancing and music. Her musicians complained the cold and damp was damaging their instruments, the Queen's fool had a cold and could find nothing even mildly amusing about their present predicament, everything smelled of wet wool

164

and the courtiers were bored and frustrated. Thus it was a bad-tempered and aching cavalcade that wound its way up the east coast towards Aberdeen.

But by the time they reached there the weather had cleared. They met with a loyal address from the burgesses of the city and a thunderous welcome from the crowds. Their spirits rose, but there were still dissatisfactions.

There was no sign of Lord Huntly, who should have been there to welcome the royal party.

The Queen and her ladies settled into the house set aside for them and she began a satisfying round of government and local business, justice ayres, charity almsgiving and entertainments by students and children. As the days passed there was still no sign of Lord Huntly and the Queen's mouth would set in a grim line whenever his name was mentioned. 'His absence does not endear him to me.'

Now, a week after their arrival the day's duties were done and the Queen was relaxing with her immediate friends and ladies round her. They were laughing at the Queen's fool, who had recovered from her cold and was doing some mock wrestling with the youngest page.

There was a noise at the door and the chief usher entered. 'Will Your Grace receive my Lady Huntly?'

The fool gave a squeal of fright and hid behind the Queen's chair. 'A witch, a witch,' she whispered loudly and was hastily shushed. This was not a time for frivolity, but there had been suggestions from some of the local women that the Countess of Huntly had familiars to do her bidding.

'Ask her to wait.'

He bowed and backed out. The Queen turned to Lord James. 'Shall we see her?'

'It would be wise. Perhaps she has some explanation for her husband's absence.'

Lady Huntly was admitted. She was followed by ten or more of her people who crowded into the room. There were clearly others waiting outside. The guards on the door, at a signal from Lord James, pushed these people back into the outer hall and closed the door on them.

'Lady Huntly,' said the Queen. 'You wish to have words with me.'

'Your Grace.'

'Where is your husband?'

'Alas, he is ill and could not leave his bed. But if Your Grace stays long enough in our country he hopes for a meeting. Your Grace's road to Inverness passes Strathbogie where he will await Your Grace's pleasure.'

'Lord Huntly is waiting for *me* to go to *him*?' the Queen said and there was something in her soft voice which caused those round her to stiffen.

'Alas, Your Grace. As I say, illness...'

'I am told,' said the Queen in the same soft voice beguiling with its French accent and gentle musicality, 'that your husband travels to a different place every night and sleeps there, for fear of his life. Why should that be?'

'He has many enemies,' said Lady Huntly. Was there a swift glance at Lord James?

'If he is well enough to travel every day to a different place, why then is he not well enough to travel here to greet me, his Queen?'

Again the silence save for a slight shuffling of feet and a sigh from one of the girls standing demurely beside the Countess.

'You may tell Lord Huntly that I would have him wait upon me with an explanation.'

Lady Huntly bowed her head.

'You will go and do that now,' said the Queen in dismissal.

'Your Grace, there is more.'

166

'Is there? What more can you have to say to me?'

The Countess gathered up her skirts and fell heavily onto her knees. She raised her voice and suddenly there was real anguish in it.

'I plead with you as a mother. Spare my boy. John is young. He regrets already his action. And Lord Ogilvy did not die.'

'That was chance,' said the Queen.

'He did not die,' repeated Lady Huntly. 'My son did not intend to wound him seriously.'

'That is not what I heard,' said the Queen. 'There is bad blood.'

'There was the honour of his sister.'

'Oh?'

'My daughter the Lady Jean has been pursued in a most unseemly fashion by a kinsman of Lord Ogilvy and it was necessary they should know such a liaison was not to be. We have no wish to align ourselves with the Ogilvys.'

She almost spat out the name. She reached up to take the hand of the girl standing next to her.

'My daughter is only a child. Her brother was protecting her honour.'

Jean Gordon, thought Lord James. The one I had thought might serve the Queen as one of her ladies. The girl, as richly dressed as her mother and sisters, was staring fixedly at the ground with a faint blush on her cheeks. She looked barely sixteen. A pretty girl. Perhaps she had not been averse to the attentions of one of the Ogilvy clan, even though their families were not friendly.

Well, her parents have destroyed any chance of the girl's attendance at court, the father by his insolence in not being here, and the mother now staring proudly at the Queen, even from her kneeling position.

The Queen was speaking.

167

'Your son will receive a fair trial. But he must show his good faith and return to ward in Stirling. We will better believe in his innocence when he does not confront us with more crimes.'

Lady Huntly lowered her head.

'I will tell him.'

'You will tell him? You know where he is? You are shielding the miscreant?'

'I do not know, Your Grace, but there are men who do, who will not tell me.'

The Queen indicated with an impatient jerk of the head that the audience was over. The Countess was helped to her feet by her daughters and they all retreated from the room. She left behind a room where the air was fraught with tension.

Chapter Twenty-Seven

They left Aberdeen three days later and turned west towards Inverness.

The Queen, her fury nurtured by Lord James and Maitland, was determined to go to Strathbogie Castle and confront Huntly. 'He will see he cannot defy my wishes.'

'No,' said Lord James. 'It would be too dangerous.'

The Captain of the Queen's guard agreed with him. They were both adamant that she should not travel anywhere near Huntly's stronghold.

'It may be true that Huntly is waiting to welcome us,' said Lord James. 'But my scouts bring me stories of an excessive gathering of Huntly's people there.'

'I would fear for Your Grace's safety,' said the Captain.

So it was decided that although the more southerly route would take longer, they would avoid all the Huntly castles. With the improved weather they made good time. It was now September and the leaves were beginning to turn golden and red. The going underfoot was dry and as they rode through the glens the Queen and her ladies sang the songs they had learned from their hosts in Aberdeen.

Just after passing the hamlet of Ballater they were halted by the raised hand of the Captain in the front. He had heard a whistle from up ahead. He reined in his horse and waited till Lord James rode up to the front to see what was amiss. The guards closed in round the Queen.

An outrider appeared from amongst the trees.

'There were men up ahead. They fled when we were almost on them. I think they were preparing an ambush.'

'Armed?'

'Yes.'

While the Queen's guard stayed with her Lord James rode forward with some of his men. About a mile beyond, as the outrider had described it, in a narrow defile they came upon signs of disturbed undergrowth. Dismounting and examining the ground where it widened beyond the rocky outcrops they could see where there had been a gathering of many horses and men.

One of his men suddenly dived into the gorse which lined the road and emerged holding by the hair a struggling boy, his hand clamped over the boy's mouth so that he could not cry out. He could barely breathe.

'They left something behind.'

'Well spotted. Is he the only one?'

The boy had given up on his struggles and drooped on his knees in the mud. They listened. There was no sound save the cry of a hawk high above them.

Lord James nodded to his man. 'Bring him.'

He sent a man back to tell the cavalcade to move up. They continued on their road, cautiously. They paused overnight at the house of a laird, eager to welcome the Queen and her ladies, while the men camped round about, or slept in the wagons which carried the Queen's gear. The guard was strengthened and everyone was alert.

When it was dark and the Queen had settled for the night, Lord James took his lantern and two of his men and went out to the outhouse in which the boy was being held prisoner.

He crouched in a corner, whimpering.

'We'll not hurt you, lad,' said Lord James. 'If you tell us what you were doing there.'

'Nothing,' said the boy.'

'Who is your master?'

The boy stared at him. 'He's lost his wits,' growled the man who had been guarding him.

170

'Come on, now, boy. Who is your master?'

Lord James nodded to one of his men who stepped forward and casually, without effort, seized hold of the boy's arm and twisted it up his back. He screamed as his shoulder dislocated.

'Your master, boy?'

The boy was no hero. 'Lord John Gordon.'

'And what was his plan?'

The boy was crying, tears dripping onto his muddy shirt. There arose from him the stink of urine.

'I don't know.'

'You must have heard them discussing what he planned to do. Was he going to kill the Queen?'

The guard made to grab the boy's other arm.

'No.' A shriek. 'They were going to kidnap her. Kill everybody else.'

'And then what?'

'She would marry Lord Gordon who would be king then.'

Lord James nodded to his man, who let go of the boy.

'Keep him close guarded. Bring him with us.'

The next day, riders were seen on the tops of the hills out of range of arrows and pistols, just sitting watching them, making no move to approach. Overnight there was a disturbance among the horses. An attempt was being made to steal them, the attempt fortunately prevented, for now there were more men than ever standing guard round the Queen and her people. None of the courtiers would wish to be accused of negligence where the Queen's safety was concerned and men who had been living softly in Edinburgh for months now reverted to the tough warriors they had had to be in the past. If Lord John Gordon chose to harry them on their journey, they would find him and perhaps he would not survive long enough to stand trial.

171

Soon they reached Darnaway Castle, the seat of the Earls of Moray, though the earldom was vacant since the death of the last earl, the Queen's uncle.

As they approached through the heavily wooded countryside a scout returned to say that there was a large body of men waiting. Campfires burned round the castle and makeshift tents of canvas and brushwood filled the area. Groups of small highland ponies were tethered round about.

'Hostile?'

'They saw us but did not approach or disband.'

'Huntly livery?'

'No. Drab.'

Lord James was conscious of many eyes watching him from among the trees as he rode forwards. A man wrapped in a highland philabeg stood in his path, his hand raised in greeting.

'Who are you?' called Lord James.

'Robert-Mor Munro, chief of the Munros. Who are you?'

'James, Earl of Mar.'

'Then you are welcome. We have heard of you.'

'By what right do you welcome me to the seat of the Earl of Moray?'

'By right of arms. We come to the aid of the Queen.'

'How will you aid her?'

'It is said she will not be welcome in Inverness. I bring my people to make sure that she will not suffer any insult when she arrives there.'

Lord James dismounted and walked towards the other. They eyed each other warily. Then the clan chief smiled and struck his hand on his breast. 'I give you fealty.'

They talked for an hour and then Lord James, satisfied that Munro was loyal to the Queen, sent back word that she could approach.

They entered the castle. The highlanders crowding enthusiastically in the Hall to see the Queen, had taken possession of the castle, and the servants, many of whom were likely of the same clan, had done their best to make the Queen's quarters at least comfortable.

There the Queen issued a new proclamation. Lord James had agreed to renounce the Earldom of Mar and in return the Queen raised him to the Earldom of Moray. Darnaway was now his.

This indeed would be a blow to the Earl of Huntly. While the earldom was in abeyance he had the governance of the lands and received the revenue. The lands of Moray were among the wealthiest in the country, covering as they did the vast swathes of flat fertile land that bordered the Moray Firth, to say nothing of the rich fishing grounds off the coast. Truly Huntly was being punished for his insubordination.

At the same time the Queen pronounced that Lord John Gordon, who had failed to heed the instruction to give himself up to the law, was put to the horn. He was now an outlaw.

The next day they arrived at Inverness.

Inverness Castle belonged to the Queen. On her orders it had been rebuilt by Huntly in his capacity as Sheriff of Inverness. The new keep was visible from a distance, standing high on its hill with the river winding round the north side and on the south the steep slopes easily defended.

As the party approached they could see that the portcullis was down and the ramparts lined with armed men. The Queen's herald rode forward and up the hill till he was within hailing distance of the gatehouse.

'Open for Her Grace, the Queen of Scots.'

Nothing happened.

He called again.

'Open your gates to admit the Queen of Scots.'

173

In response a man in full armour appeared on the top of the keep.

'Name yourself,' called the herald.

'Alexander Gordon, Keeper of this Castle.'

'Another of Huntly's sons,' muttered Lord James to his sister.

'I seek entry to this castle in the name of the Queen.'

'Entry is denied.'

There was a stir at that among the watchers. The Keeper was refusing the Queen entry to her own castle. This was not only insolence. It was treason.

Suddenly those guarding the Queen realised that she was within distance of well-aimed arrows from the castle, should any be released and at a word she moved back to lower ground and safety.

'Aye,' said Robert-Mor Munro. 'It is no more than would be expected of a Huntly. We will not stand for it.'

'Can you take the castle?'

'We can.'

He must have sent round word of the Queen's predicament for within days more men appeared, men of the Clan Fraser. Their seventeen-year-old chief, barely old enough, as the Queen's men remarked, to shave, knelt and pledged fealty to her. One by one his men also knelt. They enthusiastically declared themselves willing to make war on Huntly and all the Gordons and fight to the death if necessary.

There was an uneasy lull, while the fighting men gathered in force round the hill. Perhaps the Keeper decided he was outnumbered, perhaps he feared that if an attack came the castle would be destroyed, or, as became clear, of the men in the castle only Alexander Gordon himself was prepared to oppose the Queen. Whatever the reason for his capitulation without bloodshed, as evening came, the castle portcullis was raised and the gates opened to admit the Queen's troops.

Her guards swept into the castle while she rode after them. She stayed mounted and watched as her men dragged the steward of the castle into the courtyard.

'We found him in the storerooms.'

'Locked up, Your Grace,' said the steward, falling to his knees. 'They beat me and locked me up because I refused to take arms against Your Grace.'

The Queen nodded. She believed him. He was sent to prepare the Queen's rooms ready for her occupation.

Lord James came down from the castle keep. 'We have Alexander Gordon in chains. We'll take him back to Edinburgh to face trial.'

'No,' said the Queen. 'Hang him. Hang him from the castle walls. Let him be an example to any who would commit treason against me.'

She dismounted and followed Lord James up to the battlements. Alexander Gordon, his face bloody, his body wound round with chains, his arms twisted behind his back, glowered at her.

'Have you anything to say to me?' she asked.

'Nothing, madam.'

She turned and walked away.

As soon as she was gone they dropped a noose over his head and looped the other end of the rope round the stone battlements. Then at a signal from Lord James two men lifted him bodily and tossed him over the wall. The onlookers saw the rope twitch a few times and then was still, save for an occasional creak as the body below them swung gently in the wind.

Chapter Twenty-Eight

They brought word to the Queen that Lord Huntly was dead, died of apoplexy on the battlefield at Corrichie. The rising of the Gordons in the north was ended. The Queen's troops led by Lord James, commanded in the field by among others his brother-in-law Patrick Lindsay, had won. These men who only a few years before had been fighting against the Queen's mother were now among her most enthusiastic supporters. A woman she might be but her ruthlessness with the Gordons proved she was her father's daughter and fit to lead them.

Since the Huntly lands were now all forfeit to the Queen, Lord James Stewart was able to take possession of the lands of Moray along with the earldom. He relinquished the title of Earl of Mar, it was given to Lord Erskine and both men, now considerably richer, were well satisfied.

The Queen refused an audience to Lady Huntly who came to plead for the life of her other sons. The errant John Gordon, who had given the Queen cause to wage war against his father, was captured, along with his brother Adam. They lay in the Tolbooth in Edinburgh for months. Adam was eventually pardoned, as being no more than a boy, and the Queen pardoned the eldest son, Lord George Gordon, since he had been in the south when the rising took place and had not taken part.

But the full force of the law fell upon Lord John Gordon. He was to be executed.

'Let it be carried out,' said the Queen. 'No mercy.'

The court sat and watched as Lord John was dragged forward. Most men going to the scaffold, and concerned with their immortal souls, would say no more than a brief prayer, for it was too late to plead for mercy. But Lord John was not going to go quietly, with dignity. Offered the chance of a speech from the scaffold he looked directly at the Queen and shouted 'I die for love of you. I suffer for that love.'

The Queen shrank back into her chair. Moray nodded to the axeman. Lord John was pushed down onto the block, where he writhed and twisted. The axeman paused. One of the guards gave Lord John a kick in the side. He groaned and lay still.

'Get on with it, man,' muttered Moray. Perhaps the cries of the doomed man unnerved the executioner. Perhaps the presence of the Queen made him nervous.

The axeman steadied his stance, raised his axe and brought it down hard, but he struck only a glancing blow on the neck of the prostrate man. Blood spurted and Lord John screamed.

'O, mon Dieu,' muttered the Queen. The onlookers watched aghast as the executioner raised his axe and again brought it down, but the dying man was twitching and again the axe failed to sever the head. A third stroke was more fortunate and the head rolled into the waiting straw.

'The Queen,' cried Moray.

She had fainted. She was brought round sufficiently to be half-carried, half-walking. A litter was sent for and she was conveyed back to the palace, screened from the crowds who had gathered.

She lay prostrate in a darkened room for two days, crying and sleepless. Whenever she closed her eyes she saw again the bloodied neck of the executed man. She vomited up anything that they tried to make her eat.

'Is that how they execute men in this country? In agony?' she cried.

'Has she never seen an execution before?' Moray asked Mary Seton.

177

'No. How could she have? She had no enemies to be made an example of.'

'But she must have seen death.'

'Only decently, in beds. Not that barbarism.'

Chapter Twenty-Nine

The boards with their snowy covers were set with all that would be necessary for the Queen's dinner. The silver candlesticks shone and the glassware sparkled. Venison and fowl were roasting in the kitchen while pies, sweet and savoury, subtleties of spun sugar, and fine wines, all were waiting in the pantry.

At the top table there was drawn up one of the Queen's chairs of state, sent for the purpose from Stirling Castle, and over it hung a great red and gold cloth of state. Margaret twitched at the end of it to make sure it was straight. This was one of the spoils of Strathbogie Castle after the death of Huntly.

The New House was ready to welcome the Queen.

Margaret found William in his library, where he had retreated, complaining that the dust raised by cleaning the rooms not normally used had aggravated the tightness in his chest.

'I hope the weather improves,' she said.

'This rain will blow over.'

'Is all ready for the hunt tomorrow?'

'The hounds are at their best. If the Queen's mount tires we have others equally fine. Don't fuss, Mother.'

'It's a great honour.'

'Expensive.'

'Nonetheless.'

There was a flurry of noise outside. He looked from his window which overlooked the stables.

'Master Knox.'

'I'll go down.' Margaret moved towards the door. William began to cough. 'Shall I fetch Agnes?'

'No, let me be.'

'William...'

'Let me be,' he almost shouted at her. 'Get ready to welcome the Queen. I will be there.'

John Knox was shaking the rain from his cloak when she met him in the hall.

'I'm glad you could come, John.' She spoke truth. They were of an age and he was stimulating and amusing and she could sweeten his temper when she encouraged him to relax and talk about his time in England. But she hoped he would not argue with the Queen.

'The girl,' as she had said to Knox on more than one occasion, 'cannot help her upbringing.'

'Aye,' he would reply. 'We can hope that the next twenty years with us will eradicate the damage of the first eighteen years with the papists.'

Now she held out her hand and he clasped it between his. He's looking better, she thought. 'You had a good journey to the west?'

He frowned. 'They brazenly celebrate the mass still in parts of Galloway. I had the priests imprisoned. Now she's summoned me here to answer for it.'

'She told me she wanted to debate with you on the matter.'

'I will debate with the devil if necessary.'

'John, my dear, you must not upset her.'

'I can only speak plain. If she is upset, then perhaps it is her conscience reproving her.'

'It is not your job to act as her conscience.'

'Who else is coming?'

'Not many. She's bringing Mary Seton and Mary Livingstone. Jamie's here. One or two others. She wants this to be a quiet visit, some hunting, some resting.'

'I anticipate a private flyting then.' She laughed at that and called a servant to show him to the chamber set aside for the older men.

Her daughter-in-law was looking for her. Agnes looked blooming as always though now she had little fretful lines on her brow. She was pregnant once more. Whatever the state of William's health, he obviously did his duty in bed.

'I wish we had organised some entertainment.'

'The Queen will bring her own musicians. We cannot match hers. We should not try. She wants a quiet private visit.'

Soon the Queen was with them, professing herself delighted with the house and the countryside and the prospect of good hunting. But she expressed herself disappointed in one thing.

'I wish we could stay at your castle on the island,' she said.

'It is not large enough for all your people,' said Margaret.

'But I have such memories of staying in a castle on an island. It was summer and everyone was very kind. I was only a little baby, but I remember.'

'It was a different island. A different castle. We were at war then. It was feared that King Henry would order your kidnapping,' said Margaret. 'So you were sent there for safety.'

Tomorrow the Queen would have her hunting and if she wanted to travel across to the castle they would organise that too. If she saw that as romantic, well, that was all to the good. It would keep her amused.

Knox spent part of the evening in serious conversation with Mary Seton.

181

'The other girls call Mary Seton "the nun",' the Queen, watching them, confided in Margaret. 'Is that not a good name for her?'

'I do not know her well enough. She is so quiet.''

'She is very devout. She is a good Catholic. I hope Master Knox will not corrupt her. You know, he is the most dangerous man in the kingdom. My uncles told me so.'

'Perhaps at a distance they did not see so clearly.'

'That is true. They told me he was an old man who should sit at the fire like other old men. Now I know he is not.'

On the following evening the Queen's party were taken across to the island in the largest of the boats, lavishly decorated. She strolled round the courtyard admiring the buildings. Such a high keep! Such a pretty circular tower! What was it used for? And she would climb up to the roof and look at the view, look out over the loch and the surrounding moorland and to the hills on the north bank of the loch where she had been hunting in the early morning.

'It is enchanting. Like a castle from the tales of King Arthur. What you should have here is a maiden in need of rescuing.'

Margaret nodded and smiled and reflected that she was glad they did not live there any more, but in the New House, dry, warm and comfortable.

Before supper that evening John Knox sat with the Queen for two hours, talking. The others kept a tactful distance. Discussions touching on the soul were not to be overheard by anyone. From time to time Knox's voice was raised and the Queen was shaking her head vigorously. Once she was seen to lay her hand on his arm in emphasis of what she was saying and though the words were indistinguishable, all could hear the emotion in her voice as she spoke. The two of them seemed oblivious to anyone else in the room.

182

At the other end of the Hall the Queen's musicians were playing soft airs. One of them struck a chord on his lute and then began to sing in a deep voice, a melancholy song in his own language.

Margaret leaned forward to whisper to Lord James. 'Who is that?'

'His name is Rizzio. Italian. The others call him Signor Davie.'

'I am surprised the Queen allows such an ugly little man near her.'

'She is kind to the unfortunate.'

Margaret gave up straining to hear the Queen's conversation with Knox. The voice of Rizzio was drowning it out. He did have a pleasing voice. She could understand why the Queen retained him among her musicians.

'Warn the maids to keep clear of him,' murmured Lord James. 'He tried to bribe your steward earlier to supply a girl for his bed.'

'I was not told.'

'The men will keep an eye on him.'

'Discreetly. We do not want to offend the Queen. We certainly don't want trouble in our house.' Margaret decided she had better not tell Agnes of this exchange. The girl was so near her time she should not be worried.

Suddenly the Queen stood up. 'Faugh,' she said. 'There is no arguing with the man.'

'There's no arguing with the truth,' he responded, struggling to his feet.

The Queen's cheeks were flushed and her eyes were sparkling. He too was smiling. They like each other, thought Margaret and watching them later as the two sat side by side listening to the music, still talking in low voices, she wondered. Surely the Queen was not flirting with Knox? Surely he was not responding?

183

The next day there was more hunting. As they were mounting in the stable yard, the Queen sent her page to fetch John Knox.

'Your Grace,' he said, when he arrived, slightly out of breath, for the summons was unexpected.

'I am sorry you will not ride out with us today,' said the Queen.

'I present a poor picture on a horse, Your Grace.'

'I wanted to talk with you about my sister. I want you to intervene with her husband.' If Knox was surprised by this sudden reference to a matter hitherto unmentioned he did not show it.

'Jane and Argyll must not separate. You must tell him so. It is not fitting that a member of the royal family should be living in such disharmony with her husband. Make him behave.'

'I cannot make any man behave.'

'Discipline him. Does your church not do that?'

'I would hesitate to suggest such to my Lord of Argyll.'

'Nonetheless, it is my wish that you do this.'

She looked down at him and there was a smile on her lips. 'Do this for me, please.'

Then she indicated with a nod that he should step back and with a flick of the reins led the hunting party out of the stable yard.

Margaret, standing in the doorway, sympathised with the stunned Knox. 'It is not a good idea to intervene between husband and wife.'

'If she wishes me to do it, I will try.'

She stood aside to let him into the house. 'She will have her reasons, which might not be obvious. Take care, my old friend.'

Chapter Thirty
1564/65

When Margaret heard that the Earl of Lennox had been allowed to return she was astonished.

'Queen Elizabeth pleaded for him,' Lord James told her.

'Why?'

'I cannot tell.'

Margaret remembered the previous times Lennox had set foot in Scotland, the time when he was summoned by Mary of Guise and Cardinal Beaton. He had done nothing but cause trouble then. At Pinkie Cleugh he fought on the side of the English and there were many could not forgive him for that.

'Surely someone should warn Mary.'

Lord James shrugged. 'I did try and tell her. But she took the view that if her dear sister Elizabeth wished it then it must be all right. I could not persuade her otherwise. And what could I say? That the man is an enemy of Chatelherault? That he has a claim to the throne? To fear assassination? She would not listen to me.'

'What does Chatelherault think of this?'

'He tried to stop it. But she would not listen to him either.'

'Why does he want to come back now he's married to a kinswoman of Elizabeth? He can hardly think Scotland is a more comfortable place for him than the English court.'

'Don't forget, Mother, what matters to Mary more than anything is that Elizabeth names her as her successor. That is what we are working towards and Mary will do whatever Elizabeth wants.'

When word came that Lennox had not only been welcomed at court, but that he and Chatelherault had made a public declaration of amity, Margaret continued to feel more than usual unease.

'Mary stood over them while they assured each other of perpetual friendship,' Jamie told her. 'It was farcical She is the only person who could not see it. Neither man was happy.'

Margaret returned to Lochleven to help her daughter-in-law through the latest confinement and stayed on across the winter. William's health was poor with the winter weather, which was proving particularly severe.

At Martinmas Margaret took her son's place for the hearing of the estate's accounting and for several days the tenants came and went, bringing details of their dealings during the last year, paying their rent in kind, while the steward sat beside Margaret making notes. The house was full, for the auditing of the accounts was a big day in the life of any estate. Tenants could meet up, discuss farm talk and drink ale and eat meat at the expense of their landlord. Margaret, listening to the stuttering application by a young man to take over the tenancy on behalf of his father who had died, could hear the buzz of talk in the next room. She enjoyed these occasions as much as the tenants.

But her mind was always on what was happening in Edinburgh. She wrote to Jamie. Beware of Lennox, she wrote. He never did anything from simple motives. Marrying Margaret Tudor's daughter took him one step closer to the English throne. His ambition knows no bounds.

She read over what she had written. Then she tore up the paper and dropped the pieces in the fire. Her son knew all that. He did not need her to tell him. But she had sensed his unease when he told her that Mary was not listening quite so amenably to his advice as she had done in the past. It would not do for him to lose his influence.

It was time she was back at court.

When the spring came and with it better health for William she wrote to the Queen requesting leave to return to court. A response arrived. She was bidden to come to join them at Stirling.

She was welcomed in the Queen's outer chamber by a smiling usher, who knew her well.

'I will send in word,' he said, beckoning a page.

They waited. After a time the door opened and a small dark man came out. Signor Rizzio, she recollected.

'Lady,' he said, without preliminary. 'I regret that it is not convenient at present. Perhaps tomorrow.'

'I am here by the Queen's request,' said Margaret, eyeing the other's chequered red and purple velvet jacket and gold rings. He had not been so richly dressed when he was at Lochleven. Royal musician must be a lucrative post.

'Her Grace is ill. It is not convenient.'

Margaret, feeling anger welling up in her, could not bear to be speaking to him a moment longer. She turned and walked out of the chamber without a backward glance. She made her way to the room where the Queen's ladies were relaxing.

'Why would he not allow me in? If she is ill what is he doing there? She should have friends round her.'

'Signor Rizzio controls all access to the Queen nowadays,' said Mary Seton. 'Who knows whether he even told her you were here? Wait till tomorrow morning and present yourself again. Rizzio will still be in bed.'

'Aye, ordering our people about as if they were his slaves.' This remark came from Mary Beaton.

'But why?' asked Margaret. 'I do not understand. I thought he was only one of her musicians. No word of any of this has come to Lochleven.'

'They don't broadcast it. She has appointed him the secretary for her French correspondence. M. Paullet died, you know. We think she gives him a free hand to deal with business matters concerning her estates in France. No doubt he's lining his own pocket. He's very clever.'

'Clever!' said the usually gentle Mary Seton. 'He is not clever enough to see what enemies he makes.'

The next morning Margaret was admitted to the Queen's bedchamber by Mary Livingstone.

'My dear,' she said, grasping the girl's hand. 'You are to be married. I am so glad.'

'Thank you. But you know my family are not happy with my choice. A younger son and not legitimate, but we love each other and the Queen approves. She is giving me my wedding gown and reception.'

The Queen's room was in semi-darkness.

'Who's there?'

'Margaret Erskine.'

'Come over.'

The Queen was curled up on the bed wrapped in a heavy quilt though the room was stiflingly hot. Margaret took her hand.

'Why do I have to suffer like this? Every month, cramps and pains.'

'Have you taken the medicine?'

The Queen shuffled round onto her back. Margaret helped her to sit up and handed her the cup by the bedside.

'It helps, I suppose.'

The Queen's face was white and drawn. Margaret took the empty cup back from her and took her hand.

'The doctors say if I have a child it will cure this.'

'They often say that.'

'Is it true?'

'Sometimes.'

Tears sprang into the Queen's eyes. She gripped Margaret's hand more tightly.

'What chance have I of a child when I do not have a husband?'

'You are young. There are many men eager to marry you.'

'Marry my crown. And who is there? I had hopes of Don Pedro of Portugal. He is handsome, is he not? But now they say he is mad.'

The tears were now coursing down her cheeks.

'And there is Mary Hamilton to be married soon and I think Mary Fleming will marry Maitland though she says not but he woos her so romantically. Even Master Knox has married again. His new bride is younger than I. And out of his station.'

She stirred and half sat up, tears momentarily forgotten in a surge of anger. 'She is kin to the Stewarts. What right has Knox to marry my kin? Are they happy?' This was said fiercely.

'Yes,' said Margaret. 'Very happy.' She knew full well this was not what the girl wanted to know.

Mary fell back on the pillow and clutched at her belly and moaned. 'Even my cousin Elizabeth has her lover. Oh, how can I bear it?'

She turned over onto her side. Her voice came muffled to Margaret. 'Soon no one will want me.'

'They will.'

'Not for myself. Not for *me.*'

'Here, I will rub your back. That always helped my daughters.'

She gently kneaded and rubbed, feeling the young flesh taut over the bones. So young and so despairing. When she heard the Queen's gentle breathing, she stopped and pulled the covers up over her. When she was sure the girl was asleep, she stole quietly from the room, sending in one of the maids to sit with her mistress in case she woke.

She joined the Queen's ladies in the outer chamber. As she entered one of the women came forward, hands outstretched. Margaret did not hesitate. She would be friends with everyone.

'Lady Huntly. You here?'

'The Queen asked me to come to court. She bears no ill-will.'

'I heard she has pardoned your son George and restored the family estates.' Not all of them, Jamie had told her, but enough to give back some dignity to the family. Jamie had been against this. Apart from any other reason, the Huntlys still persisted in protecting the Catholic Church in the north and adhering to the outlawed faith. They still considered themselves to be above the law in that respect. The Queen always declared she had no wish to upset the country's settled religion, but pressure, Jamie said, was always coming from her relatives in France, to say nothing of the Pope himself. Who knew but she might be convinced there was some support in Scotland itself for its return if the Huntlys persisted in holding to it in the north?

'My daughter Jean has come to be one of the Queen's maidens.' She signalled and the Lady Jean Gordon came forward and curtseyed to Margaret. At a nod from her mother the girl went back to her place by the fire with the other girls.

'It was just in time,' Lady Huntly confided to Margaret, drawing her into a window embrasure. 'You'll have heard about the unfortunate liaison she formed with one of the Ogilvys.'

This, Margaret recollected, had been mentioned before as one of the causes of the girl's brother's fight with another of the Ogilvys. So it was continuing. She felt sorry for the girl. If their affection for one another had lasted this length of time, it was hard that they should not marry. And after all, what were the Huntlys now but declared traitors only partially admitted to favour, and still to prove themselves worthy of it?

'I have been away from court for so long,' said Margaret. 'Who else is here?'

'We were joined last week at Wemyss Castle by the Master of Lennox. The Queen finds him amusing.'

'Lennox's boy? Henry Darnley?'

'Yes. He has come north to help his father sort out matters relating to their estates. The Queen herself asked that he be allowed to come.'

'What's he like?'

'Pleasing enough in his manner. Good-looking in a soft sort of way. He seeks favour with everyone.'

Lord James agreed with this assessment. He sat beside his mother at the meal that followed, held in the Great Hall to accommodate all the lords and their families arriving with the intention of spending two weeks hunting with the Queen and then celebrating Easter with her.

'Darnley brought generous gifts for all of us. He gave me some very fine stones which I'm having set in a necklace for Anyas.'

The man himself was seated at the top table beside Lord Erskine, presiding in the absence of the Queen who was still ill and keeping to her bedchamber.

'He very obligingly came with me to hear Knox preach. But he has since attended mass with the Queen.'

'You do not like him?'

'There is nothing there to like or dislike.'

Lady Huntly was right. The lad was good-looking and his clothes, the puffed sleeves and the lacy collar of his shirt overlarge and pleated in the English style, suggested a measure of vanity. And tall. Lady Huntly had not mentioned that. Even seated he had to bend his head down to hear what Lord Erskine was saying.

On his other side Annabella Erskine was eating determinedly without speaking to her neighbour. Had Darnley offended her? But then, most people did.

The voice of Signor Rizzio on the other side of the Hall could be heard, raised in excited argument with his neighbours. Beside him Lord Robert Stewart, the Queen's half-brother, seemed to be vying with the young George Gordon to see who could drink the most. Others of the younger men were beginning to gather round. Lord Erskine sent one of the ushers down. He bent over Lord Robert and spoke. Lord Robert glanced at Lord Erskine and made a face. Then turned back to Rizzio and they both laughed.

A reprimand sent and ignored.

This is what happens when the Queen herself is not here, thought Margaret. From time to time she caught Lord Darnley throw a reproving glance over to where the two were sitting. Darnley must think this a very uncouth court after the English court, where it is said that under Elizabeth there is total decorum.

The Queen was back at court next day, recovered. Although it was Lent the high spirits of the young people would not allow them to be serious. There was hunting and hawking in the royal parks round Stirling in the mornings and music in the evenings.

Lord Darnley was attentive to the Queen and it was obvious she found him amusing. Rizzio was also by her side. One so handsome and one so ugly, they made an odd pair but it was evident that between them the Queen was delighted and as the days passed Margaret became aware that there always seemed to be the trio of them, the Queen, Darnley and Rizzio, together in a way that excluded the other courtiers.

Darnley, as fine a lutenist as Rizzio, joined him in playing duets. They finished the piece and bowed to the courtiers applauding politely. They turned back to the

Queen who smiled on them. Darnley gestured towards Moray who was at the other end of the Hall. Margaret, straining to hear, just caught the words. He was remarking on those who dress in black like priests to seem more serious. In Elizabeth's court it would not be allowed. And the Queen laughed. And then, as Margaret bent her head to listen to what her neighbour was saying, she heard a murmured reference to an old crone. She had no doubt who was being referred to. As she glanced up she caught the Queen's eye and Mary looked away, somewhat shamefaced.

The court musicians took up their instruments and the dancing began. Darnley led Mary in a sprightly gavotte.

When it was near midnight the Queen rose to signal the end of the evening's entertainment. Margaret caught her words to Darnley. 'Join me in my chamber. A game of cards perhaps?' The Queen looked round the room and signalled to Lord Robert Stewart and to Patrick Lindsay. They swaggered after her.

As Margaret left the Hall she caught up with Jamie.

'I would have words.'

He nodded and joined her shortly on the wall walk. The sentry took himself discreetly off to a far corner and turned his back. They could be sure not to be overheard. It was late and down below them the torches flickered as men and women passed under them, soberly or otherwise, making for their quarters. Above them the sky was filled with stars. It was a still night and they kept their voices low.

'My son,' said Margaret. 'What of the negotiations for the Queen's marriage?'

'Slow.'

'She must be married soon.'

'Yes.'

'Beware Darnley.'

'He dislikes me and I despise him. But you do not think Mary would be foolish enough to consider him for a husband?'

'Not yet perhaps.'

'Can you imagine the rule of Scotland in the hands of such a man? He is a fool and a coxcomb. In France they call him a fine young cockerel.'

'They know him in France?'

'They are watching everyone who comes near our Mary.'

'He has one advantage which is not given to everyone.'

'What?'

'He is tall.'

'Tall? Mother, what has that to do with anything?'

'Do you not think even a queen will consider how she looks by the side of a man? And Mary herself is so tall. How many men about the court can match her in height?'

'Mary would not be so foolish as to let that weigh with her in her choice of husband. She has too much pride.'

'Pride, perhaps. But every woman has some vanity, queen or not.'

'Ever since that limp turd Darnley came, the Queen has lost all common sense.' Lady Annabella expressed herself in her usual fashion. No one made any comment. It was a quiet family meal and the fish which was served was unlikely to raise the spirits or encourage lively conversation. As it was Lent there had been no meat at table and the fowl which took its place was being saved for the Queen's banquets.

Jamie quietly ate. He hardly seemed to notice what he was eating most of the time, his mind far away, and only Lord Robert was drinking wine. The others drank small ale. But Margaret, glancing at Robert now and again, could see that he was watching his brother covertly, as if wary of being attacked.

'You have not gone hawking?' she asked.

'No,' he said shortly.

'Robert is out of favour,' said Lord James. 'He has sown bad blood, have you not?'

There was no answer.

'Robert has been showing Henry Darnley the map of Scotland and telling him who owns what estates.'

'He asked me.'

'And why should he be interested?'

'I don't know. It wasn't just yours. It was everybody's.'

'But Darnley was particularly interested in the extent of my lands. So Robert obligingly told him all. And what did Darnley say to that? Tell the Lady Margaret, Robert. Tell her what Darnley said.'

'He said it was too much.'

'Too much, and what do you think he meant by that?'

'He meant you are too wealthy.'

'So Darnley has been turned against me, because I am too wealthy and I have been turned against Darnley because he is showing too much interest in my personal affairs. It was a good day's work, Robert.'

Robert muttered something they could not hear, threw down his napkin and left the room, his meal unfinished.

'Gone to gamble with the stable lads,' said Annabella. 'And with that Rizzio. He'll take them into the town and they'll find some drinking den and they'll be there all day and all night, whoring, and be unfit for their work tomorrow.'

The meal was finished in silence. Afterwards Lord James followed his mother to her chamber.

'I'm leaving court for a while. I'll take myself off. I have plenty of business elsewhere.'

'Is that wise?'

'I will say I have no taste for the popish celebration of Easter. That is true enough. Let the Queen consider how well she can manage without me.'

She nodded.

'And, Mother, you will be my eyes and ears here.'

'That goes without saying.'

Chapter Thirty-One

The crucifixes, candles, statues, everything in the chapel had been draped in purple and all day and for most of the night of the long week before Easter the Queen's chaplain and his priests and several of the Queen's household came and knelt for hours before the draped altar while the choir sang the old anthems. Those of the reformed religion living in the castle passed through the close, tight-lipped and with their eyes averted as if by ignoring it they could make it cease to happen.

On Easter Thursday a mass was held in the crowded chapel. Then the chapel was stripped of all its morbid drapes and silver and gold adornment and the tabernacle doors left hanging open to show the emptiness within.

Throughout Easter Friday the priests and the others knelt in the chapel praying. Then came the day of silent waiting. The Queen herself knelt all night through the vigil from sunset on Saturday. As the first rays of the sun began to light the undersides of the clouds in the east, the Paschal candle was lit in the porch, the deacon processed through the chapel chanting and they all one by one lit their candle and the mass began.

The bell began to toll in the Church of the Holy Rude, on the hill down from the castle. In the austere church, its wall paintings now whitewashed out, Margaret sat with the rest of the congregation on a hard bench listening to the preacher denounce the activity in the the Queen's chapel. His sermon was fierce and erudite but she felt her mind wandering. Why was the Queen deliberately, it seemed to her, flouting the sensibilities of the people? Was Lord Darnley encouraging her? And Rizzio. How much influence was he wielding? As a foreigner he could be allowed some measure of adherence to the old ways out of respect. Not that he as a man had earned any respect, but there were diplomatic reasons for granting foreigners the right to their own way of worship.

Jamie had been right to absent himself. The overblown ritual which was infuriating the others, might have hardened his heart against the Queen, and he could not afford that, not if he was to stay as her principal adviser.

As they passed back up the hill towards the castle a few of the townspeople who had not been in the church with them shouted out, 'Is there popery up there?'

'Return to your homes,' was Lord Erskine's sharp response.

Some of them looked as if they would argue the point, and one man even raised a stave in a gesture which might have been meant to encourage the others to storm the castle gates, but Lord Erskine stopped in his stride and glared at him, and respect for the Erskines or perhaps just common sense caused the man to drop the stave and the others to turn away and wander off down Goose Green to their houses.

When the Erskine family returned to the castle the Queen and her court were still in the chapel, from which came the sound of the choir singing.

'This can't go on,' murmured Erskine to his sister.

'If Darnley and Rizzio could be removed she would recover her senses and be more discreet.'

It was two days after Easter that Darnley began to show the first signs of illness. He was unable to rise from his bed in the morning and his man brought word to Lord Erskine that he required a physician.

The Queen, who was breaking her fast in her bedroom with a few of her ladies, was told of this. She sent for Darnley's man.

'What ails him?' she asked.

'Shivering, pains in the head, aching all over.'

'Is he vomiting?'

'No,' said the man, hesitantly.

'Purging?'

'Not while I was there.'

She dismissed the man and leaving the table with the food almost untouched, sent for her dresser.

'I must go to him.'

'No,' said Margaret sharply. 'You cannot go to a man's quarters. My brother will have sent a physician.'

'My own man must see him.'

'It will be your own physician my brother has sent.'

As soon as she was dressed, the Queen led the way, her ladies hurrying after her. Lord Darnley's room was on the third floor of the old palace, overlooking the vast sweep of the merse westwards, but the shutters were still closed and the room was in semi-darkness lit only with one candle and the pale blue flames of a newly lit fire. It stank of stale wine and piss.

'My friend,' Mary approached the bed, ignoring the protests of Margaret and Lady Huntly behind her. The younger women, unmarried, had been prevented from following. Only the matrons could be with her and they were horrified: it was most unseemly that the Queen should be in the room of an unmarried man.

'My dear,' said Lady Huntly, taking the Queen's arm. 'We must leave.'

Mary shook her off.

She knelt by the side of the bed. 'Henry, what's wrong. Have you been poisoned?'

'Your Grace.' The doctor had arrived. He took her elbow and lifted her back onto her feet. He was an elderly man who had been one of the Queen's physicians ever since she arrived in Scotland. 'I must examine my patient.'

She submitted with ill-will and allowed herself to be led from the room by Lady Huntly, Margaret following and closing the door at their backs.

'I want a French doctor. I do not trust the Scottish doctor. He may be bribed.'

Lady Huntly and Margaret glanced at each other. Clearly the Queen was too distraught to know what she was saying.

'Come,' said Lady Huntly. 'There is nothing you can do. He is in good hands.'

But Mary would not be persuaded to leave. She ordered them to bring a chair so that she could wait outside the patient's door. Lady Erskine, having been sent for by Margaret, came and tried to reassure her, but it was as if Mary was not hearing her. The irritation in Annabella's voice merely caused a distant frown. All her concentration was focussed on the sounds coming from Lord Darnley's room.

She leapt to her feet when the door opened.

'I have prescribed a sedative. It is well that he sleeps. When he wakes there will be herbs and perhaps some bleeding. The humours sit ill with him.'

'Humours? Not humours, sir,' cried the Queen. 'He has been poisoned.'

The doctor held up a hand. 'Now, who would want to poison him?'

'Just about everybody,' Lady Huntly muttered to Margaret.

'It is not poison,' said the doctor. 'There are others in the castle and in the town suffering from the same ailment and they all respond with rest and time. There is nothing for Your Grace to worry about.'

But the Queen could not be argued with. She returned to her bedroom, but only to change her dress for a simple one of linen and a shawl to wrap round her shoulders. Then she returned to the sick man's room and insisted on gaining entry.

His man looked aghast at Lady Margaret who had come trailing after the Queen. She shrugged. Let her in. There is no arguing with her. The Queen was admitted to the sick man's chamber and the door closed behind her.

'Who else is in there?'

'A nurse, and a chamber-woman to clean up,' answered the man.

It was chaperonage of a sort.

All the plans for the next week had to be changed to accommodate the absence of the Queen, who refused to leave the sick man's room, except to eat. She hastily swallowed anything that was put in front of her and hurried back to the patient. It was in vain for her ladies, hovering over her while she ate, to warn her that she herself might succumb to the illness which ailed the man and then where would Scotland be? She grew even paler than usual, but whether from confinement in a small space without light or sunshine, or from not eating enough, or from worry, none would venture to say.

She allowed none to nurse him but herself. Indeed, no one else wanted to nurse the sick man. His illness brought out the worst of his temper. He kicked out at one of the women who was attempting to change his bed and his own man had to retreat on one occasion, having had a full chamber pot thrown at his head. But then, he said, he was used to such treatment, whether his master was well or ill.

When Lord Erskine received a letter from his man of business in Antwerp commenting on tales of the strange behaviour of the Scottish Queen, he erupted in a temper. The letters from there had always contained a mixture of gossip and comments on the news from various countries. But now this!

'They are gossiping all over Europe,' he told his wife and Margaret. 'It is a disgrace. What can she be thinking of?'

'She is thinking of Darnley,' said Annabella. 'And God only knows what is going on. The nurses are not there all the time.'

'Shut your mouth,' he said, turning on her. 'As far as anyone is concerned there are several other women there and the doctor is in constant attendance. Do you hear?'

She shrugged. 'If you say so.'

Moray was in Edinburgh by now. Lord Bothwell had been in trouble again and his people were creating disturbances there. Moray had been obliged to muster extra men to reinforce the watch. Now that all was quieter he proposed to return to Stirling.

He wrote to Margaret to ask for the truth about the situation there. The Queen's behaviour was the talk of Edinburgh. The common people were sniggering behind their hands and Master Knox in his sermons was waxing furious about the immorality in the court.

And yes, he wrote, my correspondents in London and Paris and elsewhere have the same news, exaggerated or otherwise. She is making herself the laughing-stock of Europe. I dare not begin to think what Queen Elizabeth makes of it.

When he arrived he received a cool welcome. A message awaited him that the Queen was busy but would see him later. After he had cleansed himself of the dust from the journey he sought out Maitland in his room.

Maitland greeted him. 'You know what the wits are now saying?'

'About the Queen?'

'No, about me.'

'Tell me.'

'They are saying that Master Machiwilli now has all the time in the world to woo his mistress, since his services are no longer required by the Queen. I have no objection to being called after Signor Machiavelli, whose writings I admire, except what they say is true. I have been displaced.'

'By Darnley?'

'By Rizzio, mainly with the enthusiastic support of my Lord Darnley, whose illness is not so severe that he cannot talk and since his talk, I am told by those unfortunates who require to wait upon him, is of betrayals and conspiracies and hatreds of his person, our poor mistress has had her brains, such as she had, addled. As addled as the eggs in this dish here which I have been unable to eat.'

'Does she entrust more than her French correspondence to him?'

'It has gone well beyond that. Whatever advice we give her is taken to Rizzio for his opinion. Tell me what a lute player brought up in the slums of Naples can know of the governance of Scotland? I grant you, he is a very talented musician.'

He pushed the dish of food away from him.

'You should not have gone away, Jamie. Between us we might have managed to hold firm. Now she has given me a task which I admit is not to my taste. I am to go to England and inform Her Majesty Queen Elizabeth, our Queen's dear sister, that Mary intends to marry Lord Darnley.'

'Is it so then? It is decided?'

'What else can she do? She is compromised in the eyes of all decent men.'

'Can we stop her?'

'How? She will not listen to anyone.'

'There will be few who would favour such a match.'

'He struck Chatelherault the other day. He had only gone in to sympathise with the invalid. I grant you I often feel like striking the old man myself, but refrain in respect of his age.'

'We must prevent this.'

'Jamie, I will not be heard to conspire. The Queen will interpret a conspiracy against Darnley as a conspiracy against herself.'

'I will talk to her. See if I can make her see sense. As for being compromised, that will pass. Look at Elizabeth and Dudley. She has not lost her authority because of that scandal.'

'She had more authority to start with. Our Queen is charming, but she is a foolish girl. See what you can do. I wish you luck.'

The Queen continued to nurse Darnley and sent word that she was too busy to see Lord James. He did not show his annoyance, but was careful to act as if nothing was amiss. He avoided dining in Hall so that he did not have to associate with Rizzio, or any of Darnley's cronies. His days were spent riding out, either visiting his estates in the vicinity, or hawking with the other men.

Margaret, sitting with the Queen's other ladies, embroidering a new coif for herself, tended not to join in the subdued talk. The less that was said the better; careless words could not be quoted back to her later. The younger women were not so careful.

They were universal in their dislike of Lord Darnley.

'He sneers at me,' Mary Seton said. 'Because I am not pretty.'

'He pawed at me on Easter Day when I met him on the stairs,' said Mary Livingstone with a moue of disgust.

Lady Huntly said quietly to Margaret, 'He is a bad influence on the young men. I am sorry to see my son in his company.'

Margaret had observed this for herself. To her regret she knew that her daughter's husband, Lord Patrick

Lindsay, now come into his estates and title with the death of his father, was often in Darnley's company but she could not say that Darnley was to blame. Lindsay had been a sot long before Darnley came on the scene.

She sorted through her threads and chose a black silk. Threading her needle she listened and nodded and murmured sympathetic noises.

The women paused in their work and lifted their heads to the sound of shouting from the neighbouring room. They could hear Moray's voice but his words were indistinguishable. But the Queen's words were clear.

'You dare to argue with me. What was your purpose in mustering men in Edinburgh at Easter? Answer me that. You seek to usurp my throne. I do not believe you. You have always sought to rule. I see that now. You have found you cannot rule through me as a cat's paw so you would rule by yourself. You would turn the people against me. You would set the crown on your own head.'

Her voice dropped and the women could hear nothing further. There was the sound of a door slamming and then silence. Lady Huntly beckoned to one of the pages who were seated round the fire at the far end of the room.

'Take a message to Her Grace. Ask if she wishes one of us to wait on her.'

He was back in a moment.

'Please, my lady, Her Grace has gone to Lord Darnley's chamber.'

The women looked at one another, sighed and returned to their sewing.

It was several weeks before Darnley recovered. As the spring wore on he could be seen in the privy garden, walking slowly, leaning on the Queen's arm, while she fussed with a shawl over his shoulders. The Queen's ladies and maids kept a discreet distance, or watched from the windows of the palace, full of foreboding.

When the Queen called a parliament in June to seek consent for her marriage to Lord Darnley, Moray did not attend. He pleaded illness.

'Diarrhoea,' Margaret told the Queen, who hesitated to ask further.

To give credence to this he took himself off to Lochleven, ostensibly to rest. He needed to think things through.

Chapter Thirty-Two

Moray was plotting rebellion. 'I have been assured,' he told Argyll, 'that if Mary and Darnley are taken and sent to England, then Elizabeth will order they are kept under close guard there.'

'Kidnap them?'

'If necessary.'

'And then what?'

'Darnley will be for the Tower, where his mother already is, for defying Elizabeth. He is too close to the English throne. She doesn't want him married to Mary and his refusal to return to England last month when she ordered it has enraged her beyond measure.'

'And Mary?'

'Separated from Darnley she will see sense. We can bring her back in time and find her a more suitable husband.'

'Can Rizzio be taken also, to disappear, never to be heard of again?'

'He's of no importance. He'll sneak back to Italy where he belongs.'

They were in the castle at Lochleven. Moray felt more secure there. It was only partly out of respect for his half-brother William Douglas that Moray did not stay in the New House. There was also the consideration that the castle afforded maximum secrecy. Argyll had landed on the island in the dark. Now, around them the castle was silent save for the footsteps of one or other of their men walking overhead, posted as sentries to look out for anyone approaching the island. Already there had been one scare when a small boat carrying some men fishing had ventured too close and been ordered to stay away.

'Elizabeth will back us. She fears that with Darnley as her husband Mary will return the country to Rome. And if that happens then England's Catholics will be encouraged. Elizabeth's throne will be in danger. She herself has no doubt of that.'

So they plotted. The kidnapping would be done when Mary travelled to Falkirk. She was to be godmother to Lord Livingston's child and the baptismal ceremony would be held at his seat, Callander House.

'Darnley will be with her. She goes nowhere without him. Our people will intercept them, take the Queen and Darnley and carry them to England.'

They separated then, Argyll back to the west, while Moray took to his bed in case the Queen should send people to check the truth of his story.

All was planned and put in place, but the plot failed. Their men went to the ambush spot and waited but no one came. By enquiry of a swineherd in a nearby hamlet they learned that a large body of riders had passed through at five o'clock that morning. Soon word came to Lochleven that the Queen had been warned of the plot, none knew how, and travelled early under heavy guard. She was now safely in residence at Callander House, beyond the reach of the conspirators.

Moray, realising that if the Queen had truly discovered the plot then she would know who the plotters were, went into hiding, reassured in the knowledge that Argyll safe in his impregnable stronghold in the west would raise his troops, ready to fight if need be.

Mary, frightened by the threat of the kidnap plot and assuming that religious issues were once more at the back of it, published a proclamation that she did not intend to make any change to the settled religion. This did not satisfy John Knox or his colleagues, for they recalled all too vividly such statements by her mother, statements which were made lightly and were not intended to be kept.

Her uncles in France, they knew, were sending money and urging her to restore the Catholic religion. Knox was in the pulpit every day now, fulminating against the proposed marriage.

The Queen, in a rage, sent for him.

'What have you to do with my marriage? Who are you to comment?'

'A citizen born within this country, madam.'

He absented himself on the day the banns were read in St Giles', in Canongate Kirk and in the Chapel Royal at Holyrood.

After that, the Queen's herald took up his position at the Mercat Cross and unrolled his parchment to cheers from an exuberant crowd. Forgotten now was the gossip about the Queen's behaviour.

He read out the proclamation that Henry Stewart, Lord Darnley, Duke of Albany, was now King of Scots. There was a rousing cheer. Wasn't the long lad a Scotsman like themselves, a Lennox, and it wasn't his fault he'd been reared in England.

Hadn't they looked a fine couple, he and the Queen, when they walked among them? It was true he was said to be a Catholic, but there had been last week's proclamation that the Queen would not upset the settled religion. And the people had seen Lord Darnley worshipping in St Giles'. And soon no doubt there would be an heir to the throne, nay several heirs for were not the couple young and healthy?

But there were some in the crowd who did not see it this way. 'Only parliament can proclaim him king and parliament has not met. So how can he be king?' someone shouted.

209

The cry was taken up by others. 'Aye, how is he the king?'

The herald hastily rolled up his parchment and retreated into the Tolbooth for safety, while the constables pushed their way through the crowd to the men and women who had shouted. There were some who silently backed away and disappeared up closes and through gardens, hastening to spread news of the proclamation. Not everyone would greet the news with joy.

The Protestant Lords were waiting to see what would happen next. And those who had already indicated to Moray that they would support him began in their turn to arm their men.

The Queen issued another proclamation. She called her lieges to arms, for a rebel army was being formed with the intention of marching on Edinburgh.

Chapter Thirty-Three

'She has done everything to destroy good relations,' Moray said to his mother. 'All the goodwill I sweated to build up over years, years, with England has been shattered in an instant. I hope Lennox considers having his son on the throne worth the loss of his English estates and the imprisonment of his wife.'

'He will,' said Margaret. 'If my memory of the man is anything to go by. He would sacrifice all for that.'

The wedding of Queen Mary and Lord Darnley had been celebrated at Holyrood with a week of ceremony and celebration, condemned by Knox in language that earned him a fifteen-day prohibition against preaching. Many of the Lords pleaded illness or other causes for their absence.

Margaret's brother had been in attendance. 'What else can I do?' Erskine asked. 'My first loyalty and that of my house must be to the crown, whatever head it sits on.'

Within a week of the wedding Moray had been put to the horn and declared an outlaw. Margaret herself had been dismissed from the court. As the mother of an outlaw she was no longer welcome there. She returned to Lochleven, where she found Jamie with his closest friends preparing to ride north to gather men to their cause.

'She offered me safe conduct to go and talk to her,' he told Margaret. 'But I am not such a fool as to take it. She may intend amity, but Darnley does not and I doubt if I would reach Edinburgh alive.'

He left to join Argyll and the other Protestants who were prepared to take up arms against the Queen. They sent messengers round Scotland to post up their complaints on the doors of churches and civic buildings. The posters which appeared overnight were avidly read.

The complaints were several and varied, designed to appeal to different sections of the community: that Mary and Darnley proposed to reinstate the Catholic religion; that the marriage had not received the consent of parliament and was therefore invalid; that there were too many foreigners being employed at the court. This last received particular sympathy for everyone remembered the extent of the late Queen Dowager's reliance on Frenchmen to help her rule, so that Scotsmen hardly had control of their own country.

With the appointment of several Catholics to important posts in the Queen's service and her instructions to the burgesses of Edinburgh to replace their provost with a Catholic of her choosing, it was clear that the Protestant religion was under threat.

The rebellion was short-lived. The people in general were too loyal to their Queen to countenance a popular uprising. The Queen sent for Lord Bothwell, who returned from Paris and in him her army had an experienced commander.

There were no engagements of the two armies. The opposing forces were small in number and made up on both sides of men with little stomach for fighting their fellow Scots. They skirted one another and moved round the country, each seeking men and support, but Moray and his friends had to accept that they had failed. A brief occupation of Edinburgh by Moray's own troops was disastrous, for Lord Erskine had ordered his gunners at the castle to fire on the rebels and they had been driven out by the hostility of the townspeople.

Painful as was Lord Erskine's actions his loyalty was understandable. Less forgivable was Patrick Lindsay, riding with Darnley. Lindsay, it was true, was kin to Darnley, but then so were many of the people who dreaded seeing him wed to the Queen.

The family at Lochleven were too close to Moray to hope they could remain forgotten for long. Agnes came rushing out into the garden to find Margaret, who was trying to amuse the grandchildren by blowing dandelion clocks.

'There's a herald arrived from the Queen.'

Margaret scrambled to her feet scattering flowers from her lap.

'Warn William. I'll speak to the herald.'

The herald was waiting in the hall. 'You bring a message from the Queen?'

'My lady.'

'My son is ill but you can see him.' She led him up to William's room.

William was half-lying, half-sitting and his breath was coming in short stabs. His face was drawn and white. Agnes was on her knees beside the bed holding his hand and whispering his name. He stirred slightly but did not open his eyes.

The herald, uncertain, placed his letter on the quilt. Margaret picked it up.

'I see,' she said. 'The Queen asks that we surrender the castle to her.' She folded up the paper. 'We have sorrow in our lives. My son is in peril of death.'

The herald shifted awkwardly. He was only young, a recent recruit to the college of heralds.

'The Queen believes you are protecting the Earl of Moray.'

'We are not.'

'She's sending soldiers to search the castle for ammunition which she believes he is storing there.'

'There is no ammunition stored at the castle, nor here in the house. I do not know where the Earl of Moray is.

213

I understand he has fled. Can you convey this message to the Queen? If necessary I and my daughter-in-law here will wait upon her personally to reassure her that we wish her no ill-will. We would seek her forbearance at this difficult time.' She drooped her head onto her chest and brought out the final words in a choked voice.

The herald nodded and with a final uneasy glance at the sick man on the bed, he left. They waited till they heard his footsteps descend the stairs. Soon they could hear his horse's hooves on the brick of the stable yard and, gathering speed, fading in the distance.

William turned over onto his back and Agnes helped him to sit up. 'Are you all right?'

'Aye,' he grunted.

'She'll have us all killed.'

'No, she won't.' said Margaret. 'She hasn't entirely lost control of her senses. I know her. Allow me to handle this. You and the others need only plead ignorance of Jamie's movements and plans.'

Soon the message came back. The Queen herself would visit Lochleven.

Once more the house was made ready to welcome her. But there was none of the excitement and pleasure of her previous visits. Now all was tense and quiet. Her party arrived. It was the new-made King who strode in first. His lip was curled in a sneer. He walked past the bowing men and curtseying women, peeling off his riding gloves, without as much as a glance in their direction.

'I hope there is a good explanation for your failure to hand over the castle to us,' he said, halting before Margaret and without a preliminary greeting.

'The illness of Sir William, Your Grace,' she said. She kept her gaze on the floor. She had no illusions about this young man. He had been known to knock over a servant who dared look him in the eye and kick the lad almost to

214

death before he could be restrained. There had been nothing in his behaviour to suggest he was above assaulting a woman.

'Dying, is he? That's what the herald told us.'

'We pray not.'

'Hmmph.' He gestured to his man who helped him off with his riding cloak. To Margaret's eye the well-padded doublet suggested extra protection. Fear of daggers, perhaps, and if so, perhaps with just cause. What was it Jamie called him? A poltroon, that was it.

But the Queen following behind him smiled at Margaret with eyes that were bright and sparkling. She was glowing with colour and health and vitality.

'Lady Margaret,' she said in her soft sweet voice. 'I am sorry for your troubles. Sir William was always a good servant to me.'

'A good and loyal servant, Your Grace, as are we all.'

'Save the Earl of Moray,' snapped the King.

Margaret shrugged and spread her hands in a gesture of impotence. 'Your Grace, what can a woman do when her son will go his own way?'

The Queen nodded and passed into the inner room in the wake of her husband, where a meal was laid out for them. While they ate the soldiers searched the house and then took the boats and went over to the island. They returned to confirm they had searched the castle, and that there were no rebels there and no ordnance.

'Very well,' said the Queen. 'My decision is that Sir William and his family may continue in possession of their property, provided you do not shelter any rebels.'

'We can safely promise that, Your Grace.'

'Lord Moray's estates are of course forfeit.'

'That is understood.'

215

The Queen called for her horses. 'Lady Douglas,' she turned to Agnes. 'I will pray for the health of Sir William.'

And then they were saddled up and gone and all was quiet.

'Did you see him?' asked Margaret. 'The King. He was as nervous as if he expected Jamie to leap out from a cupboard and stab him.'

The two women went back up to Sir William's room.

'They've gone,' said Agnes.

'I heard them go.'

'They did not find anything. It has all been well hidden.'

Briefly the women told him what had been said. The castle was still theirs as long as they dissociated themselves from the rebels.

'It could have been worse,' he said, pushing aside the bedclothes and reaching for his breeches. 'Can we get word to Jamie of what has happened?'

Moray was in Dumfries, where he lingered for a few days, hoping he would hear from Queen Elizabeth that he had her support. When a message came from her that she would not interfere and could give no aid, he gave up and slipped over the border to Carlisle and into exile.

Chatelherault left for France and Argyll made sure he himself was beyond the law in the wilds of the west coast. Margaret received a hastily written letter from Master Knox. He deemed it sensible to absent himself from the capital for a while and was travelling to his wife's people in Ayrshire.

The Queen appointed a new council mainly from her Catholic supporters, including those two erstwhile troublemakers, Lord Lennox and Lord Bothwell.

Chapter Thirty-Four
1565/66

Queen Elizabeth has given me leave to stay in Newcastle wrote Jamie. *She will not give more aid than that. Meantime I find that the people well remember Master Knox from his time as preacher here, and I am made welcome for his sake, if not for my own.*

Margaret dropped the letter in the fire. She would have to find a way of returning to court. It was essential that means be found to have Jamie pardoned and returned from exile.

They spent the winter at Lochleven quietly, careful not to draw attention to themselves. It would be best if the Queen forgot about them. None of them spoke of matters outside their immediate concerns. It was safest. Who knew whether any of their own people had been suborned to spy on them.

Jamie's wife, Anyas, turned up with one small cartload of possessions. Their Edinburgh house had been stripped of all its furniture and furnishings, forfeit to the crown.

'They even took the baby's cradle.' Where some women might have been in tears Anyas was angry.

'Don't worry,' said Margaret. 'It will all be auctioned in due course. That is the normal procedure. We will buy back what is yours. The loss of some furniture is the least part of it.'

As the seasons turned and the Yuletide celebrations, such as they were, had thankfully finished, and satisfied that the family at Lochleven would be left in peace, Margaret rented a house in Canongate. Here, within sight of the palace, she set herself to the immediate task of returning to court and in the long run, Jamie's pardon.

It was hard to think of Darnley as King, when you could see him swaggering through the town, in heavily jewelled sleeves with slashings to show the linen beneath and embroidered breeches, with his long thin legs in their close-fitting beribboned tights. Coxscomb, muttered the people of Edinburgh, shoved aside from going about their legitimate business by the King's progress through the town. And for what? For no good reason, save to show himself off and demonstrate his disdain for the ordinary people. Forgotten now was their approval of the marriage.

Even worse was to hear the servants as they closed the shutters at night remarking on the passage of the King and his cronies on the prowl round the streets, looking for women to waylay before ending the night in some inn or whorehouse.

'My dear,' said Lady Huntly, who had become one of Margaret's regular visitors, 'it is a relief when he goes off hunting. He will spend a week, sometimes more, away and then the court becomes quiet and peaceful again. Hunting is more to his taste than governing Scotland. He leaves that to the Queen and then complains she tells him nothing. And she complains he is never there. And he complains that she spends all her time with Master Rizzio, then they quarrel and he goes off again.'

'And does she? Spend all her time with Master Rizzio.'

'He is certainly more amusing company than the King.'

'And the Queen? Is she well in herself?'

'The morning sickness is beginning to pass, but she still does not wish many people near her. The pregnancy is making the pains in her bones worse. Once she has the child she will recover her strength. But her council! My dear, I have to say all of them put together do not have the sense of your Jamie. And I say that even though my son is now one of her advisers, may God help her. Ruthven is a sick man and as for Bothwell, all he is good for is subduing the border reivers which he should be good at, being no better than one himself. That does not require wit, only brute force.'

'Would there be a place for me at court?'

Lady Huntly considered. 'If you were to catch her in a weak moment and appeal to sentiment, she might allow you back. She has lost so many friends, you know. They give different reasons for their absences but the truth is they cannot bear to be in the company of the King. Be careful not to mention Moray's name. That is forbidden. Being the one closest to her, his betrayal was the worst.'

Margaret dressed in her simplest black and attended services regularly at St Giles'. There she could be guaranteed to meet at some time or other the Queen's ladies and others of the court.

'Oh, Lady Margaret, she is still angry with Maitland. He dare not return to Edinburgh,' wailed Mary Fleming one day as they walked down the hill from the cathedral. 'And my father will not let me visit him at Lethington, even though we are to be married. If the Queen does not relent maybe my father will refuse to let me marry.'

'Come in for some refreshments,' said Margaret.

'But then,' said the girl, choosing a marzipan sweetmeat, 'when you see the Queen with her husband you wonder if marriage is such a good idea.'

'Maitland is a good man,' said Margaret, knowing that Mary Fleming, innocent, pleasure-loving Mary, would have no knowledge and probably would not care that Maitland was considered one of the most devious of all the royal advisers. 'Would he be willing to visit me here, if he were able to come quietly, without being noticed?'

'I am sure he would.'

219

'You could meet him here. Would you like that?'

Mary Fleming would like it very much.

Maitland came and before leaving him and Mary Fleming alone in her parlour, Margaret had a long talk with him.

Margaret wrote to her daughter Euphemia. *Come and stay for a while. Bring your husband with you. I am getting old and cannot bear to be thus estranged from kith and kin. William and Agnes are coming for he has business in town. Let us be friends.*

Phemie came, bringing two of her children. Patrick, she told her mother, had gone off hunting in Ettrick with the King, but would return in a day or two.

He came and Margaret greeted him as if there had never been any ill feeling. She had not seen Patrick, Lord Lindsay, for some time. He had held the title now for nearly two years since the death of his father, but it seemed to her that whereas some men will grow into their responsibilities, Lord Lindsay with the extra wealth and power was himself only more so. He was still the ruffian he had always been.

He was now, she calculated, in his mid-thirties, being ten years older than Phemie. He was losing his good looks, with a network of fine red veins marring his cheeks and swollen black weals under his eyes. He looked older, almost a contemporary of herself.

He was close to the King and for that Margaret needed him. Newly returned from a hunting, he was full of his friend's grievances. The King was hard done by. Mary never consulted him. She never trusted him with state papers. In fact, she had had a seal cut with his signature so that his consent was affixed to documents without his knowledge.'

'I have heard,' said Margaret, 'that the seal you speak of is being used by Master Rizzio.'

'Who said that?' Lindsay asked sharply.

'I do not remember.'

'It is not good that so many of the lords stay away from court,' put in William from his place at the head of the table. 'There are men here in Edinburgh who are anxious for the future. They see the reins of government in the hands of foreigners. It is said she takes counsel from no one but Master Rizzio.'

'Rizzio. Rizzio. Everywhere we go we hear the name of Rizzio on everyone's lips,' said Agnes. 'Is the man some sort of monster that everyone fears him so?'

'No one fears him.' Patrick Lindsay had raised his voice. 'The man's twisted in body and mind.'

'They say,' said Margaret, 'that the Queen is closer to him than she is to the King.'

'That's vile talk,' said Lindsay. 'Just the sort of thing I would expect from old women with nothing to do but gossip.'

'Patrick,' murmured Phemie.

'Well, it's true,' said Patrick. 'Do you think the King would stand by and watch himself being usurped by a lute player?'

'But he does seem to be standing by.'

'It's vile defamation.'

Margaret pressed home. 'We know how the Queen behaved with the King when they had known each other less than six months. If that is in her nature, then what is to stop her behaving in the same way again with another man?'

'Mother, she's pregnant.'

'You're calling the Queen a whore?' Patrick was almost beside himself. 'You're calling the King a cuckold?'

'Why,' she leaned forward and spoke softly, 'Why does the King not do something about it?'

Lindsay slammed his wine cup down on the table and pushed his stool back. 'I'm not staying to listen to such poison.'

221

'Sit down, Patrick,' said William gently.

Lindsay scowled at him, but he sat down.

'Listen to me,' said William. 'Some of us care little how the Queen comports herself as long as she does it discreetly. But there are other matters in which Master Rizzio has a hand. There is to be a summons issued to call a parliament.'

He now had all their attention. The Three Estates had not met for some time.

'There are believed to be two items on the agenda which should concern us. One is to declare forfeit the entire estates of all the rebels. Jamie will not be spared just because he is the Queen's brother. The other is that the parliament is to consider the old church property. There is talk of confiscating all of it to the crown. All of it.'

The old church property was still providing a substantial income to many of the lords. The appointment to the livings by the King of his sons and to the sons of his friends, still held good. There was hardly a noble family in the country who did not benefit from the substantial church lands.

'They can't do that.'

'They can. Our cousin Morton has been in touch with all of us who have such property to warn us that this is coming. And you should know that the person pressing hardest for this is Master Rizzio. He has an eye to acquiring some of that wealth for himself.'

There was a silence round the table while they all thought about this.

'Morton suggests that there must be a way of persuading Signor Davie that this is not a good idea,' added William.

That night, Margaret sat down to compose a letter to Jamie.

Seeds are being sown, she wrote. *Pray that we may reap the harvest.*

William Maitland, she thought, that Scottish Machiwilli, you would be proud of me.

Chapter Thirty-Five

When the Queen held an audience as usual one Wednesday morning, Margaret, wearing her best air of humility, knelt and asked leave to return to court. The Queen looked at her sternly. She's trying her best, thought Margaret, glancing up and down again. Mary looked tired and old. These nine months of marriage had aged her. Margaret could almost grieve for the happy child Mary had been on her arrival in Scotland.

'I can never forgive your son.'

'I know that, Your Grace. What he did was very wrong. Would I had never borne him, but I have been punished too for I will never see him again.' She was able to put a vestige of a sob in her voice.

The Queen's expression softened. It was as Lady Huntly said. The Queen did not blame the women merely because their men were traitors. Any initial coolness would not last for long. In fact, she seemed to have the capacity to forget grudges easily. An attribute, Margaret could have told her, that was not wise for a monarch.

Margaret pursued her opening. 'Your Grace will soon be a mother yourself. Would that your son will obey you as mine did not.'

It was enough. Mary held out her hand. Margaret was back at court.

Lady Jean Gordon, the late Lord Huntly's daughter, who must at one time have thought her chance of joining the court had been destroyed by the actions of her menfolk, had fitted in well with the Queen's other maids-in-waiting. She was a devoted adherent to the old religion and attended mass and this made a natural bond with the other Catholics.

She was quieter than the others and more cautious and this, combined with a ready intelligence and understanding made her a natural listener to the problems of the others, no matter whether trivial or serious. But like many quiet people, she found it difficult to display her own emotions, so it was with surprise that Margaret, walking unexpectedly into the little room set aside for the Queen's maids, found her crouched by the window in tears.

'What is the matter?'

The girl straightened up and dried her eyes.

'I am being foolish.'

'No. What has upset you?'

'I should obey the Queen in all things. My mother has told me that.'

'What does she want you to do?'

The girl hiccupped.

'Marry Lord Bothwell.'

'Marry...? My dear, that is nonsense.' Of all the men at court who would be most unsuitable for this girl, Bothwell must surely top the list. He was no better than a brigand.

'The Queen says I must.'

'Whose idea is it?'

'Hers, I think. Lord Bothwell has not shown any inclination towards me. He has hardly spoken to me.'

'You do not want to?'

'Of course I don't. I want to marry Alex Ogilvy. I love him and he loves me. How can I marry another man?'

Yes, the old romance. This girl would have no better fortune than herself, but then what girl did have a choice in her future husband?

'What does your mother think? And your brother as head of the family will have to agree.'

'My mother says I must do as the Queen bids me. George has given his consent. He wouldn't refuse Bothwell anything. And I believe Bothwell has promised him that the Huntly title will be restored to him.'

'But you are Catholic and Bothwell is Protestant. Do your family not care about that?'

'That counts for nothing.' The girl was crying now and Margaret took her in her arms.

As she soothed the girl, she could not but reflect that Bothwell would come off very well indeed. There would be a large dowry and he was known to be financially straitened all the time, always in debt, financially incontinent. It was a pity this girl had to be sacrificed to his ambitions.

'It is to be announced tomorrow evening after the banquet for the English ambassador.'

The next evening the music was particularly lively, the food more than usually lavish, for of all the ambassadors to be impressed the Englishman was the most important. Mary never forgot for an instant that if Elizabeth died childless she herself had a claim to the English throne. She was using all her charm to demonstrate to him that she was a suitable successor. Not least of this was her obvious pregnancy. She was demonstrating that she was fecund, ready for the day when Elizabeth's crown might become hers.

The dancing had finished and the couples were making their way off the floor, some to join the Queen and the ambassador on the dais, others to put their heads together in noisy talk in the corners of the Hall.

The centre of attention in one group was George Gordon who, some reckoned by sheer good fortune, had been in the south when his father rebelled against the Queen. Today he had been restored to his late father's title. He was now Lord Huntly. It was rumoured that along with the title, the Queen would restore to him all the Huntly estates in the north and add to them the Moray estates, now confiscate. Conspicuously celebrating with him was Lord Bothwell.

The Queen on the dais stood up and clapped her hands.

'Attention, please. I have an announcement.'

The conversations stopped and everyone waited, alert.

'I have to announce a betrothal. Two of my dearest friends will be united. My Lord Bothwell?'

Bothwell separated himself from the group of men near the window and moved to stand beside the Queen. There was a stir in the room.

Mary took his hand. 'My very loyal friend,' she said. She turned to her ladies-in-waiting.

'My Lord Bothwell will marry the Lady Jean Gordon.'

Jean Gordon did not move, until Mary Beaton gently pushed her forward, hissing something into her ear. Like a sleepwalker Jean moved to the side of the Queen who took her hand and put it into the hand of Bothwell.

She held both hands high.

'This will fulfil our dearest wish. The wedding will take place soon.' She kissed Jean and then Bothwell.

This was not altogether welcome news. Between them the combined estates of Huntly and Bothwell would run from the Orkney Islands down to the border. There were many who viewed that with unease.

The Queen clapped her hands again and nodded to her musicians who struck up a lively and celebratory tune. Bothwell bowed to Jean and led her onto the dance floor. Neither of them spoke during the dance.

Jean's mother, Lady Huntly, was not there. She had been confined to bed all day with a severe headache and arthritic aches. Later that night Margaret made her way to Lady Huntly's rooms.

She was awake and said she had slept well during the day and no doubt would be well enough to rise in the morning. She sighed. 'Truth to tell, Margaret, I did not want to be there.'

'If you do not approve could you not have stopped it?'

'How? The Queen wants it. My son wants it.'

There was a knock at the door and Jean herself came in. She had heard her mother's last words.

'You know I do not want this,' she said.

'It is a good match.'

'I want to marry Alexander Ogilvy.'

Lady Huntly made a derogatory noise. 'A mere laird is no match for the daughter and sister of the Earls of Huntly.'

'Then I will enter a nunnery.'

'Don't be silly,' said her mother. 'It is not in your nature.'

Margaret expected the girl to begin to cry then, to seek sympathy, but she did not. She stood there, composed and cool.

'Very well. But remember it is against my will.'

She left the room then, quietly.

Chapter Thirty-Six

Margaret was careful in her visits to the court. She did not go there every day and when she did she sought out the women around the Queen. She avoided the men who were closest to the King. The King himself hardly saw her: she was just one more middle-aged woman dressed in black, beneath his notice. She only went into Hall when there were no grand occasions such as the receiving of ambassadors. These were fewer now, for the Queen pleaded her belly to receive them privately and the King had no taste for the intricacies of diplomacy.

She sat with the Queen's ladies, those who were off duty, read aloud to them while they stitched, sorted their silks, gossiped with them, provided soothing hot drinks when they had monthly cramps and listened to their woes. She was ever ready to walk with them in the gardens if dry and in the long gallery if wet, or shoot with them at the butts when they were in the mood for exercise and always, always, she was listening.

More than one of the women suggested she move into the palace. She could share a room with one of them, but she always declined, citing the need for her to run her own household for the sake of her family.

Each evening as she left the palace and walked home, sometimes in the dark, hearing the hours cried and greeting the men who opened the wicket in the town gates to let her through, she reflected that each day at court was one day nearer the return of Jamie.

The wedding of the Earl of Bothwell and Lady Jean Gordon was celebrated. The Queen, generous as ever, gave the bride a wedding gown and paid for three days of feasting. The couple went to Bothwell's castle at Dunbar.

Now February gave way to March and longer days and milder weather.

She wrote urgently to Jamie.

You will have heard by now that the parliament is to meet on 7th March and you will be summoned to attend in order to answer charges of rebellion. There are many plots afoot here. There are rumours that certain people are to lose their influence with Mary, but how or when I cannot discover. I believe our fortunes are about to turn.

But no sooner had she dispatched the messenger with this letter, than she received one from Jamie himself to tell her he was on his way home, but secretly. He arrived the next day. He came to her house late in the evening and slipped in, unseen by any who recognised him.

'The others are travelling home too. Argyll, Rothes and the others.'

'You are not afraid?'

'No, Mother. I think I can be confident that all will be well.'

The next day they watched from the window as the Queen rode up the High Street to the Tolbooth to open the parliamentary session. There was no sign of the King.

'They are saying he is angry because parliament still refuses him the Crown Matrimonial,' said Anyas, her arm round her husband's waist.

'Then he's a fool. Does he think that if he had the Crown Matrimonial and the Queen were to die, and the bairn with her, then the lords would stand for him as King? He wouldn't last a day.'

'Come back from the window, Jamie, you might be seen.'

Their servant, instructed to hang about the Tolbooth and listen, brought them the news. It was as they expected.

At the first session the rebel lords were summoned to appear on 12th March to answer charges.

The following Saturday Margaret spent the evening with Lady Huntly in her room, dining quietly. She left early. As she went along the passage from the ladies' quarters she was aware that something was amiss. There were more guards about than usual. None of them paid her any heed. Then she realised that most of them were not in the red and yellow royal livery, but in Morton livery, with groups in Ruthven livery.

When she arrived at the door into the close she found it barred and guarded on the inside by men, also in Morton livery. One of them recognised her as kin to Lord Morton but he would not let her through.

'I am sorry, my lady, but we have orders to allow no one in or out.'

'Why? What has happened?'

He shrugged.

'Is the Queen in danger?'

'I don't know, lady. I just follow orders.' But he winked at her. He knew. They all knew.

She turned and went back up the stairs. But at the top instead of turning right to take her back into the main residential part of the palace, she turned left, towards the royal apartments.

The corridors were dark. Many of the torches in their sconces had been put out and that was unusual. Only here and there one flared, sending eerie shadows up walls and across ceilings. She picked her way up the staircase towards the Queen's apartments on the second floor of the tower. This way took her past the King's quarters on the first floor. From his room came the murmur of voices, the King's high-pitched tones among them. She tried to steal softly past.

Then, sharply, at her back. 'Who's there?'

231

A man wearing Ruthven livery was standing on the turn of the stair.

There came a scrape of chairs. 'What is it, man?'

'A woman.'

Patrick Lindsay came out. 'It's all right. It's only Lady Margaret.'

Lord Ruthven's voice could be heard. 'Then she can do us a service.' So, something was afoot to bring Ruthven from his sickbed. He had excused himself from attending court for weeks back, pleading illness. It was true he was a sick man. He himself believed he had cancer and would talk about it to anyone with patience to listen.

It was Ruthven who followed Lindsay from the room. To her surprise he was wearing armour breastplate. What did he fear when death was so near him anyway? 'We want you to fetch Master Rizzio. He is upstairs dining with the Queen.'

Margaret bent double and clutched her stomach. 'The privy, my lord. Please.' And she groaned.

There was some laughter from inside the room. Half a dozen men at least.

'Please.' Her voice rose in panic.

'All right, go.' And then a muttered *Stupid old hag* before he turned back into the room. Before he could change his mind Margaret scuttled down the stairs. Once out of their sight she straightened up.

She made her way back up to the ladies' bedchambers by a different staircase. There were no guards here. She slipped behind a curtain in an alcove on the turn of the stair and hunkered down to wait.

She was beginning to doze when the screams woke her. There was the sound of running feet and more screams. These were not the screams of a woman, but of a man, calling to God in a foreign tongue, echoing through the corridors of the palace.

She waited. Nearby there were footsteps and the sounds of agitated women. Several people ran down the stair, not seeing her. When she judged there were enough people around she slipped out of her hiding place.

From the gallery she could look down into the lobby below her. Men were gathered round something on the ground. One of them raised a purse which clinked and stuffed it into his pocket. One of his fellows made a grab for it and they began to fight. She recognised some of them. Servants of the lords for the most part. As the group parted for a moment she saw what was absorbing their attention. Her gullet heaved. The body of Rizzio lay there. His clothes were slashed to pieces, revealing gaping wounds in his belly with his guts trailing out. Blood was seeping into pools round him. His head looked as if it had been almost severed from his body.

Swallowing hard she moved away, sliding along the wall so as not to be seen by the men below her, but they were intent on stripping the body in their search for valuables and were paying no attention to anything or anyone else.

She ran upstairs. Anything to get away from this. She met Lady Huntly, wrapped in a cloak.

'Rizzio,' she gasped.

'I thought as much,' said the other woman. 'Morton's men have taken control of the palace. They have threatened my son and Bothwell. They're locked up in Bothwell's room. I think my daughter is there too.'

'We must go to the Queen.'

The two women crept through the palace past weeping women and helpless-looking men, men of insufficient station to be able to command any resistance.

As they passed Rizzio's room they saw his own servants looting among his clothes and jewels. He was a flamboyant dresser and they found plenty to amuse them

233

and satisfy their greed. One man, drunk from the flagon of wine which he had in his hand and was pouring into his mouth, was marching round the room with one of Rizzio's lacy ruffs loose over his head, the ends flapping down his back like ribbons. Another man was sitting on the floor picking the jewels out of a crucifix with a penknife.

There were guards across the Queen's door.

'Make way there,' said Lady Huntly.

They did not move. 'We have orders to admit no one.'

'I am not 'no one'. I am Lady Huntly. I demand to be allowed to pass.'

There was no answer. The man looked over their heads.

'Is the Queen a prisoner?'

No response.

It would have been foolish to stand there arguing, and undignified. Back in the ladies' quarters they gathered the others round them, quietened the hysterical sobs and hiccupping of the younger women and told their story.

'We must keep calm,' Lady Huntly told them. 'I do not think they will harm the Queen, not in her condition. Go back to your rooms and wait for the morning. All will become clear.'

Suddenly they could hear the tolling of a bell and one of them opened a window. There were crowds of people approaching the palace. Torches flickered. There was the cry of orders given and stamping feet. The militia had been called out. The people milled about but someone must have calmed them down, for soon they all retreated back inside the town walls and all was quiet.

The women refused to separate and spent the rest of the night huddled in one room. Margaret stayed with them. Even if she would be allowed to leave the palace she had no wish to.

234

Just as the window was beginning to pale in the early morning light the door opened and Lady Jean Bothwell rushed in. She ran into her mother's arms. 'I created such a fuss they let me out,' she said. 'I have a message from Bothwell. You are to tell the Queen that as soon as he can he will come and rescue her, whatever happens.'

When it was light a trembling page brought a message for Lady Huntly. She was to attend at the Queen's bedchamber with no more than two other ladies and a servant. She took Margaret with her, and Mary Seton.

They found the Queen huddled on the bed. The face she now raised to them was white and her eyes glittered. Her sister Lady Argyll was with her.

In a low voice Jane told them what had happened, how the King and other men, Ruthven, Lindsay and others had burst into the room and dragged Master Rizzio out.

'The equerries could do nothing to protect him. He had already been stabbed even before he was clear of the room,' she whispered. She indicated a heap of clothing in the corner, clothing recognisable as the Queen's chamber gown, now vivid with red streaks. With a nod Lady Huntly gestured to the bed-woman to take it away.

The Queen raised her head. 'One of them pointed his pistol at me and would have killed me and the baby had the gun gone off. I will remember him. I will be revenged.'

'Is this true?' whispered Margaret to Lady Jane.

'I don't know,' she said. 'I was crouched on the floor. I did not see. I was terrified.'

As well you might be, thought Margaret. The murderers seemed to have no care who might witness their crime.

'And was the King really one of them?'

Lady Jane nodded.

'I will have vengeance,' said the Queen in a low voice.

235

But if the King himself was one of them, what need for the assassins to fear vengeance?

Lady Huntly whispered the message she had been given by Bothwell. He will help you escape. All is not lost.

They passed the long day. They were prisoners, with guards at all the doors, but at least they had some privacy. The Queen paced up and down, sometimes crying in a rage and sometimes weeping for the death of Rizzio. Now and again she knelt in prayer, muttering the words of the Viaticum. Rizzio had died unshriven. This gave added agony to the Queen's grief.

Some food was handed in by one of the guards. Margaret asked him, Please, could she go and find some clean clothes for the Queen. This was Sunday and it was not decent for her to be dressed in clothes which were still streaked with the blood of the dead man. The man considered, eyeing her suspiciously and she shrunk into herself, a quiet harmless old woman. He let her pass.

As she made her way through the palace she saw that things were beginning to calm down. There were still guards but they were more relaxed, standing at ease and talking. She was able to have quiet words with the servants who were now moving about, doing their duty as if this were a normal day. There were cleaning-women and porters carrying food from the kitchen, bringing with them rumour and counter-rumour. Rizzio's body had gone, thrown, it was said, into a common grave. Someone was scrubbing at the bloodstains on the floor.

First it was said the King himself had arranged the murder of Rizzio. Then it was said he was not involved and had spent the night in the Queen's bed comforting her. Bothwell and Huntly were found to have fled. Some thought they were involved in the plot, some thought not.

In the deserted wardrobe rooms she rapidly collected everything the Queen might need. In addition to the clothes which the Queen would normally be expected to wear to mass, for this being Sunday even murderers might respect the Queen's normal habits, she also tucked into her bundle a dark simple gown. She rummaged and found a pair of breeches, for the Queen had sometimes dressed as a man in happier times to wander through the streets of Edinburgh incognito. The Queen's belly was not yet so large, they would still fit, and if there was hard riding to be done, they would be better than a gown.

On her way back she was startled by a hiss and in a minute a letter was thrust into her hand and the bearer of it melted back into the shadows. Tucking it into her bodice she continued up the stairs.

She found Lady Huntly and Mary Seton in the outer chamber. The door to the Queen's bedroom was closed. Lady Huntly gestured with a jerk of her head towards the bedroom and held her finger to her lips. They could hear the King's voice. He was pleading with Mary. Her voice was softer and they could not hear her replies. Phrases came to them as the King's voice, generally loud in normal circumstances, now rose and fell. *Never expected. Never intended. Young and imprudent. Mea culpa. Crown matrimonial that was all.*

'He's betraying the conspirators,' whispered Lady Huntly.

'How can she allow him near her?' Margaret whispered back.

Margaret remembered the letter and she pulled it out. It was addressed to Lady Huntly.

'It is from my son,' she said. 'Oh, what idiocy. He proposes to smuggle in a rope and the Queen can climb down it to where horses will be waiting. The fool. As if the Queen could climb down in her condition and anyway, the windows are all being watched.' She crumpled up the letter

237

and threw it on the fire. 'If that is the best they can do for us then we must fend for ourselves.'

The King did not stay long. The Queen admitted the women.

'He's terrified of Ruthven and the others. He thinks having killed David they might kill him next. As for me, their plan is to hold me as a prisoner. They propose to take me to Stirling.'

'Plead illness, Your Grace. We must give out that you are ill.'

'Tell them I am in labour. They will not risk the loss of the child.'

Margaret showed the Queen what she had collected and thrust everything under the bed. The Queen's eyes gleamed as she climbed back into bed and curled up as if in pain. She would fight back. She would find a way out of this.

They sent word that her midwife and physician must attend. They came quickly. The midwife waddled into the room followed by the doctor.

'What's this? What's this? Too much excitement.' The beldame thrust her hands under the bedclothes and began to feel about. She stood back and regarded the Queen thoughtfully.

'We thought it were as well,' said Margaret, 'for her not to be moved. Is that your opinion also?'

'She should be left in peace. For the safety of the bairn.' The woman winked. 'She is bleeding and threatened with a miscarriage. Tell them that.'

When they had gone the Queen pulled herself out of the bed.

'Your Grace,' protested Lady Huntly.

'It's all right,' said the Queen irritably. 'There's nothing wrong with me. Can you get word to Lord Bothwell? I will write a note. If he and his men can wait for me near Seton Palace I will find a way of escaping from here and will join them there.' Hastily she scribbled a note and had just passed it to Lady Huntly who concealed it in her chemise, when Lord Lindsay came bursting in, furious.

'They had no right to allow the physicians here. I don't believe the truth of what they say.'

Lady Huntly squared up to him while the Queen curled herself up again on the bed, whimpering. 'Sir, the Queen cannot be moved. Her labour may have begun. Would you risk the death of the child even if you care nothing for the life of the mother?'

Margaret stepped forward and stood beside her friend.

'Son-in-law, you will leave this chamber. It is no place for you.'

Somewhat abashed, he stopped ranting.

'You,' he stuck his finger into Lady Huntly's breast. 'You are dismissed. You,' he glowered at Margaret. 'You can stay.'

'And you, hold,' he said as he followed Lady Huntly from the room. He started to search her, pulling at her gown. But even he hesitated to probe too deeply into the underclothing of a respectable woman old enough to be his mother. He did not find the letter.

He turned back. 'You will see Lord Ruthven,' he said to the Queen.

'I will not.'

'Lord Morton, then.'

'No.' She gave a small scream as if in pain. Defeated, he left.

As the day wore on and the physician and the midwife relaxed in the outer chamber, deterring any who would come near, the palace resumed its normal workings, or as near normal as it could. The guards on duty in the presence chamber were removed and two of the Queen's equerries were allowed to remain there.

'Margaret,' whispered the Queen, 'is Jamie in Edinburgh?'

'I believe so.'

'Would he be willing to come and see me?'

'I am sure of it. It grieves him to be estranged.'

When Moray, summoned, came to a side door of the palace, the guards on duty there had mysteriously absented themselves. In the pay of the assassins they might be, but not everyone was comfortable with what was being demanded of them. It was one thing to kill the hated foreigner, it was quite another to hold the Queen a prisoner. Some of these men had fought side by side with Lord James in the late religious wars and if his lady mother had a deep purse that encouraged them to turn a blind eye for a few minutes, well, that was not much to ask.

Margaret closed the door behind Jamie, but not before she had seen the Queen hug Jamie to her, weeping. 'Dear brother. Dear brother.'

He left an hour later.

'All is well?' asked Margaret.

'Better than well. We are friends again.'

It was given out that the physician and the midwife would stay with the Queen overnight. Her exhausted ladies would try and get a night's sleep; and some food, for none of them had eaten much or slept much in the last forty-eight hours.

Margaret slept overnight in Lady Huntly's room. The next day they joined the other ladies to process as usual towards the Queen's bedroom. But when they arrived they found the rooms empty.

The Queen was not there, nor was the midwife, nor the doctor, nor any of the equerries.

At first they thought she had been taken away in the night as a prisoner, but from the sudden eruption of fury of

Ruthven and the others they gleefully realised the truth. The Queen had escaped.

Across the day they were able to piece together what had happened. It appeared that during the night the Queen with her few companions and the King (for he too was gone) had made their way down the backstairs to the kitchens and cellars and there made their escape through a door which must have been deliberately left unlocked.

Men with horses had been seen waiting near the Canongate Kirkyard. There were reports of riders, moving fast, on the road to the east, heading for the dawn; and the numbers had swollen the further east they travelled.

'She will be at Seton by now,' Margaret told Moray when she had run up to the house. She found him still being shaved.

'By God,' he said, signalling to his man to carry on. 'The only person who could have done this is the King. She has him on her side now. My little sister has learned some craft in the years I have trained her. Come, Mother, we have an appointment to keep.'

Rapidly he dressed and they made their way to the Tolbooth. There they met Argyll and Glencairn and others of the rebels. They gave their names in and said they were here to answer the charges made by the parliament. But since the King the day before had given orders that the parliament was to be dissolved, the members had gone home and there were now no accusers. The men were free, the charges dropped, rebels no more.

Chapter Thirty-Seven

'The planning was all the Queen's,' Lady Huntly told Margaret. 'She persuaded the King to organise the horses. The physician and midwife needed no persuading, nor did her servants. So she has gone and we can expect vengeance.'

'Who would have thought she would have the wit?'

'When a woman is carrying a child she becomes like a serpent in the protecting of it.'

The next day a declaration was read at the Tolbooth to an expectant and excited crowd. All good men and true lieges were to assemble, armed, at Dunbar Castle in order to defend their King and Queen against the rebels. Which rebels this time, murmured some.

Less than two weeks later Margaret stood at her window beside her family watching as the Queen rode through Canongate at the head of a force of several thousand men and up the hill towards the castle. The bells of all the city's churches were ringing in acclamation. The Queen who had been in such danger was now free and once more in charge. Beside her rode the King and any doubts as to his loyalty to her were stilled.

There were the young Lord Huntly and Lord Fleming and her faithful servant Lord Seton. Anyas leaned out of the window and waved as her father the Earl Marischal rode by, raising his bonnet to acknowledge her.

There, some way back in the cavalcade rode the Earl of Bothwell at the head of his troop of men. Since he had clearly organised the wholesale muster of the army he was being uncharacteristically modest. The rebels, Morton,

Ruthven, Lindsay and the others, knowing themselves betrayed by the King, had fled.

The Queen took up residence in the Royal Palace at Edinburgh Castle. She refused to return to Holyrood.

'I cannot bear it,' she told Margaret. 'How could I walk the rooms where such horror happened?'

The Queen gave Jamie permission to move his quarters into the castle. 'And Argyll? Can I trust Argyll?' Jamie nodded. Of course. As brother-in-law to the Queen, Argyll had her best interests at heart, he assured her.

When Lady Jane heard that her husband Argyll was to be brought back to court she lost her temper. 'I will not live with him as man and wife,' she shouted at her sister. 'I want a divorce.'

But the Queen refused to allow this. 'Your own behaviour is not all it should be. You should be kinder to him.'

'Just because you cannot divorce your husband,' began Jane, with a sneer. The Queen slapped her face. 'Get out of here.'

Jane went and sulked round the court.

No one expected the Queen to admit that those who advised her against marrying the King had been right. How could she say so? But she welcomed back to court those who had come so close less than a month before to being exiled forever as traitors.

If there were those who thought that the lords who were now being hunted as rebels might within a few short months be back in favour again, they kept those thoughts to themselves. And if some were beginning to wonder if this Queen would ever know her own mind from one week to the next and whether this was a sensible basis on which to govern a country, then they too kept a discreet silence and awaited events.

'But Mary,' said the King when he heard Moray was to return, 'Moray was to blame for the murder of David. He was one of the plotters.'

'He was not. I have his word for that.'

'He will want you to pardon them.'

'I may yet pardon those who did not actually strike the blows.'

The King went white.

'You would not.'

'If I allow them to return you had better stay close to me, otherwise who knows what might happen?'

Margaret, who was playing chess at some distance from the fire where this conversation was being held, heard most of this, for she had sharp hearing. Again she felt a surge of admiration for the Queen. She knows how to keep the King loyal to her at this time. He is such a coward. He betrayed his friends to save his skin, now he fears them and very likely with good cause. They would be seeking vengeance.

'Checkmate,' said Margaret.

Lady Huntly tipped her king over.

'If it makes you more comfortable, husband, then my Lord Moray, along with my Lord Bothwell and my Lord Huntly, shall not dine with me. I will have no arguments at my dinner table. I want my household to be peaceful and it appears to me that there will be no peace if they are together. But you, husband, shall dine with me every day.'

And she smiled at him.

Go on, thought Margaret, keep him sweet.

'And more perhaps,' she added. 'Once the bairn is born and I am myself again.' The King was appeased. Her refusal to sleep with him was an insult to his manhood.

And so the court settled down uneasily to await the birth of the baby and there were hearty prayers said that this bairn would be a boy.

244

Chapter Thirty-Eight
1566

Moray stood in the porch of the Chapel Royal at Stirling along with the other Protestant lords. They would not set foot inside while the mass was being served. No matter that representatives of most of the royal houses of Europe were crowded into Stirling for this event. There could be no pretence that the Protestants approved of what was happening.

The baptism of the prince, now six months old, was being carried out with full Catholic rites, despite the protests of the Kirk and the lords. The prince would one day rule over a Protestant nation; it was not right that he should be baptised into a faith which was anathema to the people, and, it might be said, to Queen Elizabeth who was standing godmother. This child, through both parents, was the closest in royal blood to the English throne. Moray could feel in his bones that this augured ill for the future.

Lord Bothwell beside him stirred as the singing of the Chapel Royal choristers swelled and enveloped them in sound.

'She could not persuade the King to be here.'

'So I understand.'

'He's sulking yonder in his chamber. Bleating to anyone who will listen that she uses him ill.'

Moray knew this in the same way that Bothwell knew it. There were few of the Queen's council who did not have men – and women – willing to report to them every move of the King. And of each other. Argyll, resplendent in red, for she had given a gift of new clothes to all her lords in celebration, growled that it was not only kings who had trouble with their wives.

The others smiled at this. Argyll's wife, the Lady Jane, was carrying the baby prince, her nephew, inside the chapel in express opposition to his wishes. But then it looked as if nowadays she went out of her way to defy him. She had not stopped asking the Queen for permission to divorce him.

'Why then do you not sit in his chamber and sympathise with him?' taunted Bothwell.

Argyll turned his back. Moray was silent. Argyll was his brother-in-law and old conspirator, Bothwell was his enemy and new conspirator. There were uneasy alliances being made now in the shifting sands of Scottish politics. Let them quarrel over the trivial and the foolish as long as they held fast to their secret agreement, recently made at Craigmillar when the Queen was staying there to recover from her confinement:

That they would act to relieve the Queen of her marriage.

That they would do nothing to dishonour the Queen.

That the Queen would not regard her marriage at an end unless ended by the Pope.

That there were no grounds for the Pope to end the marriage.

And so, full circle, that they would act to relieve the Queen of her marriage.

His thoughts were interrupted by the sudden fanfare from the trumpeters stationed round the walls of the castle. The bells of the town started ringing. The baptism was done and the baby had been named Charles after the King of France and James after his grandfather. He had not been named for his father.

The three days of pageantry, the banqueting, masques, fireworks were not much to Moray's taste, but he attended most of them for appearance's sake. It was a pity that the whole atmosphere of the proceedings was so very French and Catholic and that one of the masques offended the English visitors. He could see that bridges would have to be rebuilt to soothe the feelings of Queen Elizabeth. Many of the Protestant lords left the castle early.

But residence in the castle allowed him to talk at length with his mother, who had been at Lochleven these last few months convalescing after an illness but had now come to Stirling to witness the baptismal festivities.

They dined quietly with Lord Erskine and his wife on a day when most of the court had gone riding out in a display of splendour round the town and villages.

'She's taking the baby back with her to Edinburgh,' Erskine told them.

'But the bairn is safer here under your protection.'

'Aye, but Annabella here is kin to Lennox, and the Queen no longer trusts any of the Lennoxes.'

'She has no right to impugn my honour,' snapped his wife. 'As if I would do anything to harm the child.'

'Mary is becoming mistrustful of everyone,' put in Margaret. 'She is frequently distressed, cries for an hour, and will allow none near her except her closest and oldest friends.'

'Sensible woman,' growled Erskine.

They were silent while the serving man placed a platter piled high with roast venison on the table. Moray recognised the man as an old retainer of the Erskines. The family were generous to their people: it was unlikely the man could be bribed to spy on them. But you never knew. He turned the conversation to more general matters. Erskine nodded slightly. He understood.

The court left Stirling on Christmas Eve, the Queen to rest at Seton Palace and the others to disperse to their homes. At the same time the King left, but travelled west to

Glasgow where he considered himself safe, to stay at Dumbarton Castle, well inside Lennox territory.

Chapter Thirty-Nine
1567

On Twelfth Night they were all back in Stirling again for the marriage celebrations of Maitland, who had at last won the hand of Lady Mary Fleming. At the celebratory banquet which followed Margaret sought out her son.

'What word of the King?'

'He has the pox. Why?'

'He has been writing to the Queen. Great scrawling letters accusing her of neglecting him. He begs her to visit him in Glasgow but she has said it is not convenient. When she was at Seton she had a slight accident with her horse and could not ride. At least that was the reason she gave.'

'As long as he remains there he is safe.'

'Would that he would stay there for ever. The Queen is in better spirits when he is at a distance.'

She clapped her hands as one of the pages dressed as a swan came over and flapped his wings at her. She tossed him a marzipan bonbon and he glided away.

'Yes, that is obvious.'

She followed his gaze to where Bothwell was leaning over the Queen and she was laughing up into his face.

'My Lord Bothwell is often with the Queen,' said Margaret.

'Indeed. But never alone, I think.'

'No, never alone, though the ladies keep a discreet distance. But...'

'But?'

'The atmosphere sometimes...' she hesitated again. How could she say to her son that sometimes the atmosphere in the Queen's chamber was so heavily overladen with sexual awareness that even prude Lady Mary Seton, 'the nun', could feel it and on more than one occasion had excused herself from the Queen's presence.

'It is like the time before she was married. When she was nursing Lord Darnley in his illness. But yet it is not like.'

It is not like, she thought, because then the lust evident in her every movement was not reciprocated. Now it is. But she left her statement hanging in the air.

They were silent, watching the lutenists who had now taken to the floor to serenade the wedding couple seated on the dais garlanded with flowers, Maitland looking very uncomfortable indeed.

'Come to my room tonight. I would have more speech with you.'

Later, in the privacy of his room, with his own man standing guard outside the door to prevent anyone who might be tempted to linger and eavesdrop, he made Margaret comfortable in a chair by the fire. Her knuckles and wrists were aching, she said, aggravated by the cold weather. She tucked her hands under the cover. Apart from that she had recovered from her illness and he suspected that by the time the spring came she would be as vigorous as ever.

'Are you well enough to return to the Queen's service?'

'Yes, it is agreed.'

'Good. She needs some older women round her to keep her steady.'

'Is it true she is going to pardon Morton and Ruthven for the murder of Rizzio?'

'Yes, the council agrees. They can return from exile as long as they stay away from court.'

'I imagine such discussions are easier in the absence of the King.'

'The King goes in fear for his life. With justification. He is safe as long as he stays where he is, well protected by his father's people.'

She looked at him shrewdly. 'Perhaps there are more than the men he has betrayed would prefer that he be not so well protected.'

'Perhaps.'

'Is there any reason why he does not stay in Glasgow forever and leave you and the Queen to rule in peace? And the Privy Council of course.'

'It will not do. The Queen wants rid of him.'

'How?'

'By persuasion of course. How else? But how can he be persuaded when no one ever sees him. So, Mother, could the Queen encourage him out of his lair? I avoid talking to her about it. I feign indifference.'

'A promise of the Crown Matrimonial?'

'He would not believe it and it's a promise we could not fulfil.'

'The promise perhaps that he can return to her bed?'

'Better.'

'A suggestion that one boy in the royal nursery is not enough?'

'Can she enact the part of a loving wife, do you think?'

Margaret remembered the hours after the murder of Rizzio when the Queen successfully detached the King from the conspirators by acting just so, the loving, frightened wife. It had succeeded then. But could she be persuaded to go through such a charade again. Why should she want to?

'She could safely use the excuse of his illness to avoid sharing his bed,' she said. 'But what could persuade her even to pretend to want him back?'

'If she had him under her eye she could be sure he was not plotting against her.'

251

'*Is* he plotting against her?'

'Of course. He is continually plotting. The latest is that he is trying to recruit an army from France to invade and place him on the throne.'

She was aghast.

'That won't happen, will it?'

'Of course not. You could also tell her that he plans to kidnap the prince. Oh yes, he's doing that too. Mother, tell her all of this. Persuade her to encourage the King away from Glasgow.'

A few weeks later Queen Mary travelled to Glasgow to bring home her invalid husband. Sir Simon Preston, the owner of Craigmillar Castle, only seven miles south of Edinburgh had been prevailed upon to make accommodation ready for him.

'You were good enough to accommodate me during my convalescence there,' said the Queen, reaching out a hand to help the elderly courtier to his feet. 'Your parkland is so beautiful. I am sure the King will recover his health there.'

'As Your Grace wishes,' he answered. Some of the Queen's ladies had to stifle a laugh. His reluctance was palpable.

'Whose idea was it?' he muttered as he backed out of the Queen's presence.

Maitland had his reply ready.

'Lord Bothwell, you will recollect, was there with most of the council when the Queen stayed with you, and all were particularly impressed with the comfort.'

'You were there too,' said Sir Simon.

'I was. But alas I do not have the influence over the Queen which my lord appears to exercise. You have him to thank for this honour.'

252

'Why?' asked Margaret of Moray later. 'Why is Bothwell so keen that the King go to Craigmillar?'

'I have not asked him.'

'Will you be there?'

'Not I. Nowhere near.'

The entourage from Glasgow took several days to travel the sixty miles, for the King was unable to ride and had to be carried in a litter. No matter how slowly they went he grumbled and complained of being thrown about.

All the planning counted for nothing. He threw a tantrum when he was told he was to go to Craigmillar. He refused to go there. If he could not stay at Holyrood Palace then he would go to Kirk o'Field. He had been offered lodging in one of the new houses there, an empty one which belonged to Sir James Balfour. Sir James, it appeared, was one of those who still felt able to be of service to the King.

'The King is a fool,' said Moray. 'He will be next door to Hamilton House and God knows Chatelherault bears him no goodwill.'

'Does that upset the plans?'

'There are no plans, Mother.'

Since the house was barely furnished, Mary sent word that the stewards were to take from Holyrood anything that was needed for the King's comfort. They were to furnish a bedroom, including a bath, for his illness required that he bathe in warm water several times a day. They were also to prepare a bedroom for herself.

Margaret and the other ladies welcomed the Queen back to Holyrood Palace two days later. The King, Mary told them, was comfortably lodged in Balfour's house at Kirk o'Field.

'It is very pleasant there, even at this time of year. His room has a balcony that overlooks the fields and when he is strong enough there is a pleasant garden for him to walk in.'

'Did you have much difficulty in persuading him to come?'

'Yes. But I persuaded him with promises. Oh Margaret,' the Queen looked drawn and her mouth twisted in a grimace. For a moment she almost looked ugly. 'What promises I had to make. God forgive me.'

'It is for the best.'

'Of course it is. At least if I have him under my eye I know what he is doing. I cannot rest a minute when he is out of my sight.'

Margaret helped Mary off with her hood and rubbed her temples with eau de cologne. 'It is difficult to feign affection when there is none.'

'I have promised to spend time there with him whenever possible.' She gave a short barking laugh, so very different from her usual light chuckle.

'I have quarters on the floor below him. He seems to think that this is the proper arrangement. That he as King should be on the upper floor and I on the floor below. I had not realised that the arrangement at Holyrood annoys him. Useless to explain it has always been thus since the days of my father and grandfather when their queens had the rooms above. He reads grievances into everything.'

Margaret made no comment but took the tray of food from the serving girl, for the Queen was to dine quietly tonight with only a few of her ladies and courtiers. These were now beginning to drift into the room and the Queen's demeanour soon lightened.

'Is Lord Bothwell to join us?' asked Mary Seton.

'Lord Bothwell has gone to Dunbar.'

The next two weeks passed quietly. Whenever her duties permitted the Queen made the short journey to the King's lodgings, taking with her those of her courtiers who could tolerate being in company with the King. Several times she spent the night there, but not, as everyone knew, in the

King's bed. His illness made that impossible. The visits were spent in pleasant occupations: playing cards, conversation, music, chess. His doctors told him he must live quietly until he recovered from the pox. And he did seem to be recovering. Stories of increasing restlessness and temper were relayed back to Holyrood.

It was clear what he wanted: back to Holyrood, to be given the honour and power of a king, and Mary back in his bed. Eventually the doctors pronounced him cured and there was no reason why he should not return to court. He would return on the first Monday of Lent.

Sunday was a day of carnival before the austerity of the next few weeks. In addition to the usual festivities Master Bastien Pagez, one of the valets whom Mary had brought with her from France and of whom she was particularly fond, was being married. The Queen attended the wedding feast in the morning. In the afternoon she and several of her council, Bothwell, now returned from Dunbar, Huntly, Argyll and others, said farewell to the ambassador of Savoy at a formal dinner held in the house of the Bishop in Canongate.

'Where is Jamie?' she asked Margaret as they went in.

'He has gone to St Andrews. His wife has had a setback. The doctors think she might lose the baby. Jamie has gone to be by her side.'

'I am sorry. Let me know if she needs anything.'

The dinner ended at six o'clock.

'It's early,' said the Queen as they returned the short distance to Holyrood.

Tomorrow would begin the fasting and abstinence but today the carnival atmosphere in the streets was irresistible. People were milling about and there was a great deal of laughter and hailing of the royal party with good wishes. 'It is a pity the King could not be at the wedding today. He would have enjoyed himself. We shall go and see him and spend some time with him.'

'Your Grace, they are not expecting us,' said Maitland by her side.

'We will surprise them,' said the Queen.

'Everything will be packed away already, ready for His Grace's return here tomorrow.'

'That does not matter. What a gloom you are tonight, Maitland.'

'But Your Grace does not intend to stay overnight?'

'Perhaps.'

Her squire gave the order and the party separated, the Queen and some of her friends to go to Kirk o'Field, those ladies who professed themselves tired, Margaret among them, to return to Holyrood. There they found the wedding festivities for Bastien and his bride still going on, and they found the energy to join in.

It was towards midnight that Margaret, exhausted by the day's events, was making her way from the ballroom of the palace when she met the Queen and her party entering.

'Your Grace, we had not expected you back.'

The Queen indicated Lord Bothwell by her side. 'We were reminded that I promised to be at the masque for the wedding.'

'I'm sorry, Your Grace. It is over.'

'Never mind,' said the Queen who looked in high spirits, almost windblown, exhilarated by her ride through the darkened streets. 'I will just say a word.'

At that moment the bride was escorted out by her ladies, giggling and joking. They paused when they saw the Queen, who stepped forward and swept the bride into her arms and gave her a kiss. Laughing, she released her and told her she was a lucky girl to be marrying the man she loved. The girls curtseyed and went on.

256

The Queen looked after them. 'I don't think it is appropriate for a Queen to attend the formal bedding ceremony,' she said wistfully.

'No indeed,' said Bothwell heartily. 'Well, I'm for bed myself.' And with a deep bow he left them.

'Lord, I am tired,' said the Queen. 'We'll to bed too. Tomorrow we will be busy. The King comes home.'

But he never did come home. That night an explosion ripped through the house at Kirk o'Field, killing some of the servants; the King himself was found strangled in the garden.

Chapter Forty

Told of the death of her husband, the Queen collapsed. On the advice of her doctors, her ladies carried her to Seton Palace. Every day they wrapped her up warmly in her cloak and stout boots and persuaded her out into the fresh air. No other activity was permitted. The doctors were clear. She had to have quiet. Now, cold as it was and with every day the east wind blowing in snow over the firth, snow which the low February sun did nothing to melt, the gardeners were out as early as they could be to clear the paths on which the Queen walked slowly, with her head down, speaking to none, while her ladies trailed behind her, ready to step forward if she wanted conversation. She seldom did. There were times when they had to walk one on either side of her to support her, for she complained of pains in her legs and side and once she had fainted.

'How do I know who my friends are?' Mary took Margaret's hand. 'You are my friend, I know you are. And you.' She turned to Lady Huntly who walked on the other side of her.

'And always will be, my dear child.'

There were only the women. The Queen wanted no men round her. Which of her advisers could she trust? Which of them could she call on for advice? Who was not involved in the plot?

One thing she was clear about in her own mind: she had been the intended victim. She had so nearly stayed at Kirk o'Field that night. Who could hate her so much? She withdrew into her own thoughts.

They stayed only four nights at Seton. Long as the walk out from Edinburgh was, some people found their way there and were gathering round the gates, calling for the Queen. They were beginning to talk, the servants reported, as if they believed the Queen to be guilty and in hiding.

'Guilty of what?' she wept.

None dared frame the word: murder.

It was best that she return to Edinburgh and some semblance of normal life, as normal as was possible while the court was in mourning.

And gradually, as information came in from the Edinburgh baillies who were investigating the explosion, it became obvious that whether or not she was intended to die also, her husband was undoubtedly the focus of the atrocity.

Her ladies could not hide from the Queen that within days of the murder there were posters going up round Edinburgh on church doors and on trees, accusing Bothwell of the murder and Balfour in whose house it had happened.

These posters were torn down by Bothwell's men, for he had now flooded the capital with his retinue. They crowded the streets and stood at the doors of the taverns and churches. Some townspeople, braver than the others, elbowed them aside and dared them to cause trouble. Children threw mud and stones.

More posters went up, this time accusing her secretary Joseph Rizzio, appointed by her after the death of his brother. A quiet man, lacking the flamboyance of David Rizzio, he had offended none, only scribing the Queen's French correspondence. Now these posters accused him of murder, in revenge for his brother's death.

'It is not possible,' shouted the Queen. 'He is loyal to me, he would do nothing to harm me or mine.' There were those who said the new posters were prompted by Bothwell himself, but Joseph was no longer seen in the royal apartments and the correspondence with her French relatives ceased.

259

'Your Grace must be seen to be impartial. It is best that you keep your distance from the lords who are under suspicion,' was Margaret's advice. Lady Huntly was more reticent, for Bothwell was clearly the main suspect and since he was married to her daughter and her son was a close confidant of the accused man, she did not want her family drawn into the matter.

The few of the Queen's advisers who were admitted to her presence pleaded with her to have the crime investigated. Maitland managed to extract from her an agreement that the Privy Council should offer an award for information, but beyond that she would give no instructions. She seemed to be suffering from a paralysis of the will.

Margaret could see the girl was more like her father than she realised. There had been times when he too had suffered agonies of melancholy and indecision.

None of them, not Maitland, nor Argyll, nor Erskine would take upon themselves the authority to carry out the investigation. They left it to the people who had jurisdiction in the area, the Edinburgh authorities. The citizens who had been near Kirk o'Field that night and who might have been able to give information that would help, kept quiet, for many had no doubt that the people involved in this crime were too close to the Queen to want an investigation. If some of the men who must have been moving about in the dark that night had been recognised, no one dared name them, not openly.

As the first week passed, then the second, the Queen withdrew further into herself and could only lie listlessly on her bed. Sometimes she permitted the women to rub her arms and legs with fragrant balms to ease the pains, but as often as not she failed to respond, lying on her back with tears in her eyes.

Every day there were clusters of men waiting to see the Queen and every day they were sent away by the ushers.

The Queen was too ill to see anyone. The Queen was overcome with grief.

One, more persistent than most, was the Earl of Lennox. Loudly grieving for his son, his voice could be heard even beyond the presence chamber in the bedroom and beyond to the tower room where the Queen was lying curled up on her daybed.

He was demanding vengeance. He was demanding that the perpetrators of the crime be brought to justice. He had no hesitation in naming who was to blame. The Earl of Bothwell had murdered his son and he wanted the Earl hanged for the crime.

Moray tried to reason with his sister. 'Mary, you must investigate. You are the Queen. You must display your authority.'

She clung to him. 'You at least had nothing to do with it, had you brother?'

'How can you ask?' he said. 'Of course it was none of my doing.' After all, he had been nowhere near Edinburgh.

The half-hearted investigations begun by the Burgh Council faltered to a halt.

Even when Lady Huntly came to her in some anguish the Queen just listened listlessly.

'My daughter is ill and asks to be excused attendance on Your Grace today.'

Her words were measured but there was a slight quaver quickly suppressed. 'If Your Grace pleases.'

'What's the matter with her?'

'A slight indisposition. Some fish that perhaps disagreed with her.'

'I will send my own physician to see to her.'

'Your Grace is very good, but that will not be necessary,' said Lady Huntly firmly. 'The worst is now over. We have attendants enough.'

But as Lady Huntly left the room, Margaret caught a glimpse of her face. The old lady had relaxed her court look and now looked drawn and anxious. Quietly, one eye on the Queen who was now lying staring into the fire while the ladies around her quietly stitched their embroidery, Margaret rose from her seat on the outskirts of the circle and followed Lady Huntly.

She caught up with her in the passage from the tower to the main building. 'What ails Jean?'

Lady Huntly paused and as she turned to Margaret there were tears suddenly sprung into her eyes. 'I don't know, but she is very ill. I made light of it to the Queen for it would be too cruel to burden her with more than she can bear.'

'What do you fear?'

Lady Huntly looked at her in anguish. She shook her head. She did not dare put her fears into words.

The two women made their way to Bothwell's quarters. They found Jean in bed with her hand being held by one of the chamber-women and another sponging her forehead. As they entered Jean suddenly twisted on the bed. She vomited into the bowl, which was covered up by the nurse and carried to the privy. Lady Huntly took her place at her daughter's side. With a nod of the head she dismissed the other chamber-woman.

Lady Huntly wrung the excess water out of a new cold cloth and applied it to her daughter's forehead murmuring soft words of comfort. Whether the bout of sickness had eased the trouble, or whether with her mother there the girl felt more reassured, her face had gained a bit more colour.

'Where is your husband?' asked Margaret.

'Gone hunting. Shooting at the butts. Gambling with his friends. Who knows? I don't, and don't much care.'

'My dear,' said Lady Huntly.

'I never wanted to marry him in the first place and now he does not want me. He never did, only my dowry.'

'He is your husband and you must stand by him.'

'Why? When he has asked me to divorce him.'

The other two women were shocked into silence.

'He wants a divorce,' Jean continued. 'They've both been here, him and my brother, trying to persuade me. I told them I would not and they could not force me.' She laughed bitterly. 'I will never live with him again. As soon as I am well I will go home, to Strathbogie. And I think I must be more careful in what I eat.'

'You are tired,' said her mother. 'Of course you will go north if you want to. Sleep now. I will make the arrangements. The Queen will excuse you, I am sure.'

'The Queen will be delighted to see the back of me.'

The two older women glanced at one another. Pointless to pretend they did not know what Jean was speaking of.

'I will never divorce him. We are man and wife in the sight of God and whom God hath joined no man can put asunder. I will have to be dead for him to be free of me.'

Her voice was weakening.

As the two women rose Margaret leaned over to smooth the girl's hair and straighten the coif which held it in place.

'Tell me,' she said softly. 'The Earl your husband claims that on the night of the King's death he was safely in bed with you. Was that true?'

The girl looked straight at her.

'If he was in someone's bed, it wasn't mine.'

Margaret bent forward and kissed her. 'Take care,' she said, reflecting that the girl would have to be very careful indeed and the sooner she was in the north and well away from the court the better.

263

Chapter Forty-One

'I'm better out of it,' said Jamie. 'I'll ask leave to travel to England. There needs to be some explanation made to Elizabeth about what is happening here, else she will receive distorted views of it.'

'Distorted?' asked Margaret. 'Is the truth any worse?'

'Can you find a way to warn Annabella's brother there will soon be a reward out for him?'

'Her brother? You mean James Murray? Why is there a reward? What's he done?'

'He's been making the posters.'

'Has he? How do you know?'

He didn't answer her, but continued to scribble notes for his steward and others, matters to be dealt with once he was gone. 'There will be bloodshed,' he continued. 'Lennox will have his revenge on Bothwell.'

'Would he dare, were Bothwell to be wed to the Queen?'

He paused and looked up at her. 'Has it come to that already?'

Briefly she told him of the sickness of Lady Bothwell.

'He wants her out of the way. She will not agree to a divorce. He'll stop at nothing.'

'Poor lass. For her own safety she should agree.'

'She won't. Her religion goes too deep.'

He sat back. 'So,' he mused. 'If there is no Lady Bothwell, he would want to marry the Queen. Would she have him, I wonder.'

'It's likely he mistook some flirtation for more than that. There is a lustiness about him that brings out responses in women.'

'Is there now?' He looked amused. 'But I hope that Mary has learned sense by now. Even she must see he is not a suitable consort for her.'

'He will pursue her and in her present state who is to say what she might agree to.'

'Then we must try and separate her from him.'

'And bring him down?'

'Lennox will do that for us. It is best I be seen to having nothing to do with it.'

He rose. 'I must prepare to travel,' he said. 'Whatever happens, I do not want to be here. I do not wish to be embroiled in any of this.'

'Go well, my son.'

But, Margaret reflected as she lay in bed that night, it would not be such a bad thing if the Queen were to marry my Lord Bothwell. Universally hated by virtually the whole of the nobility, his promotion could be the signal for the Queen herself to be brought down.

And then Jamie would come into his own once more.

The Queen roused herself to express displeasure when he asked leave to travel to England.

'It is time someone went to explain matters to Queen Elizabeth. She hears from her ambassador that Scotland is approaching a state of anarchy. I must go and reassure her. I will explain that you are pursuing your husband's murderers, but quietly, so as to lull those who are guilty into a false sense of security. I think that is the best explanation I can offer her.'

'As you think fit. Go if you must.'

'I will tell your cousin you are distraught but that matters are in hand.'

265

'Tell her what you wish.'

'But my dear, while I am away do not rely on Lord Bothwell too much for advice. It were as well you do not admit him to your presence more than is necessary.'

She snatched her hand away. 'Why not?'

'It is not good for your reputation.'

'Are you saying he was involved in the killing?'

He was silent.

'You are his enemy. You have always hated him.' Her voice was rising and the ladies gathered at the far end of the room raised their heads in concern.

'Go,' she said. 'Go now. How can I trust you? Who can I trust?'

She turned away and gazed rigidly from the window while he stood undecided, but as the moments passed he sighed and withdrew.

But when he was gone the Queen sank down onto cushions and wept. In her excitement she began to choke and then to vomit while the ladies called the chamber-women to clean up. With a moan she threw herself down on the bed and buried her face in the pillow. She was still shouting but her words were muffled by the bolster.

'Wicked. Wicked. How can they say it?'

The next day Margaret picked her way through the Grassmarket past the street traders and luckenbooths, easing her way round the knots of people talking in low voices.

Overhearing snatches of conversation, Margaret could hear that sympathy was with the late King. The tradesmen, those who benefited from his custom could be expected to be sorry for his death, but many more forgot that while he was alive they saw his behaviour as an insult to the Queen. Now he was dead he was the poor wronged lad. He was, they reminded themselves, only twenty years old and maybe no more than a daft laddie. They all remembered

266

what a handsome boy he had been when he first arrived to woo the Queen.

Some were asking loudly that since Bothwell was obviously the killer, why was he not brought to justice? Others more circumspect, would look round anxiously and shush the speaker. My Lord Bothwell's men were everywhere. They ignored the talk. They knew it could not touch them or their master.

The torn remnants of several weeks of scathing derogatory posters hung from doors. No sooner were they put up than they were torn down again, but everyone remembered what they said.

Margaret was admitted to the castle. Telling her maid to wait for her at the gatehouse she made her way to her brother's private quarters. Erskine was not there. Annabella told her he was in conference with the Privy Council.

'The air is fraught at the palace,' said Margaret. 'The Queen is ill and everyone is tense. And frightened. No one knows what will happen.'

'Is it true that Bothwell is constantly with her?'

Margaret heard a noise from the inner room.

She was instantly alert. 'Who's there? Can we be overheard?'

'It's only my brother,' said Annabella. 'Come out, James.'

James Murray came slowly out.

'James, do you know there is a reward out for you?'

'I know,' he said. 'Why do you think I am here?'

'He's safe here,' said Annabella.

'Does Erskine know?'

'No. He came well disguised. My husband is too busy to notice. Besides, they do him an injustice.'

'No, they don't,' protested her brother. 'I made the posters. Why should I deny it? Many people thought them very fine.'

'You must not stay. They will arrest you. He'll take ship for the low countries.'

'Aye, let him do that. For if Bothwell gets hold of him his life is worth nothing. But before you go, James, here's something for you to put in your posters. The Lord Bothwell has ambitions to wed the Queen.'

'We all know that,' he said, and there was a sneer in his voice. Well, thought Margaret, I think I am privy to knowledge and it turns out it is common gossip already. Perhaps events are moving faster even than Jamie knows.

At that moment they heard Erskine's voice from the landing. Like a ghost, Murray was gone out by a door onto the stair.

'Right,' said Erskine, bursting in. 'Get ready to pack. We are ordered to Stirling.'

'To Stirling?' yelped Annabella. 'I don't want to go to Stirling.'

'You have no choice. I am being relieved of my command here. I am to take the prince to Stirling. Does she think... but it is not her, is it? Hullo sister, we know who is behind this, do we not?'

'Who will be governor here?'

'One of Bothwell's affinity. We can be sure of that. God's blood. God's blood, why do we have to put up with this?' He turned on his heel. 'Within the week,' he said. 'We are to be gone.' He left and they could hear him shouting instructions to the garrison commander.

The two women looked at each other.

'Has Bothwell such power?' asked Annabella.

'He will have,' said Margaret grimly.

They were thinking the same thing. Did Bothwell really think that he could rule Scotland. He would need to do it by force. It was inconceivable that the lords in the north, Moray, Lovat and others, in the west, Glencairn, Ochiltree, and the Douglases and Maxwells in the south would stand by and allow him to do it.

'At least the prince will be safer at Stirling.'

A week later the prince's household, accompanied by Lord Erskine and his household and protected by several hundred arquebusiers, made their slow way through Edinburgh and out of the western gate towards the distant castle of Stirling. The townspeople lined the streets to watch them go and for the most part the crowd was silent.

The huge requiem mass which marked the official ending of the court's period of forty days of mourning for the King was the signal for the Earl of Lennox to bring a private prosecution against the Earl of Bothwell, accusing him of the assassination.

When the day came for the trial, Lord Bothwell left Holyrood and rode up to the Tolbooth, followed by a large contingent of his men. It took only a short time for the High Court of Justiciary to find him not guilty, because Lord Lennox did not appear to give evidence. Bothwell swaggered back to Holyrood and strode through the palace to kneel at the Queen's feet.

'You see?' he said triumphantly. 'There was no case to answer. There will be no more accusations.'

But those listening knew there was no case because the law allowed Lennox a bodyguard of only six men and six Lennox men in a city where several thousand of Bothwell's men were lodged could not have protected him. No wonder he stayed away. To that extent he was considered wiser than Bothwell.

Margaret wrote to Jamie to tell him what had happened. A week later she had a reply. *He must be brought down. Give him sufficient rope and he will hang himself.*

269

She could envisage a situation in which Jamie might never be allowed to return to Scotland and that could never be. He was destined for power and she would take any necessary steps to aid him to that power.

So be it. Bothwell would have to be brought down. That much was clear. If the Queen herself had to suffer, then that was unfortunate, but how could she be helped when she was so clearly unwilling to help herself?

Now all that remained was to make sure that Bothwell would be free to marry the Queen and with luck, weave a rope long enough to hang them both.

Chapter Forty-Two

'I will not grant him a divorce. Our marriage was consecrated by God and the church. It cannot be broken.'

'But it is what the Queen wishes,' said Margaret.

'She cannot wish that. She is a good Catholic, as I am. There can be no divorce.'

Jean Gordon was now lodged in the Edinburgh house of her uncle the Earl Marischal. She was refusing to cohabit with Lord Bothwell. He did not press her. Perhaps he was so busy with Privy Council affairs, where he now had complete control, freed of the inhibiting presence of Moray, that he hardly noticed whether she was there or not.

'Look at Bessie Crawford, your own laundry-woman. Flaunting the fact that he has had her. She boasts of it. And more than once.'

'Making me a laughing-stock? What of it? Look at Lady Jane. When did she last live with Argyll?'

'It gives grounds for divorce for those who wish it.'

'Your church might recognise a divorce but my church does not.'

'I have heard it said that the Archbishop would be willing to have your marriage annulled.'

'How can he?'

'There are no children after all.'

'The marriage was consummated, there is no question of that,' said Jean and her mouth was twisted as perhaps she recalled her wedding night and other nights.

'There are many unpleasantnesses you would be free of.'

'So on what grounds does the Archbishop think my marriage could be annulled?'

'It could be said on grounds of affinity.'

The girl rose and went to her kist. She took out a casket and opened it.

'See this?' She pulled out a parchment. 'This is the dispensation which the Archbishop granted us at the time of our marriage. He himself removed the impediment. How can he say it still exists?'

'But you know, dear, that the new Scottish church has done away with all those restrictions on marriage between kin further away than first cousins and you and Lord Bothwell are nowhere near first cousins. You are not really related.'

'The church thought so at the time.'

Margaret felt a surge of irritation with the girl. Sensible as Jean was, and none of the other women came near her for her common sense and steely determination, but there were times when her stubbornness got in the way of her own best interests.

Looking over Jean's shoulder at the parchment, written in Latin which she could not read, Margaret said, 'If there were no document...'

'But there is.'

'There need not be. Documents can be destroyed. Or lost. Think, if you stand in his way, what will he do?'

Lady Jean shivered but did not answer.

The skill of the doctors had pulled her through her illness, though she would have it that it was praying to God which had saved her and the masses the Queen had paid for.

'If you were divorced from him, you could remarry.'

'What would be the point? Alexander Ogilvy has married Mary Beaton. The Queen arranged that too. Is he also to divorce? Besides, even if I were divorced from Bothwell in the eyes of the world, in my own eyes I would still be his wife. As long as he lives I could never marry another.'

'We marry where we must,' said Margaret. 'Sometimes we have little say in the matter. My dear, think on this. There is your marriage settlement. Crichton Castle is yours, and other estates. He will be so anxious to be free that he will agree to anything. You would be a rich woman, beholden to none.'

For a moment Margaret thought that she had made a telling point, for there was a gleam of alertness in the younger woman's eyes.

Jean put the parchment back in her box and turned the key.

'If he married the Queen, would there be trouble?'

'I think not,' said Margaret. 'The lords quarrel amongst themselves but most of them have signed a bond agreeing to support the marriage. They know that the Queen needs a strong man by her side and everything will settle down and she will rule wisely with good advice.'

'A strong man, you think him that?'

'Most people think him that.'

'He is strong as long as he has his men at his back. Wise advice? I wonder. He is a bad enemy, and a friend can quickly become an enemy.'

'Think of it, my dear,' said Margaret, who judged that she had said enough. 'Think of it. And think what it would be like to be back in your own country, a free woman.'

Chapter Forty-Three

The long weeks of Lent came to an end and then the Easter solemnities, but as March gave way to a milder April the Queen's health did not improve. Encouraged by her ladies, she made a private visit to Stirling Castle to visit her baby son. James was now ten months old and responding to his mother's teasing with ready chuckles. He was beginning to hoist himself upright, gripping on to his nurse's hand and shuffling his feet.

'He will grow up strong and well, won't he?'

Yes, they all hastened to assure her. He was a sturdy healthy lad, a great credit to her. When the time came to part with him she wept.

The small group left Stirling to travel back to Edinburgh. She had taken with her only a handful of courtiers, Secretary Maitland, a few of her ladies and a bodyguard of only thirty men. It was fine, almost balmy weather and the woodland floors were yellow with drifts of primroses and aconites.

The journey was taking longer than it should have, for they had to stop regularly as the Queen was feeling ill. When she almost collapsed in her saddle as they were passing the house of a respectable laird it was decided she would have to rest. His wife hastily prepared a couch for her to lie on and a corner where she could relieve herself in privacy.

'Something she ate,' Margaret assured the householders. It would not do for word to get about that there was something seriously amiss with the Queen. 'And of course she is still full of sorrow for the death of her husband.'

Yes, grief affecting the body they could understand. Their sympathy comforted the Queen. The people still loved her. When she was able to leave she agreed that they could spend the night at Linlithgow Palace instead of travelling all the way to Edinburgh.

The palace was always ready for the Queen. It was the finest of the royal palaces and as she shed her travelling clothes and was helped into her nightgown the Queen expressed herself thankful to be there. They settled her in bed and she lay back and closed her eyes. With a nod Margaret dismissed the women.

The Queen sighed. 'Margaret, I am so tired.'

'It is not surprising, my dear. The journey has been hard for you.'

'Not just the journey. Tired, long-term tired, tired down into the depths of my soul.'

'Your Grace will feel better in the morning. A good night's sleep. And tomorrow we will be back at Holyrood.'

'And then it begins all over again. The lies, the accusations, the insulting posters. Did you know the last time I went out there were those in the crowd who booed at me. These kindly people today, they still love me, don't they.'

'Yes,' said Margaret firmly. 'It is only a few troublemakers in Edinburgh. They will soon forget and all will be well again.'

'There is nothing to be done to stop them.'

She closed her eyes and Margaret wondered if she had fallen asleep already.

'Will I die here, do you think?'

'Who speaks of dying?' said Margaret, startled.

'I was born in this palace. In this bed. Perhaps I can die here. And be at peace at last.'

275

Margaret studied her face. The beautiful face which men so admired had shrunk to a little pale circle, pale against the creaminess of the pillows.

'So much pain. So much grief. So much death.'

Margaret had to lean forward to catch the words. 'You are young. Let us not speak of death.'

'In my studies I have been reading Livy with Dr Buchanan. You know that?'

Margaret knew that in happier times Dr Buchanan had been reading Latin with the Queen.

'I want to be as clever as my cousin.'

Yes, Queen Elizabeth was reputed to be something of a scholar. Margaret had to smile at the idea of Queen Mary being a scholar. She was not stupid, but there were so many distractions.

'And in time you will be,' she answered.

'The ancient Romans that we read about, they were honourable. They had their own code of honour. If they were guilty, do you know what they did?'

'No,' said Margaret uneasily.

'They fell upon their sword. They died by their own hand. Do you not think that is a brave thing to do?'

'It is a sin.'

'I wanted the King dead.'

'You do not mean that.'

'I had no hand in his killing.'

'Everyone knows that.'

'Do you think one sin cancels out another?' She sighed. 'My Lord Bothwell has asked me to marry him. I do not know what to do.'

'I think that many of your nobles would be pleased if you were to marry him. He has many friends,' said Margaret.

'Yes, they have told me so. They come to me and tell me a woman cannot rule without a man and assure me that he would be the man of their choice. I tell them I have no wish to remarry yet, but still they come back.'

'Your Grace, if it were your wish to marry Lord Bothwell, I know that Lady Bothwell would agree to an annulment of the marriage if she were asked.'

'Would she? Would it be so easy?'

'When both parties wish it. And I know that Jean Gordon feels no love for her husband.'

'What of my brother? He has no love for Bothwell. What would he do if I were to marry?'

'Do not trouble about Jamie. He writes that he spends a great deal of time at Queen Elizabeth's court. He is working hard to obtain her agreement to your succession to England. I think he would be happy to be your ambassador there and in France, which as you know he loves as much as you do yourself.'

'Still, I do not wish to marry Bothwell. I think I do not want to marry anyone.'

It was, reflected Margaret as she sat on by the now silent and soon sleeping Queen, a sign of Mary's weakened state that she should so readily accept assurances that in the past she would have disbelieved.

When she was satisfied that the Queen was in a deep sleep Margaret rose and went out to the anteroom. She nodded to one of the women to go in. The woman would watch over the Queen while she slept. She made her way through the deserted corridors of the palace.

In the Hall the few courtiers who had travelled with them were grouped round the fireplace at the far end. Maitland was not there. He would be in bed with his wife who was on duty this week as one of the Queen's ladies, and had sneaked away early in the evening.

Huntly was throwing dice with James Melville and some of the others, but even as she watched from the shadow of the door she saw him rise and with a word which brought a laugh, he left them, going through the door of the Hall that led into the courtyard.

Margaret continued her patrol through the now silent palace. As she glided past the windows, still unshuttered, she looked out. She was just in time to see Lord Bothwell slip round the shadowed walls of the courtyard. He was moving in the direction of the kitchens.

Swiftly Margaret, who was totally familiar with the layout of the palace, slipped downstairs, pausing when she heard voices. She could not tell where they were coming from but they must be nearby. She stopped and tried to still her breathing. If she could hear them they could hear her.

'You're a fool,' she heard Huntly say. 'If that's your plan I'll have nothing to do with it.'

'It is the only way. It is the best way. You'll see. Everyone will accept it.' It was Bothwell's voice, soft and sounding very reasonable, as only he could.

'You're forgetting you're still my sister's husband.'

'Not for long.'

'This is madness. Think again. Find some other way.'

'There is no other way. And there is no time to be lost. Do you want the enquiry to start again?'

'Of course not.'

'Well then. I can stop it. And I will have the authority, do you not see?'

'I see your ambition is boundless.'

There was a pause.

'Aye, but I do it for Scotland.'

There was an amused grunt at that from Huntly. Bothwell went on, 'So you won't help me?'

'I will not.'

'Just carry a message to the Queen.'

'Not even that. I will have nothing to do with it.'

There was the sound of a boot striking the floor and then the footsteps of Huntly, quickly running up the staircase. Margaret waited. She heard Bothwell quietly swear. And then he too was gone and she was just in time to see him stride swiftly across the courtyard, like a ghost, and then he was gone through the postern gate.

Something was going to happen. Something that Bothwell had planned of such enormity that even Huntly, his shadow in most of his exploits, refused to have anything to do with it. Margaret made her way upstairs to her own chamber. As she climbed into the bed which she was sharing with Mary Seton, Mary turned in her sleep and murmured, 'What time is it?'

'Late, go to sleep.'

The next day it was a subdued and silent group who rode out of Linlithgow Palace.

Chapter Forty-Four

As Lord Huntly eased his horse into place behind the Queen he was heard to mutter to Maitland that he hoped for a quiet journey and dear God, a peaceful homecoming.

The Queen herself seemed oblivious to all of this. She was silent, shrunk in her own thoughts.

'You will soon be visiting your boy again,' said Margaret, drawing her horse up alongside the Queen at a wide bit of the road.

'God willing,' was the low reply. 'Would that I were a simple cottager and could spend all my days with him.' This was in response to greetings from the people of a small hamlet through which they were passing. The women curtseyed and the men bowed, but if there was less cheering and cries of *God bless you, lady* than there had been a year earlier, the Queen seemed not to notice.

They reached the banks of the River Almond where they dismounted. The vanguard climbed aboard the ferry and were carried across. Then the Queen and her ladies were ferried over, while those who would have to wait their turn walked up and down to stretch their legs.

As the Queen was handed out from the boat, one of the forward scouts came galloping back, but even as he started to speak armed men emerged from the woodland and in a moment the Queen and her people were surrounded.

Two of the newcomers seized the ropes from the ferryman. 'You'll not be moving yet, old man,' one of them said.

'What is this?' demanded the Queen but before she could answer there appeared from the midst of the men the Earl of Bothwell.

'My lord? You here?'

The Earl raised his voice so that all could hear him. 'Your Grace, there is unrest in the capital. It is not advisable that you go there this day.'

'Unrest! What?'

'There is a great deal of drink taken and rabble-rousers are going amongst the crowd spreading false rumours. The preachers have barred the city to you and will not let you enter. They are threatening to destroy the Chapel Royal if they can gain entry to Holyrood. Your people are barricading all the gates to keep them out.'

'My lord!' Suddenly the Queen was all alert. 'We will ride into Edinburgh despite them. We will speak to them.'

'You must not. I will take you to safety,' said Bothwell.

The Queen turned and made to mount her horse but Bothwell rode forward and took the bridle. The horse shied slightly. The Queen stepped back.

'I have three hundred men here to escort you.'

'I have my own escort, my lord.'

'You have but, what, thirty men? I think you would be better with my people.'

The others, those that were within hearing of this, had now fallen silent. There were matters afoot here that were not obvious. The Captain of the Queen's guard stirred uneasily in his saddle. He rode forward and spoke to the Queen.

'If you wish us to clear a way through to Edinburgh we shall.'

'I think not,' said Bothwell before the Queen could answer. 'I think, Captain, that my men outnumber yours.'

281

The Captain looked at the Queen. The men on the other side the river made to ride their horses into the water to cross, but it was pointless for the water was too deep, and even if their horses could have swum across, it would be too late. Lord Bothwell's men had closed in, making a tighter circle round the Queen.

She looked round at the silent men, then nodded. 'Fall back, Captain. I will go with Lord Bothwell. There must be no bloodshed.'

No one now was in any doubt about what was happening. Lord Bothwell was kidnapping the Queen.

'Lord Borthwick,' called the Queen.

He stepped forward.

'Your Grace?'

'Ride to Edinburgh and see for yourself what is happening. Then come and report to me at...' She looked enquiringly at Bothwell.

'At Dunbar.'

'At Dunbar,' said the Queen.

But it was only a gesture, an indication by Mary that she still considered herself to be in control.

Lord Borthwick mounted quickly and galloped away. Bothwell's men made way for him, silently. The Queen allowed her horse to be led forward, she mounted and rode away beside Lord Bothwell. The courtiers could only watch helplessly from the further bank as the party turned a bend in the road and then were gone.

Chapter Forty-Five

In early May the Court of Session in Edinburgh granted a divorce to the Countess of Bothwell on the grounds of her husband's adultery with her laundress Bessie Crawford.

'It is not a true severance,' she said defiantly to Margaret. 'None but the Pope can end my marriage.'

'It is legal in the eyes of the law.'

And in spite of her convictions and to make doubly sure, Archbishop Hamilton declared the marriage null in the eyes of the Catholic Church on the grounds that the parties were related and that there had been no dispensation, ignoring the fact that there lay in Lady Jean's box just such a dispensation which he himself had granted barely two years earlier.

A few days later, Bothwell rode with the Queen into Edinburgh to a volley of welcoming cannon from the castle. Their stay at Dunbar Castle had lasted three weeks.

The wardrobe mistress was in tears.

'My lady, please give me time to make a wedding dress.'

The Queen moved slowly through the room while the wardrobe mistress pulled out bales of gold and silver cloth, of lace and sarcenet, of velvets in blue and green.

'No,' said the Queen. She pulled an old yellow linen dress from the heap which was lying on a table awaiting repair, for the hem had been torn when she was dancing. That seemed a long time ago now.

'Here, this will do. This will do for my wedding gown.'

'You cannot,' pleaded the wardrobe mistress. 'Please, Your Grace, you cannot wear this on your wedding day.'

'I will,' and with that the Queen walked out of the room, the wardrobe mistress running after her. 'Jewels,' she said. 'What jewels do you wish brought for you to wear?'

'No jewels.'

Back in her bedchamber, the Queen plucked at the gown which she was wearing. She yanked at the sleeves, ripping the seam before her ladies had time to move forward to help. Mary Fleming would have restrained her but the Queen lifted her head and looked straight at her old friend.

'Keep back,' she said. 'Do not touch. Do you not know better than to touch one who is defiled.'

She continued to pull at the sleeves until the laces holding them in place tore through the fabric. She nodded to the elderly chamber-woman who was hovering in the background carrying a ewer of water, for the Queen now insisted that at every hour of the day or night there should be hot water ready for her use in her bedroom. It was only with difficulty that she was persuaded to dress each morning. Left to herself she would have spent the day washing.

'Help me,' she said. The chamber-woman with a scared look at the ladies who had stepped back, moved forward to help the Queen undress.

There was a hesitant knock at the door.

Margaret left the group round the Queen and opened the door. 'Yes?'

The Queen's equerry, Arthur Erskine, stood there, the two soldiers of Lord Bothwell who guarded the door stepping slightly back to allow him to pass on his message.

'The members of the council are here. They are ready for Her Grace.'

'Tell them the Queen is unwell.'

284

'Lady,' Arthur Erskine lowered his voice. 'If the Queen is not there then Lord Bothwell will preside.' He gave an anxious glance at the guarding soldiers but they both stared into the distance.

'I'll tell her but she is too ill to come.' She glanced quickly back into the room. The Queen was now in her undershift. There was no chance of persuading her to dress and attend to the Privy Council.

'Tell them the Queen's headaches have returned.'

She closed the door.

'She has gone mad,' whispered Mary Seton, helpless on the outskirts of the circle round the Queen. Margaret did not respond. She felt a great deal of pity for the girl who was the centre of attention. Margaret believed she really had gone mad.

But it was their duty to get her ready for her wedding, which would be in three days' time.

The wardrobe mistress did not dare countermand her instructions and none of the Queen's ladies felt inclined to go against the wishes of their mistress. She did her best with the yellow linen dress, washing it carefully in the softest of rain water, ripping out the old lining and replacing it with white taffeta so that the gown hung gracefully round the Queen's body, a body which many of the women could not help but notice, had lost a lot of weight in the last few weeks.

The minister of the parish church told the Privy Council he would not call the banns for the marriage save under specific written instructions from the Queen.

Before them he denounced Bothwell as an adulterer and rapist. There was collusion between him and his wife to obtain the divorce and there was still the suspicion that the King's death could be laid at his door.

'You'll hang for that, sir,' roared Bothwell, on his feet and making as if he would physically climb over the

285

table to seize the minister, but the others hustled the man away, still shouting accusations. There were many there and many more in the streets of Edinburgh who believed the man spoke no more than the truth.

The wedding took place, not in the chapel but in the Hall of Holyrood Palace. There was no fanfare, no celebration. Margaret, standing behind the Queen with the others, heard Bothwell and the Queen exchange their vows according to the new ritual of the Scottish church.

Looking at the back of the Queen's bowed head above the yellow dress, Margaret wondered what the girl was thinking. Was she thinking that this might be a ceremony of sorts, but that without the blessing of the Catholic Church it was meaningless? Was Mary, deep in her heart, convinced that this was not a true marriage?

One thing was certain. This marriage would tear the country apart.

Margaret had yesterday destroyed a letter she received from her brother Lord Erskine, from Stirling.

It has come to my notice that certain lords have signed a bond to depose the Queen and take the boy prince into their custody. I will resist this as my duty is to protect the prince, but thought you should know. Send to your son to ask him to return. If you wish to come here for safety, you may.

If you wish to come here for safety, you may. Margaret turned the words over in her head. Was Erskine supposing he would have to hold the castle against a siege if necessary? That was what it sounded like. What of Edinburgh Castle? This was now under the guardianship of the weasel Balfour whom everybody said was one of the assassins at Kirk o'Field. The cynics at court held that Edinburgh Castle was his reward for that. He held the armaments manufactory and the mint. He was Bothwell's man.

There will be civil war, she thought, as the Queen turned towards the small congregation and made her way slowly to the door, with her hand on the arm of her new husband and a look of total desolation on her face.

She would do as her brother asked. She would write to Jamie but it would be to tell him to stay away.

Chapter Forty-Six

The courtiers in the outer chamber raised their voices to cover up the sound of quarrelling coming from the Queen's room.

Some, less avid for gossip than the others, began to make excuses to drift out of the presence chamber where they had gathered. Perhaps their petitions could wait another day. They had business in the town to see to. There was something they had to do at the stables. Or the weather was so fine perhaps some practice at the butts might be in order. There had been little of that recently, or indeed of any other form of activity or amusement.

One of the ladies had heard Bothwell berating the Queen for her love of pleasure and excitement.

'Little enough she has of that now,' muttered the courtiers. 'When did she last dance, or smile for that matter.'

'Barely a widow and now an unhappy wife.' But this was said quietly for you never knew these days who was favoured by Bothwell and might be listening, nor for that matter who was Bothwell's enemy and might wish to recruit you to a cause you would prefer not to know about.

What was clear was that the business of governing the country had resumed in earnest, but without the Queen. Bothwell now presided at Privy Council meetings and government business was moving forward. Several proclamations had been issued, including a restatement of that which the Queen had given on her arrival in Scotland, a proclamation of freedom of worship for all.

'Where then, is John Knox?' was the question asked. 'He should be celebrating this.' The answer was that he had long ago left Edinburgh. He was somewhere in the west, they said, writing his History.

The door of the Queen's chamber burst open and Bothwell strode out. The courtiers stood back to make way for him as he stormed through the presence chamber with a face like thunder. One ambassador not long arrived from a small German state, not too sure of what was happening and perhaps braver than others, made an effort to move in front of him to stop his progress, but Bothwell glared at him and the man hastily jumped back.

Suddenly he paused in his stride. He turned back and looked at Margaret. 'You,' he said. 'You are no longer wanted here.'

'I am in the service of the Queen. Only she can dismiss me.'

'I am dismissing you. I say go, if you value your life.'

Well, well. It was not altogether unexpected and she was in a way surprised that she had been allowed to remain at court for so long, in view of the mutual hatred between Bothwell and Jamie. But then, she reflected, if everyone who hated Bothwell were to be dismissed, there would be few left.

One of the men near Margaret sighed. 'What will be reported in other countries of what is happening in Scotland? We are being made to look like boors.'

Maitland materialised among them to speak to the few who lingered. Behind him was Arthur Erskine, the Queen's equerry, white-faced. Maitland raised his voice. 'Gentlemen, ladies, there will be no audience today. Her Grace is ill. Please to go about your business.'

As the people dispersed Margaret and two of the Queen's ladies moved towards the Queen's bedchamber, but Maitland put out a hand to stop them. 'The Queen wants to be left in peace.'

289

Making an excuse, Margaret fell back from the other ladies and followed Erskine as he turned down the corridor that led to the equerries' room.

'Arthur.'

He paused. He bowed.

'I am sorry Her Grace is ill. Is there anything I can do?'

'The doctor is with her now. He is giving her something to help her to sleep.' He looked as if he was about to burst into tears.

She gripped his arm. 'Arthur, you have been more loyal to the Queen than most and a better servant. Tell me.'

'Just now, she called for a knife. She said she wanted to die. And when I remonstrated with her, she said she would drown herself.'

'Did Bothwell hear her?' Margaret, like many others in the court, could not yet bring herself to refer to Bothwell as the Queen's husband.

'He was there. He was shouting at her. He told her to pull herself together. Lady Margaret, I despair at what is happening to our Queen. She has changed so much, she is not the bright woman we knew. I remember how she rode behind me when we escaped after the murder of Master Rizzio. She clasped her arms round my waist and we rode like the wind and she laughed and planned and we returned to Edinburgh in triumph. Where has that lady gone?'

'I think it would be best not to tell anyone of this. That is how you can show your loyalty. It is best that no one knows how despairing the Queen is.'

He nodded and they parted.

Back in her own room Margaret told her servants to start packing. As she was putting her private papers into a small travelling writing-case there was a knock at the door.

It was Mary Fleming. She looked round the room as she came in. 'Are you leaving too?'

'I've been ordered away. It was time to go anyway.'

'I have to go too. I have just taken my farewell of the Queen.' There were tears in her eyes. 'I do not want to go, but I cannot stay. Maitland is leaving and says I must go with him.'

'He can't go, surely. The Queen needs him. What reason does he give?'

'He has told her he is ill and needs a rest. But he can no longer work with Bothwell. He says the Queen has chosen her protector and adviser and he is no longer wanted or welcome. Besides, he fears for his life. Bothwell attacked him once and if the Queen had not intervened he would be dead.'

'The Queen will be sorry to lose you.'

'I lied to her and I am sorry for it. I told her I must go because I was pregnant. She was happy for a moment, then she lost interest. I feel terrible lying, but what could I say?'

So they were all going. Argyll had left several days earlier. There were rumours he was raising an army in the west, while Atholl was raising the north. Many of the other lords had withdrawn from court, and, so it was said, were quietly mustering their men ready to fight if need be.

It was no surprise when the Queen and Bothwell issued a summons to all the lords and lairds of Scotland that they were to meet at Melrose on 15th June with their forces, armed.

And so Scotland drifted once more into civil war.

Chapter Forty-Seven

Margaret learned not altogether to her surprise, when she arrived in Stirling, that if it came to civil war, Erskine would hold the castle for the Queen but not for Bothwell.

'I will always be loyal to her,' he told his sister wearily, 'but I cannot support him.'

Margaret stood beside Annabella in the nursery, watching the young Prince James being fed. At less than a year old he was being weaned and was now opening his mouth willingly to take saps from the spoon held out to him by the nurse. He giggled and spat it out.

'He is all that matters now.'

'Erskine will die in his defence if need be.' Annabella's tone was complacent. Whatever the loyalty of the other lords, Erskine at least had no doubt where his duty lay. His duty was to protect the prince.

It was near time for their own dinner. They found Erskine already seated at the board. He jerked his head at the serving-girl. 'Leave it.' She put the dishes in front of Annabella and left the room.

'Well, brother,' said Margaret watching him spoon meat stew from the dish into his bowl. 'What is it the lords want? What would prevent this latest confrontation?'

'What's Moray doing?'

'He'll stay away.'

'I think he should be here. God's love, what do they put in this stew? Nothing but old mutton.'

'The young beasts are not ready for slaughter,' said his wife.

'The lords, as I recall,' persisted Margaret, 'signed a bond agreeing to work towards putting Bothwell in the

Queen's bed and look how it has turned out. What is it they now want?'

'They were bullied into it.'

'Hah,' said Annabella. 'Wilting weeds that they are.'

'Or bribed,' he continued, ignoring her. 'Some of the signatures were forged, or so they now maintain.'

'They reap what they sow. So now it is civil war. Again.'

'It need not come to that. The Queen will see that we have the right of it. We have most of Scotland supporting us. Argyll has gone to the west to raise his people. Fife is ours, and the Mearns. Atholl will raise the glens. And of course Lennox has thousands behind him ready to avenge the murder of his son. Aye, he will put his women in breeches and train his dogs to go for Bothwell's throat. Where's Maitland?'

'At home at Lethington, the last I heard.'

He grunted.

'If it comes to war our people will soon defeat Bothwell's rabble,' put in Annabella.

'No,' said Margaret. 'They are not rabble.' She recalled the disciplined ranks of the several hundred men who had aided the kidnap of the Queen. She thought of the quiet stalwart guard round the Palace of Holyrood, a guard who prevented the Edinburgh citizenry from approaching the castle as they had been accustomed to do in the past. These were no rabble, but trained soldiers.

'They say Bothwell's been borrowing from the Lombards to hire mercenaries,' she said.

'What else do they say?'

'That Chatelherault does not know who he is going to support.'

'God help the side he does support.'

'And if the lords defeat Bothwell, what then?' she asked.

293

'We will separate him from the Queen and try him for the murder of the King and this time he will not escape.'

Margaret continued to eat, while her brother lapsed into silence. The Erskines had the preservation of the prince, as they had had of his mother and his grandfather before that and that was what mattered.

Jamie would have no part in this civil war. Margaret knew he was waiting to be called back to Scotland, whether as adviser to the Queen, free of Bothwell, or regent to the prince, either way his day would come once more.

As warm May gave way to warm June and the countryside round about blossomed and the hawthorn berries grew red and fat and the flourish of the elder brightened the woodlands, it was difficult to imagine that not so very far away men were arming. Annabella and Margaret busied themselves ensuring that the castle was fully stocked with all the food and provisions they would need should they find themselves under siege.

The women in the castle were sewing a banner. White, they decided. It would stand out amongst the colours of all the family banners. They cut out from brown cloth and green a central tree with underneath a corpse. Margaret carefully embroidered a little boy – that was the prince - and the words *Judge and avenge my cause, O Lord.*

'That will do beautifully. That is the banner the lords will march behind.'

Then came word that the Queen was at Borthwick Castle, but that Bothwell was not with her. For a brief period they wondered, had he deserted her, had she dismissed him? There was a tentative siege of the castle, uncertain, for the lords continued to argue that their fight was not against the Queen so why were they there? Half-hearted as the siege was, she easily escaped, but soon they learned she and her troops had joined Bothwell at Dunbar and were preparing to do battle.

It was time for Erskine to decide and after an agonising two days and nights, he resolved to join the rebels. The women stood on the wall walk and watched him ride out at the head of his men, a disciplined body of fighting men, men who only a few years before had fought by his side in another cause. At the rear of the troops came some of the cannon from the castle and wagonloads of balls. If Dunbar was to be besieged, then the best equipment, the Queen's own armaments, would be used.

A hasty note from Erskine to his wife on the evening of 14th June told her he had arrived and joined the main army gathering to the south of Edinburgh ready to march to Dunbar.

His letter told them that Bothwell's former adherents were deserting him. Sir James Balfour, in whose house the King had died and who had been given the governorship of Edinburgh Castle, now quietly declared to the rebel lords that he would hold the castle for them, provided they confirmed him in his post. Greed had triumphed over loyalty. Erskine himself had been consulted for traditionally his family held the governorship. He had agreed.

And then within two days a letter came from him addressed to Margaret. There had not been a battle, but there had been negotiations during which Bothwell was allowed to leave and the Queen was in the care of the lords, being guarded for her own safety.

Margaret was to go to Lochleven and prepare to receive the Queen there. Her Grace would be in the care of Sir William Douglas, who had already received word to expect her.

Chapter Forty-Eight

When she arrived at Lochleven she found the house in turmoil. Servants were loading beds, mattresses, wall hangings, kitchen pots, pewter plates and other household equipment haphazardly into boats.

'What's happening here?' She dismounted from her horse and looking round at the chaos of tumbled bedding hastily stuffed into boxes. A boat, heavily laden and lying low in the water, was already heading out towards the island.

'She's to be housed in the castle.' William looked harassed. 'Those are the orders.'

'The castle isn't fit for the Queen. Why can she not stay in the house?'

'They think it will not be safe here. What will Her Grace say when she sees the state of the place? She will be deeply offended. We haven't been given enough time.'

And with that he was gone back into the house with the stewards hard on his heels, attempting to make lists.

Another two boats had barely pushed off from the jetty when hoofbeats heralded the arrival of the forward scout of the Queen's party to tell them she was just an hour behind him.

Hastily the family's barge was filled with cushions and the canopy fitted, for already the June sun was at its height and casting blinding reflections from the water.

Sir William stood with Agnes and Margaret at the gates of the house to welcome the Queen. When she arrived, drooping over the reins of her horse, with Patrick Lindsay on one side of her and on the other Lord Ruthven, son of the man who had been present at the murder of Rizzio, the welcoming party were shocked into silence.

A man leapt from his horse and helped the Queen down from the saddle, almost pulling her. She gazed dully at Sir William as he stepped forward to welcome her.

She was dressed in what looked like gypsy clothing: a dirty jacket and a short red petticoat over torn hose and down-at-heel shoes. She was not wearing a cap and her hair, tangled, unbrushed, was tied back with a dirty ribbon.

She said nothing. She looked over the heads of the people round her, a remote expression in her eyes. Did she ride here from Edinburgh thinking every step of the way that she was going to be assassinated, perhaps on some quiet stretch of the road where none could protect her and none could say what had happened?

Margaret, as she stepped nearer the girl, caught the faint smell of urine. 'Your Grace,' she began.

'Is the boat ready?' interrupted Lindsay.

'Surely Her Grace can come into the house to rest before we go over to the island?' asked Sir William evenly.

'There is no time to be lost.'

'Your Grace?' persisted Margaret. 'Where are your ladies?'

There were no ladies in the party, they could all see that now as the soldiers dismounted and led their horses away to find the stable block. The only women were two servants who now climbed down from behind two of the horsemen and came forward, dipping a curtsey to Margaret. She recognised them. They were cleaning-women who worked at Holyrood Palace. They looked bewildered.

'Will you not come in for refreshments?' pleaded Sir William. 'Her Grace must be tired after her journey.'

Margaret stepped forward and took the girl's arm.

'I will take her inside the house. She needs to clean herself up.'

'No time.' Ruthven nodded to two of his men who roughly shouldered Margaret aside, ignoring her furious objection, and took the Queen's arms. She was hustled down to the jetty. Sir William followed with Agnes and Margaret running after them.

'Her clothes?' Margaret hissed at one of the women.

'They would allow her nothing.'

It was a silent party that travelled in the launch across to the island. In case she should think of throwing herself in the water, Lindsay sat beside the Queen and kept a tight grip on her wrist. No one spoke as the oarsmen pulled hard and in no time they were easing the nose of the boat alongside the castle's jetty.

The Queen was gazing up at the grey stone walls of the high keep and there was something like despair in her eyes. Margaret gave a shiver. The Queen's expression was bleak. Whatever had happened in the last few days, the girl had lost hope. What had they done to her?

The castle was not much used now that the family spent most of their time at the New House. From time to time some of the family spent a few nights there, but most of the furniture, that which Margaret had gathered in the years of her marriage, had long ago been moved across to the New House and now what was there was only what was required by men who did not care what they slept on or what plate they ate from.

Now servants worked to unload the boats and make the laird's rooms fit for a queen. Sir William led the way silently to the keep. The steward who had charge of it was there to welcome them.

'Sir, we have not had time...'

'It's all right, John. We know that.'

The party made their way up the outside stair to the second floor and then on to the chamber above that. A rat, disturbed, ran across the floor. Here there was nothing save a straw pallet and a broken stool.

'This will do,' said Ruthven, and there was satisfaction in his voice. 'This will do for her.'

At that the Queen raised her head and looked directly at him. 'You will suffer for this,' she said.

'No, all the suffering will be yours.'

One of the two women (Sarah wasn't it? remembered Margaret) who had been brought with the Queen came forward and pushed Lindsay aside. 'Make way,' she said rudely.

He swore at her but it was beneath him to argue with a serving-woman and he stepped back out to the stairwell. Muttering, she and her companion began to build up the bed which was being brought piece by piece up the stair.

Margaret put her arm round Mary's waist.

'Do not worry, my dear, we will soon have it comfortable for you. Come, we'll go outside. It's warmer there, while the servants bring what you will need.'

Lindsay let them go. With a nod to the others he went back down the stairs and they could hear him calling to Sir William's servants to bring him meat and ale.

'No longer master in my own house,' murmured Sir William.

Margaret led the Queen down the stairs and out into the courtyard. There was a stone bench against the wall of the garden. She gently pushed the girl down on it. It was private here and the shouts of the men as they pulled the boat away from the jetty to make way for another were muffled by the thick walls of the castle. The sun was going down but the day was still warm.

'It has been terrible for you,' said Margaret. 'You can rest here. We will look after you.'

299

It was Agnes who brought a basin of warm water and a cloth. Margaret gently sponged the Queen's face to remove the grime. That done, she eased the Queen's hair back and ran her fingers through it to straighten out the tangles and deftly pleated it in one long thick rope.

'That's better,' she said. 'We'll find you some clothes and make you comfortable.'

'Four weeks.' said the Queen dreamily. 'Four weeks ago I stood beside Bothwell and we were married. I have been counting it up in my head. Four weeks.'

'Where is...' began Agnes, but Margaret nudged her and she fell silent.

As if she had not heard, the Queen continued in the same flat voice. 'The people shouted insults at me, they threw stones. I have lost their love.'

Over the next few days, while the laird and his people made the accommodation comfortable for the Queen, she herself was sunk in a stupor from which it was hard to rouse her. They could not make her eat.

At first Ruthven and Lindsay were constantly with her, berating her for her wickedness and demanding that she divorce Bothwell. She looked through them. Eventually even they tired of bullying someone who did not respond and they spent more time with the guards drinking and throwing dice. They were already finding it irksome to be confined to the island.

Either Margaret or Agnes was to be with the Queen day and night: that was the order. The three of them and the two chamber-women, Sarah and Bridget, settled down into a form of everyday life, for what else could they do? They were as much prisoners as was the Queen.

Sir William visited daily, courteously enquiring whether Her Grace was comfortable. Did she need anything? He was at her service. As she roused herself from her stupor she would sometimes thank him. But 'Nothing, thank you. Nothing that you can give.'

Leaving Agnes to sit with the Queen, Margaret followed him down to the jetty.

'Is she a prisoner or is she not?' she asked.

'Yes, she's a prisoner. I've instructed Drysdale to organise the men for guard duty.'

'On whose authority?'

On whose authority, indeed. Sir William shook his head. He knew that was the question being asked uneasily in the informal session of the Three Estates from whom he received regular reports, and in the law courts of Edinburgh. What right had anyone to hold a crowned queen a prisoner? The Lords had always said their rebellion was not against the Queen but against Bothwell. Why then was it the Queen and not Bothwell who was the prisoner?

William signalled to the boatman to come. 'She is a sick woman, isn't she?'

'Her old trouble, the aching in the joints and the weakness.'

'I would not want her to die here.'

'She will not die. I'll try and get her out into the sunshine.'

'Is there aught else ails her?'

'Lowness of spirits. Hardly surprising.'

But Margaret was beginning to wonder.

They were kept inside one day, for a light drizzle had begun in the early morning and persisted. They sat by the small window to obtain as much light as possible for their sewing.

There had come a delivery of clothes from Holyrood and though they hung on the Queen, so much weight had she lost, the beneficial effects of the warm summer sunshine and new clothes, few as they were, brought a healthier flush

301

to her cheeks and the temporary loss of the despair which had been in her eyes ever since her arrival.

She was still short of linen and Margaret was now stitching a shift for her. Though the Queen herself had a piece of cloth in one hand and a needle in the other, she was not working, but gazing through the window.

Margaret was idly turning over in her head memories, conversations, drifts of phrases. How to broach the matter which was troubling her?

'Your Grace,' she said, for even here the Queen was given every courtesy. 'Have your courses stopped?'

The Queen did not answer. She might even not have heard.

'It's just that while you have been here...' Margaret let the sentence fade into silence.

'Yes.' It was spoken softly.

'Could you be...?'

'Yes.'

Margaret picked up her needle and went on stitching, tiny stitches along the hem of the garment.

After a while she said, 'Then we must take care of you. Another prince for Scotland will be a fine thing.'

She glanced up and down again. The Queen's cheeks were flushed. 'Is that what people will think? They will welcome another child?'

'I am sure of it,' said Margaret firmly. 'A prince in the true line of the Stewarts.'

Never mind who his father is.

'I cannot divorce, you see that, I cannot divorce because that would make the child a bastard.'

'Yes,' said Margaret. 'Yes, I understand. But perhaps my dear, it will not do for it to be spoken of yet.'

'The servants may suspect.'

'Neither I nor Agnes will speak of it. Neither will Sarah and Bridget. They refuse to speak to anyone else

302

anyway. All the laundry is sent to the New House. There are enough young women in the place, not even the washerwomen will notice. And of course if they do it can be said that the troubles of the last few weeks have upset you. That is not uncommon.'

That night Margaret lay awake listening to the steady breathing of the Queen sleeping in the other bed. Since the girl had told what she had up till then kept secret she seemed less unhappy. For the first time she ate all the food set in front of her, with a sideways glance at Margaret. Now, she seemed to say, I must take care of myself for the sake of the baby.

Margaret eased herself over to lie on her back. She needed to think. She watched a sliver of moonlight shining through the gap in the shutters as it made its way across the ceiling. She heard an owl, close at hand, eerie, hunting prey.

What would Jamie want her to do?

She knew how to get rid of an unwanted pregnancy. Hadn't she herself used the herbs on several occasions? Had not all women?

She thought over the time in which the child had been conceived. She mentally counted the weeks. It was likely that this child was the result of rape. This child, a son as might be, with a claim to the throne would put new heart into Bothwell, now in the north attempting to recruit an army to his cause.

What would Jamie want her to do? She went over and over the question. He would not want this child born. That much she could be sure of. No one would. The idea of a child of Bothwell with a claim to the throne would enrage his enemies and cause strife for years to come.

There was always a risk to the mother when such herbs were used. It would never do for her to die in their house.

303

Jamie would not want his sister harmed. He had an affection for the Queen that went beyond the mere loyalty of kin. He must be as perplexed as everyone else what to do with her. Would he want her back on the throne unchallenged? Bothwell dead would be the best outcome and the Queen back on the throne, acknowledging her errors and relying on Jamie once more as her adviser.

What could be done that would be the best outcome for him?

Could the girl herself be persuaded to cooperate? Margaret dismissed the idea. What she was contemplating was a mortal sin. She might be prepared to damn her immortal soul, but the Queen would not.

She would have to do it herself. None must know. No one else could be trusted. She knew more than one wise woman who would supply her with the herbs without questions asked.

Now that she could speak of her pregnancy Mary seemed to relax and more and more confided in Margaret and in Agnes, who had seen with the sharp eyes of a woman who was herself still childbearing the signs but kept her counsel till the Queen spoke of it.

'Perhaps,' said Mary dreamily one day as they sat in the sun. 'Perhaps when the bairn is born I will take him to Stirling and he will join little James in the nursery. The two of them can be brought up together. Do you not think so?'

'I am sure my brother Erskine would be pleased to have the care of both of them.'

'By that time I shall be back on my throne. The madness will have passed.'

No one contradicted her.

But others were no more blind than Agnes was. Somehow among the people coming and going with stores for the castle, one had sharper eyes than the others. It became apparent rumours were abroad that she was carrying a child. A letter came from Jamie. He had heard it from the English ambassador. One rumour had it that she was near her term, but since she was known to have ceased cohabiting with her husband many weeks before his death, this child could only be the result of adultery.

Margaret kept all this from the Queen.

But the child must not live. Of that she was now certain. Something had to be done. Bothwell's brat would be a focus for men who might still support him and would encourage others to join him. Worse, it would be a focus for any man who cherished ambitions, men who hated Moray, men of Chatelherault's affinity, or men who just wanted to make trouble. If this child lived, Jamie would have to fight that much harder to regain his place.

Chapter Forty-Nine

The chamber-women worked frantically to stem the bleeding which had started in the night. The Queen screamed as her womb contracted to expel the foetus. She cried to God to save her baby, but it was too late. Agnes, hurrying in with bowls of hot water was in tears and Margaret herself, tearing cloths to replace the blood-sodden rags which were piling up on the floor, could feel it in her heart to wish the girl's ordeal was over.

Please don't let her die, she prayed. Please God the sin is mine not hers. Don't let her die.

Afterwards, she was surprised at herself. She had prayed that the Queen would not die, but it would have been better if she had. Then it would all have been over. The Queen's suffering would be ended. Prince James would be king and Jamie would be regent. That would have been the outcome.

'It is all in God's hands,' she said aloud.

Agnes, wearily closing the door to the bedroom, said. 'Yes. It is in God's hands. Amen.'

'How is she?'

'She sleeps. Sarah will stay with her. She's exhausted too but she's a light sleeper. If the Queen wakes she will call us.'

There was a noise outside. Agnes opened the door to the stairwell to admit the entry of the doctor, sent for from the mainland.

'You are too late,' said Agnes, and broke down and wept.

'Well, well,' said the doctor. 'Was it a boy?'

'There were two,' said Margaret. 'Both boys. Both dead.'

He was admitted to the bedroom. The stink of burning cloth and flesh still lingered. Margaret opened the shutters. It was already daylight.

The doctor pulled back the sheets and made a quick examination of the patient. The Queen whimpered.

'Poor lass,' murmured Margaret. 'She has had more to bear than most.'

The doctor nodded and gathered up his instruments into his bag and with a nod and a word of thanks to the chamber-women he was gone. He would carry word to the New House. Watching him from the window Margaret saw Lindsay approach, there was some brief talk and then Lindsay climbed into the boat alongside the doctor.

'Good riddance,' she thought. But he would be back. No doubt he had gone to report to his masters.

It was only the next day that Lindsay returned, with Ruthven and two other men. He looked as if he had not slept.

'We've been to Edinburgh and back,' one of his men told Margaret, eagerly helping himself to the bread and ham she provided.

Lindsay himself would not waste time. 'I want to see her,' he said.

Margaret, without lifting her head from the table told him he could not. 'She is too ill to see anyone.'

He strode over to her and thrust his face directly into hers. She flinched and drew back.

'Listen to me, Mother-in-law,' he said. 'I have documents for the whore to sign and sign them she will, ill or no.'

'Who are these people?'

'Notaries. They will witness her signature.'

307

'Gentlemen, I say again, the Queen is too ill to see anyone far less sign anything.'

Lindsay turned to the others. 'Wait below.' With a scared look at Margaret they went.

He turned back to her. 'Do you want me to break down the door?' He would have done it. She saw that. She led him upstairs into the bedroom to be met with a cry of protest from the Bridget who was sitting by the Queen. 'She's still bleeding. This is no place for you.' He ignored her.

The Queen was lying ashen on the bed, but awake.

'If you bully her,' Margaret hissed at him as he passed her. 'I'll make sure you are punished for it.'

'Get out.'

He pushed Briget towards the door. She resisted and with a quick turn of her head sank her teeth into his hand. He yelped and struck her across the face, bursting her nose which began to pour with blood. 'Out,' he snarled.

Margaret led the woman out of the room. From nowhere appeared one of Lindsay's men, who took up a position in front of the door with his arms folded.

They could hear Lindsay shouting and the Queen sobbing. Margaret tried to push past the guard but he refused to move.

Suddenly the door opened and Lindsay charged out, almost knocking his man down.

'You,' he said, taking Margaret's arm. 'Persuade her. Else she will find herself at the bottom of the loch.'

Margaret found the Queen leaning over the side of the bed retching drily. She knelt by the girl and put her arms round her. When the girl was settled back on the bed she asked. 'What are the papers?'

'Papers of abdication,' whispered the Queen.

'They cannot. They have no right to ask it of you.'

'I will not sign. I was born a queen and I will die a queen.'

'Rest,' said Margaret. 'We will talk about it again.'

'Margaret, you were always my friend. Don't let him back in.'

'I will do my best.'

But Lindsay was back the next day. They could not keep him out. Margaret had taken the precaution of having Captain Drysdale and one of his men at hand. When Lindsay came running up the stair, he was stopped.

'The Queen will see no one,' said the Captain.

'Get out of my way.'

'The Queen is under guard. No one can see her.'

With an oath Lindsay pulled out from his doublet his letters of authority. He thrust these at Captain Drysdale.

'Can you read?'

'Yes, sir,' said the Captain. He looked over his shoulder at Margaret. 'Letters of authority, my lady. From the council.'

'I suppose we cannot stop you,' said Margaret.

'No, you can't.'

He shouldered the Captain aside and ran up to the Queen's bedroom. Margaret followed him in. The chamber-women had heard the shouting and were ready for him. With a jerk of his head he ordered them out.

'You,' he said to the Queen who was sitting up in bed. She did not look at him.

'Here,' he said and threw several sheets of paper on the table. 'Here are the abdication papers again for you to sign. Sign them.'

He strode forward and suddenly grabbed at the Queen's hair, the pleat lying over her shoulder. He yanked it, jerking her out from under the covers. She screamed and there was a hammering on the door. Margaret gasped and grabbed hold of his arm.

'Stop that.'

He shook her off and pulled at the Queen's hair till she was dragged from the bed and kneeling beside the table.

'Sign,' he said, and attempted to thrust the quill into her hand. She clenched her fist and refused to take it. He slapped her.

Margaret was by this time pummelling him with her fists. 'Stop that, stop that,' she wept, but he ignored her.

'Sign.'

'I will not,' the Queen gasped between sobs.

'Then I will kill you.'

The Queen became still.

'I will slit your throat for you.'

'Patrick,' said Margaret, in what she hoped was a soothing tone. 'Patrick, perhaps when Her Grace has had time to think about it.'

'She doesn't need time.'

Margaret laid her hand gently on his arm. 'Patrick, she has fainted. See. I will talk to her. Yes, that is best. Leave your papers here.'

Lindsay let go of the arm of the slumped and fainting Queen, who lay huddled on the floor. 'You'll get her to sign?'

'I will try,' whispered Margaret. 'Leave the documents here.'

With an oath he turned and strode out of the room. At the door he turned. 'Mind you do. Else, she is a dead woman.'

In the silence the Queen stirred. 'What am I to do? What am I to do?'

Margaret called the chamber-women and they helped the Queen back into bed. Nothing was said. They were all too frightened for speech.

Chapter Fifty

Margaret wrote a note for Jamie. What did he want? Did he know of this? But her courier was back within minutes.

'Please, my lady, Lord Lindsay's men are at the boats. They say no one must leave.'

'No matter,' she said. She took the letter back from him and tore it into pieces.

If the Queen abdicated they would presumably crown the baby prince. Just over a year old. At least thirteen years, perhaps longer, before he would come into his own and until then there would need to be a regency.

Jamie wanted to be regent. He had the right by birth and the skill, and Scotland had need of a firm hand. He was waiting in Newcastle, waiting to see how matters resolved before crossing the border. He was wisely not taking sides. Not yet. So she reasoned.

Did he have anything to do with this? Was he giving instructions to those in the council who looked to him for guidance? Maitland, she knew, would always favour Jamie.

She went quietly into the Queen's room. The Queen was huddled up on the bed. Sarah was sitting beside her, holding her hand.

Margaret stood by the table looking down at the document which was lying where Lindsay had thrown it. When he had thrown down the quill he had made a splash of ink over the grey cloth which covered the table and she gently moved the paper aside so that it would not be marked.

She read through it. *Marie by the grace of God queen of Scots...* yes, here it was... *our body, spirit and senses so vexed, broken and unquiet that longer we are not able by any manner to endure so great and intolerable pains and troubles wherewith we are altogether weary...*

'I will not.' The words were whispered from the bed where Mary lay on her back looking at the ceiling. 'I will not.' She sounded angry rather than frightened. How frightened would she have to be to sign the document?

Margaret rapidly read on. The Queen renounced the crown in favour of our son. Which lords were – ah yes, here they were, the lords who were to be responsible for crowning the prince. Morton, of course, Atholl, Glencairn, others. She read through the list. Her brother was there. That was all right. Not Jamie of course. There was nothing to show he had anything to do with this.

'Leave us,' she said to Sarah, who rose with another anxious look at the Queen and left the room.

'Tell them,' said Mary. 'Tell them I will never give up my throne to rebels.'

'They thought they were acting for the best,' said Margaret. 'They thought they were rescuing you from Bothwell. They believed he had kidnapped you against your will.'

There was silence. What could the Queen say? That she had been willing to go with Bothwell and that made the lords rebels. Or that she had truly been kidnapped against her will and therefore the lords were right to try and rescue her.

'I will divorce Bothwell.'

'Will you?'

'Now there is no bairn to think of. Then there will be no reason to keep me here.'

Margaret left the room and went down to where Agnes and Bridget, the right side of her face bruised and swollen from Lindsay's blow the day before, were waiting.

'Where's Patrick?'

'Gone to bed.'

'The Queen does not wish to see anyone. She has given orders that she will not be disturbed. I will sit with her. Do not on any account allow anyone in.'

She lifted the flagon of wine and the bread and cheese which had been left by the servants and went back to the Queen's bedroom.

'Come,' she said. 'You must eat. We'll get your strength back up, ready for the day when you ride in triumph through the streets of Edinburgh.'

The Queen nodded. There was more colour in her cheeks. Her spurt of anger had done her good.

'Is he still there?' she asked.

'Yes, he's still out there. My dear, he is mad. This cannot be the will of the council, not to have you threatened with your life. Although he is my daughter's husband, we all hate him. One day he will go too far and will answer for it. He's rampaging around downstairs threatening everyone. I fear he will kill us all. He will say you died of the miscarriage and who will prove him wrong? That is why we are all so frightened. We know the truth. How is he to let us live, those of us that saw him threatening you. I fear that once he has killed you he will kill us also. What reason he will give I know not. What has he to lose? He is so obsessed with getting you to sign the paper that all reason has deserted him.'

Margaret, exhausted by this speech delivered in a voice full of anguish while she roamed round the room, attempting to tidy it, sat down and burst into tears. Now it was the Queen's turn to comfort. 'I will have justice.'

'If you live.'

'What am I to do?'

'He's holding us all prisoner. He is allowing none near you save myself. Even when Agnes just now wept and begged to be allowed back in he refused. He will answer for that to William when the time comes.'

313

'But Agnes is safe?'

'I hope so. He will be able to frighten her into silence. For the sake of her children.'

Margaret closed up the shutters. 'Sleep,' she said. 'We will work out what to do in the morning.'

She blew out the candle and closed the door quietly.

'What's happening?' asked Agnes.

'She's sleeping soundly. She already looks better. I will think what to do. I'll try to persuade her in the morning that for her own health she should allow you in. You should go to bed too. Nothing is going to happen again tonight.

'Will she sign the papers?'

'Yes, I think so. I think that is why she sleeps peacefully. She has made up her mind. She sees the wisdom of it.'

In the morning Margaret went in to the Queen. She laid the tray with the Queen's food on the table, pushing aside the papers of abdication and sent them fluttering to the floor. They both ate. She helped the Queen to dress.

'I would so like to walk in the garden,' said the Queen.

'They will not allow us out. And they still refuse to let anyone except myself near you. There are guards on the door who cannot be argued with. Poor Agnes is breaking her heart and Bridget and Sarah are beside themselves with anger.'

She saw the Queen's mouth set in a grim line. 'I escaped once,' she said. 'I will escape again.'

Eagerly Margaret seized on this. 'I will help you. How can we do it?' But then she paused and pushed aside the bread on her plate. 'But an island is different from a palace and we have no men to help us.'

'We will think of something.'

The hours passed. From the window they could see Lindsay's men on the beach below them. The two women took up their sewing for want of anything else to do. The document of abdication lay on the floor unheeded.

'My dear,' said Margaret as noon approached. 'I wonder whether the guard would be removed if you were to sign the papers.'

'I will not.'

'No, but hear me. If you sign under duress then your signature means nothing. I am sure that is the law. And when you escape you can tell everyone that it was under duress and they will believe you because all know what kind of a man Patrick Lindsay is. I will testify it is under duress.'

'They would believe you.'

'Yes of course they would. So if you sign it means nothing and would buy us time and as soon as they relax the guard I will help you escape.'

'Will you?' There were tears in the Queen's eyes.

'Of course. My dear, it is what Jamie would want me to do. If only he were here, but he is still in England and there is no way to contact him. He will not know what is happening.'

'You think I should sign?'

'I think if you do not he will kill you and perhaps myself and poor Bridget and Sarah.'

'I am not frightened for myself.'

Margaret did not answer but went on stitching.

After a while the Queen bent down and picked up the document. She read it through.

'It is iniquitous,' she said.

'Wicked,' agreed Margaret.

'But what can I do? Even if they do not kill me with poison or dagger, do they leave me here for the rest of my life? Will they starve me to death? Who will come to my aid?'

The last was a wail and Margaret started up in case it had been heard outside, but there was only silence.

'I will,' she said. 'Once you sign and Lindsay goes away and there is no more reason for the guards, then you will escape. All will be well.'

The Queen sat at the table and picked up the paper. She read what was written. She remained sunk in thought for an hour or more. Then without a word she pulled the inkpot towards her. Picking up the quill she signed her name.

'It is done under duress. You are a witness to that. I sign because they threaten me with death and for no other reason.'

Margaret sprinkled sand over the wet signature and blew it off. 'I will take it to them,' she said. 'Oh my dear,' and she leaned over and kissed the Queen on the cheek. 'You are a brave lass. All Scotland will know of it.'

She took the document and left the room. She hurried downstairs to where Lindsay and his men were waiting.

'Here it is. She has signed it.'

Lindsay took it from her and grinned. He went to the door and called for the two notaries he had brought with him.

'This is her signature?' he asked Margaret in front of them.

'Yes.'

'Swear.'

'I swear.'

'She signed willingly?' He glowered at her.

There is no need to threaten me, she thought, and answered firmly, 'Yes.'

The two notaries hesitated and then one by one signed as witnesses. They all left then, taking a boat for the mainland.

Margaret sought out Agnes.

'She has signed. But do not speak of it to her. She has asked that the last few days be wiped from her memory and yours.'

'Is she to be kept here still?'

'Until we learn otherwise.'

At the end of July the baby prince was crowned James, King of Scots in a hasty ceremony in the Church of the Holy Rude in Stirling. There were celebrations throughout Scotland including at Lochleven. When she saw the fireworks on the mainland and was told the cause, the Queen retreated to her room in tears.

Chapter Fifty-One
1568

When the boat was out of sight and the ripples on the water had settled Margaret went down to her own room. She picked up the unfinished letter to her son. She added a sentence, sealed it and summoned a messenger.

'Take a boat, then ride hard to Glasgow to the Earl of Moray. He's expecting you.'

When the courier had gone she closed the shutters. All was finished. Tonight they had done a good night's work. The Queen would find she had few friends left in Scotland and when she was convinced of this there were any number of merchant ships waiting in the west willing to carry her back to France, where she belonged. Jamie had made sure of that.

She had done as Jamie wanted. He was right. They had held the Queen for ten months but it was not to be expected it could continue much longer.

So it has ended, she thought. It is fitting. The daughter of the King I loved is a broken reed. She has fled and will be heard of no more and the son of the King, *my* son, has gained his rightful place, ruling Scotland.

It had been a good day's work. She was content.

--oOo--

Author's Note

I visited Lochleven Castle on a cold day in April, travelling in the small launch that acts as a ferry. The day after I was there, the boat could not do the crossing, because the winds were too high. If a modern motor boat can fail to make the journey, how isolated must the people of the past have found it, when they relied on oars and sail, when the mainland was blotted out by fog and the waters of the loch dark and turbulent with storms?

History records only occasional references to Margaret Erskine and then only when her story touches on that of the people around her – her lover, her father, her sons and of course Mary, Queen of Scots. I became intrigued with Margaret's story when looking at the life of her son Lord James Stewart, Earl of Moray. He would have been king had he been born legitimate. He was one of the most enigmatic and therefore the most intriguing men of the age.

It's my fancy that his mother would do anything to forward his ambitions and in pursuit of this idea I have placed her at the centre of events. She was so closely connected with the people in power that I find it hard to believe she would be sitting quietly at home, stitching altar cloths.

Of course, what goes on in her head has come out of my imagination. Save where it narrates known true events, this is a work of fiction. Readers wanting to know more should refer to the bibliography.

Bibliography

Cameron, Jamie, *James V, the Personal Rule 1528 - 1542,* Tuckwell Press 1998

Dawson, Jane, *John Knox,* Yale University Press, 2015

Fraser, Antonia, *Mary Queen of Scots,* Orion paperback edition 2009

Historic Scotland, *Lochleven Castle, Official Guide 2009; Stirling Castle, Official Guide* 2011

Knox, John, *The History of the Reformation in Scotland,* The Banner of Truth Trust, 1982 edition

Lamont, Stewart, *The Swordbearer, John Knox and the European Reformation,* Hodder & Stoughton, 1991

Lamont-Brown, Raymond, *St, Andrews, City by the Northern Sea.* Birlinn Limited 2006

Lindsay of Pitscottie, *The Chronicles of Scotland,* Constable and Company, 1814 edition

MacCulloch, Diarmaid, *Reformation 1490 - 1700,* Penguin edition 2003

Marshall, Rosalind K., *Mary of Guise* Wm Collins Sons & Co. Ltd. 1977

Mapstone, Sally & Wood, Juliette (eds.) *The Rose and the Thistle, Essays on the Culture of late Medieval and Renaissance Scotland*, Tuckwell Press, 1998

Reid, Harry, *Reformation, The Dangerous Birth of the Modern World,* Saint Andrew Press, 2009

Sanderson, Margaret H.B., *Cardinal of Scotland,* John Donald Publishers Ltd. 1986

Sanderson, Margaret N.B., *Mary Stewart's People*, James Thin, 1987

Thomas, Andrea, *Princelie Majestie: The Court of James V of Scotland,* Birlinn Limited 2005

Weir, Alison, *Mary, Queen of Scots and the Murder of Lord Darnley,* Pimlico 2004

Lightning Source UK Ltd.
Milton Keynes UK
UKHW01f2045060818
326850UK00001B/321/P